Wazeeri was concerned about the missile payload. He still had no luck in getting a nuclear warhead, and he had been spreading money around like hummus on a pita. He did have news of sarin being available, if he could get it from the Iraqi border near eastern Syria, where he had gotten the Scud, but that could take some time. He wasn't 100 percent sure how reliable the information was on who actually possessed the deadly chemical. In the worst-case scenario, they would just fire what they had, which would only do major damage to a small area, but if they hit the White House with the president at his desk, it would be enough. . . .

CRESCENT FIRE

DAVID M. SALKIN

B

BERKLEY BOOKS, NEW YORK

THE BERKLEY PUBLISHING GROUP
Published by the Penguin Group
Penguin Group (USA) Inc.
375 Hudson Street, New York, New York 10014, USA
Penguin Group (Canada), 90 Eglinton Avenue East, Suite 700, Toronto, Ontario M4P 2Y3, Canada
(a division of Pearson Penguin Canada Inc.)
Penguin Books Ltd., 80 Strand, London WC2R 0RL, England
Penguin Group Ireland, 25 St. Stephen's Green, Dublin 2, Ireland (a division of Penguin Books Ltd.)
Penguin Group (Australia), 250 Camberwell Road, Camberwell, Victoria 3124, Australia
(a division of Pearson Australia Group Pty. Ltd.)
Penguin Books India Pvt. Ltd., 11 Community Centre, Panchsheel Park, New Delhi—110 017, India
Penguin Group (NZ), 67 Apollo Drive, Mairangi Bay, Auckland 1311, New Zealand
(a division of Pearson New Zealand Ltd.)
Penguin Books (South Africa) (Pty.) Ltd., 24 Sturdee Avenue, Rosebank, Johannesburg 2196,
South Africa

Penguin Books Ltd., Registered Offices: 80 Strand, London WC2R 0RL, England

This is a work of fiction. Names, characters, places, and incidents either are the product of the author's imagination or are used fictitiously, and any resemblance to actual persons, living or dead, business establishments, events, or locales is entirely coincidental.

CRESCENT FIRE

A Berkley Book / published by arrangement with the author

PRINTING HISTORY
Berkley edition / April 2007

Copyright © 2007 by David M. Salkin.
Cover design by Steven Ferlauto.
Interior text design by Laura K. Corless.

ISBN: 978-0-425-21446-6

BERKLEY®
Berkley Books are published by The Berkley Publishing Group,
a division of Penguin Group (USA) Inc.,
375 Hudson Street, New York, New York 10014.
BERKLEY is a registered trademark of Penguin Group (USA) Inc.
The "B" design is a trademark belonging to Penguin Group (USA) Inc.

PRINTED IN THE UNITED STATES OF AMERICA

10 9 8 7 6 5 4 3 2 1

For my family and friends, who have worn or still wear that uniform: Uncle Art Salkin, Col., USAF, WWII and Korea; Uncle Joe Varoff, Seaman First Class USCG-WWII; Uncle Philip Salkin, USCG, WWII; LTC William Peace, U.S. Army, Operation Desert Storm & Enduring Freedom; Col. Mark Franklin, U.S. Army; S/Sgt. David Clemenko, USMC; Specialist Gary Jensen, KIA Vietnam; and my friends in the Philip A. Reynolds Detachment of the United States Marine Corps League . . . just to name a personal few.

Most importantly, thanks to my family—especially my wife, Patty—for never letting me give up. Writing novels while still "working for a living" is difficult—getting published is nearly impossible. Patty has a box of rejection letters to prove it. Dad and Mom, my personal heroes, thank you for a lifetime of love and good advice. My only regret is that Mom never got a finished copy in her hands, but she is smiling down on us every day. Mom, we miss you very much:

Sylvia Varoff Salkin
October 27, 1929–March 5, 2006

And finally, if the author has an angry tone in this novel, I make no apologies. More than three thousand innocent lives were taken at the hands of Islamic fundamentalists on 9/11, including personal friends. Yes, I am still pretty darn mad.

War is an ugly thing, but not the ugliest of things. The decayed and degraded state of moral and patriotic feeling which thinks that nothing is worth war is much worse. The person who has nothing for which he is willing to fight, nothing which is more important than his own personal safety, is a miserable creature and has no chance of being free unless made and kept so by the exertions of better men than himself. —John Stuart Mill

Acknowledgments

Special thanks to Thomas Colgan and Doug Whiteman at Penguin Group (USA) Inc. for this wonderful opportunity and for taking the chance on a new writer. Also, a big thanks to those behind-the-scene workers at Penguin: Bill Drennan, Stacy Edwards, Lara Robbins, and Sandy Harding.

Thanks to my unofficial team of proofreaders and butt kickers: Natalie, Penny, and Susan, for helping me dot the i's and cross the t's. And finally, to my brother and business partner, a big thank-you for tolerating my writing "when I am supposed to be working!" When they make a movie out of this, I'll try and get you a part . . .

CHAPTER 1

Tel Aviv Security Office,
Interrogation Room 3

The young Arab man was naked, tied to a chair. He had been kept awake for forty-eight hours straight, and was only semilucid. It was only stark fear that kept his eyes open at all. The lights were bright in the white-tiled room. He was seated against one wall facing a room that was bare except for a long table and a couple of simple metal chairs. He couldn't help but notice the center drain on the floor. Through squinting, blurry eyes he could make out the shape of a tooth, the root stained with blood, sitting on top of the drain.

A handsome young Israeli entered the room wheeling a hand truck. There was a large truck battery on it with cables dragging behind it, as well as a black medical bag seated on top of the battery. He entered with the squeaking hand truck, the metal cable clips scratching across the floor, and took the black bag off the battery, placing it carefully on the table. He turned around and faced the young Arab, a man maybe ten years his junior. He just stood staring for a few moments, then sat on the table and crossed his arms. His dark eyes were somewhat vacant, shaded by an evident sadness.

"My name is Dr. Chiam Avrom. For ten years after I graduated from medical school, I spent my time putting people back together. I was a medic in the army, and a trauma center doctor here in Tel Aviv. You would have been hard-pressed to find a person more dedicated to saving lives than me, Sufah."

Chiam walked over to the battery and picked up the cables. There were very small clips on the ends of the heavy cables. As he leaned against the table, he touched the clips together. Sufah flinched when the loud electrical zap sounded and the small arc of lightning jumped off the lead. Chiam continued to make little zapping noises, apparently lost in thought for a moment before looking back up at the naked, sweating man in front of him.

"I had a nice life, Sufah. My wife, Reba, was a beautiful woman—a wonderful mother. My two little girls, Sarah and Ariel, were the sweetest things God ever put on this planet. The three of them were in a school bus for a class trip, Sufah. A *school bus!*" he yelled. He arced the leads again, making that zapping noise.

"You know, when I received the call, I knew I could help them. I knew with my medical skills I could put them back together." His eyes were welling up with tears, and he wiped his nose with the back of his hand, in which he still held the lead. "But I couldn't put them back together. I couldn't even find all of the body parts. I buried what they gave me, but so help me God, I don't know whose arms and legs they were. Not my own babies."

He stood and arced the leads again. The Arab's eyes were as wide open as they could be. His feet cramped as he tried to crawl out of his own skin. He silently began praying the Koran as the doctor approached him.

"You know, if my government was making bombs in a school, and you blew it up and killed my children, I would hold *my* government responsible, not yours. But my government doesn't *do* that, Sufah. You and your friends like to blow up schools and school buses and hospitals because you like pain and death and misery. And now, my enemy, you are about to find out personally about all three."

The doctor flipped a switch and killed the power on the battery. Then he clamped the first cable to the Arab's right testicle. That by itself was enough to make Sufah scream and start fighting the restraints. The second cable was clamped to the skin near the end of his penis, so the current would have some distance to travel.

"A *school bus,* you piece of shit," Chiam spat.

When he flipped the switch, the screaming reverberated off of the white-tiled walls, floor, and ceiling. The smell of burning flesh reminded Chiam of that day at the school bus scene—mangled arms and legs and torsos and heads lying all over the street. At least they were all together, he thought. His beautiful family—gone in a flash because they were Jews in a Muslim part of the world.

In his office down the hall from interrogation room 3, Major David Cohen was reading intelligence reports with another officer from his intel unit.

"Damn it! Isn't that room soundproofed?" he grumbled. "Who can work in this noise?"

His fellow officer answered him quietly. "It *is* soundproofed, David. *'The doctor is in.'"*

The major stood up. "Well, that screaming has been going on for ten minutes. We'd better get in there before there is no one left to question."

The intelligence officers walked down the hall to room 3 and walked in. The doctor was sitting on the table expressionless, looking at the man in front of him. The Arab was hoarse from screaming. He sat in his own excrement, sweat running down his soaked body. His eyes were out of focus, searching the room wildly for anything that resembled help. His head bobbed around on his neck like a broken toy. Mucus and blood ran from his nose and mouth. The man was clearly in shock and teetering between consciousness and unconsciousness.

"Doctor, why don't you have a cup of coffee. We would like to chat with this man for a moment. We'll call you when we need you again."

The doctor stood and left without speaking, leaving his battery and bag where they were. The major motioned to his captain, who was holding a bucket of water. He threw it on the prisoner, who coughed and spit, his head still moving erratically. The major slapped his face gently and spoke calmly to him.

"Look at me, Sufah. Focus. That's it—focus. Look at me."

The man looked up at him as best he could. He was drained of all physical and mental strength, and was confused and exhausted.

The major reached into his breast pocket and took out three small color photos. There was a beautiful young woman in the first photo and two adorable little girls in the next two. They looked to be about four and six.

The Arab looked at them without speaking.

"This used to be Dr. Avrom's family, Sufah. I was at his wedding. Did you know that? I was at his home when his first baby came home from the hospital. It was Chiam Avrom who saved my life when a sniper's bullet hit me ten years ago. I was a captain then. Chiam was my medic, and a damn good one."

The major took out a cigarette and lit it. He puffed it twice and placed it in Sufah's mouth. The Arab tried to inhale some smoke but started coughing horribly. The cigarette fell to the floor near his feet, in a pool of his own urine.

"Oh, well. That stuff will kill you anyway, won't it?"

said the major. "So where was I in my little story? Ah, yes—the doctor. A very talented man really. And then you and your people decided that blowing up little girls and their mommies was a valiant thing to do. You are so brave! It must take great courage to blow yourself up knowing you are going to kill babies and small children when you pull the cord. You know what I think? I think it is bullshit. That man there saved countless lives in his short medical career. He was a talented man. After you people killed his family, he came to me. He made me promise him that when I found out who was responsible, he could have some time alone with him.

"You know, I can get in big trouble for this. But how can I say no to the man who saved my life? In a few minutes, I am going to let him back in here. I think he went to get a blowtorch. Perhaps we should have a chat and avoid him coming back. Does that sound like a good idea to you?"

Sufah was pale and in a cold sweat. He nodded a slow yes and tried to fight back his tears.

"Maybe you are smarter than I thought you were. Very well. We are going to show you pictures. Lots of them. You are going to tell us who these people are, and how they are connected to each other. You are going to tell us who the big bosses are, and who the little bosses are. You are going to tell us everything you know. And if you bullshit us, Sufah, we will know. And then I will call my friend the doctor to come visit you again with his blowtorch. He will be angry for at *least* three lifetimes, so I suggest you do your very best. He *will* kill you, but it will take a very, very long time. And even though I keep kosher myself, I will make sure you are buried in pig intestines. We might even shove a few up your ass. It would be a shame to miss out on all the virgins and Paradise wouldn't it? Now . . . let's clean you up and get you something to drink and eat. We'll even find some clothes for you. And then we have lots of work to do."

CHAPTER 2

New Jersey FBI Office

Agents Still and Hollahan walked into the briefing room with their morning coffee. The "Marine Corps mud," as it was often referred to, was black, and strong enough to resurrect the dead. The two men exchanged glances when they entered the room and saw only Special Agent in Charge Walker sitting in the room.

"Where's everybody?" asked Still.

"Have a seat, gentlemen," said Walker.

Still, ever the jokester, looked at Hollahan and batted his eyes.

"I love it when he calls us gentlemen," he said with great drama. He slowly dropped his big frame into a black leather chair. Still was such a dark-skinned black man, he was almost as dark as the chair. He kept his head shaved, a habit that started during his first tour in Vietnam those many years ago.

Walker cleared his throat and apparently was trying to find a way to start. His hesitation, obvious only to men who had worked with him for years, was slightly disconcerting.

"This is gonna be great, I can tell already," said Hollahan. Hollahan, a ruddy-faced Irishman with reddish hair now turning gray, had the face of a boxer. The flattened nose and scar tissue over the eyelids were testament to a rough childhood. Like Still, he had served in Vietnam, although most of his time was spent flying above the jungle, not running around in it like his partner.

"Last time someone cleared his throat before he started giving me 'good news,' it was my dad showing me my draft notice," said Still. Still's hands were as big as anvils, and his muscled forearms had the tattoos of the army Green Beret.

Walker, slightly red in the face, began. "The two of you did a tremendous job on the Bulovski case. Tom Ridge himself knows your names. As you are aware, the FBI, CIA, NSA, DoD, and the like are all stretched very thin."

Still leaned toward Hollahan, about to crack a joke about "all those initials," but a stern look from Walker silenced him and he sat up straight again.

"Iraq, Afghanistan, and antiterrorist homeland defense operations right here at home have us buried. Most agents are working way too much overtime, and everyone's stress levels are starting to take a toll. We have been extremely fortunate since nine-eleven that another major domestic attack hasn't been successful, but let's be honest: every day we wait for the news about one we missed. POTUS [president of the United States] is starting to worry, and we are getting new direction. I have been asked to loan you out. Like I said, you two did a helluva job with Bulovski."

"*Ohhh, shit*," said Still with a sigh. "I knew something bad was coming as soon as he cleared his throat."

"This would be on a volunteer basis only, Bob. The operation isn't ours. It's being arranged through CIA, but that's all I can tell you for now. Truth is, I don't know much about what's being planned. What I *can* tell you is that I have reviewed the jackets on the other agents who have been requested, and they are some of our best people. I'm not blowing smoke up your ass. If you two are going to be out on loan, I will be up the proverbial creek. Frankly, I need you here, and I told Homeland Security the same thing. Their assurance that I will get help here to replace you doesn't give me warm fuzzies."

Hollahan looked at Still. "He called you 'Bob.'"

"I'm a dead man," grimaced Still.

"Look, guys, I've worked with you two for more than ten years. I know you like to joke to relieve the stress, and that's fine, but what you are going to be doing is nothing to joke around about."

"I thought you said you didn't know what we'd be doing," said Hollahan.

"I don't. But I do know with *whom* you'd be doing the stuff I don't know about."

There was a pause as the two waited for a name.

"Well? Who?" asked Still.

"Sorry, can't say. Let's just say he isn't FBI and he doesn't work inside the United States. In fact, if he did, you two would probably have to arrest him." He didn't smile when he said that.

"Super. Just super. You loanin' us out to the spooks?" asked Still.

"Actually, you would be officially 'on loan to the United Nations,'" said Walker.

"You shittin' me? That clusterfuck outfit could screw up a wet dream. That's it, man: I want no part of this," said Still, and he sat back in his chair with his arms folded.

"Bob . . ."

"There he goes again with the first name. What's that? Second time now in ten years?" asked Still.

"Hear him out, Bob. We've used the U.N. for cover on Ops before. What do you know?" he asked Walker.

"I know more than I am supposed to, only because I know the people involved. You would be working with some of the most talented people I've ever seen. A couple of these guys are in Langley, some are 'former spooks,' and a few are guys I have crossed paths with over the years and are more than just a little scary. Bottom line, POTUS wants serious results, regardless of the path taken. We are moving some of our operations overseas, where the U.S. Constitution doesn't apply. I can promise you that you won't have to serve outside this office for more than a year, unless you want to. You will be making considerably more money than you are now, but let's face it, the dishwasher in the diner makes more than we do anyway. So that's it. I am supposed to ask you to attend a meeting in Virginia. After that, it's up to you. All I need to know is whether you are interested in attending."

"Well, gee, after the way you sugarcoated it and all, how could we say no? Do we get to whack bad guys?" quipped Still.

"Actually, yes—probably more than you've ever drawn down on in your entire career."

That got their attention. Both of them had had their share of action in their careers, and Still actually liked it.

"They gonna have hyphenated names?" asked Still.

Walker sighed. "Yeah, and probably towels on their heads, too," he added sarcastically. "Now behave or I'm sending you to sensitivity training."

"Okay, I'll be good. Now, where do I sign?"

Hollahan shook his head at his longtime partner. "We'll go listen to what they have to say in Virginia."

Walker stood and extended his hand. "Fellas, I'm gonna take off my boss hat for a second. I had more than just a couple of good friends in the towers on September eleventh. If I were thirty years younger, I would have reenlisted on the twelfth. If you do end up doing this job, do it right. There are a lot of people counting on you to keep them safe in their beds at night, and there are a lot of very good agents looking down on you hoping you will get a few scalps for them. Officially, I am here to do my job to the best of my ability within the confines of the powers of my office. Unofficially, I am a very pissed off American who is pretty goddamned tired of seeing our young people coming off of planes in metal boxes. Fuck the media and their liberal bullshit. Someday they will wake up and understand that there are a billion people in the world who want us all dead. You go make sure that doesn't happen."

Walker shook both their hands and walked out, saying, "There will be an e-mail to you later today with your meeting instructions."

Still and Hollahan looked at each other. "Ya know, that's probably the most I ever heard him say at one time in the ten years I been workin' for him," said Still.

Hollahan rubbed his chin. "It's what he said at the end. This operation is gonna be a hit, not an Intel gathering. I'm not sure why the CIA would want us for wet work. They have bad guys on the payroll for that shit. Why us?"

Still sat down on a table and smiled, his perfect white teeth (except for the gap between the two fronts) standing out against his very black skin. " 'Cause they always trying to fuck with the black man," he said with a laugh.

"What about me?" asked Hollahan, smiling.

"Hmmm . . . Hollahan . . . that a Jewish name?" he joked.

"Let me ask you something, Bob, no bullshit. I'm fifty-six years old. You're what? Fifty-five? Aren't we a little old for this shit? This is a younger man's game. You think we can keep up with a bunch of gung-ho twenty-five- and thirty-year-olds? I'm thinking of talking to the pension board."

"Bullshit, man. They know how old we are. Hell, if it's CIA, they even know how many times you crap in a week. We ain't gonna be dropping into the jungle and shit. I'm sure we'll be doing more the analysis end of the job. Let's go to Virginia and see what the man has to say. Keep an open mind, 'cause if I go, I want you coming with me."

"I'll go to Virginia and hear them out, Bob. I'm just not promising anything."

They continued down the hall in silence, each lost in his own thoughts as they pondered the future.

CHAPTER 3

Hindu Kush Mountains between Pakistan and Afghanistan

A dozen men in long robes and hoods sat at the mouth of a cave that overlooked the long valley leading all the way to the Khyber Pass. To the east lay the Northwest Frontier Province of Pakistan, an inhospitable place for all by the local tribes. To the west were Afghanistan and the infidel American troops. The dozen men were close enough to occasionally hear dull "whumps" in the distance when the Americans lost their patience and dropped ordnance from a B-52.

The men sat quietly, having just finished their morning prayers. They watched the sunlight stream over the mountains as it made dramatic shadows on the rugged landscape in front of them. Muktar was the first to speak. He was a lean, hard man of about fifty, as best as anyone could guess. His heavily lined face and poor dental health made him appear much older. Being a mountain tribesman, he had no idea what his actual birthday was. There would certainly never be any cake or balloons in his honor once a year.

"I have heard news of the Great Satan," he began. The

others looked at him thoughtfully. Muktar was not a big talker, but he did have lots of "ears" all over the valley. His people had lived in the Hindu Kush for a thousand years. The very name "Hindu Killer" was a subject of much debate. Was it named for the genocide of the Hindus at the hand of the Muslims who arrived there centuries later, or for the thousands of Indians who died in the snow as part of the slave trade? No one could say for sure, except to say that the area belonged to the Muslims now. Muktar's people had been in those cold mountains and could recount tales of both events, passed down through the generations. Muktar, like most of his tribesmen, couldn't read or write, but relied heavily on the oral histories and traditional folktales that kept his people's culture alive.

"What have you heard?" asked Ibrahiim. Ibrahiim bin Abdul bin al-Bustan was the leader of the Harakat ul-Mujahidin, a terrorist organization dedicated to eradicating all Indian influence from the Kashmir region of Pakistan. Of course, that was only for starters. When the area was cleansed of these infidels, they would keep working until the world was completely cleansed of all nonbelievers. Al Qaeda backed them financially and with weapons training. "The Base," as Al Qaeda translates, provides training and financial support to many terrorist groups that are anti-Israel, anti–United States, or are radically Islamic fundamentalist. A perfect world of the faithful, without the distractions of Westerners or nonbelievers, was the ultimate goal. Muktar and his people were just another weapon in the Al Qaeda arsenal.

Muktar scanned the sky and stood up. He motioned for the others to go back into the cave. As old as he was, he could still hear rotor blades before everyone else. They all walked quietly into the cave and followed the narrow, twisting passage deep into the mountain where they had several cavernous rooms, complete with oil lamps, bedding, and tables. There were various maps and papers stacked on the tables. As they settled back down to begin where they left off, they could all hear the American helicopters flying nearby. With the equipment the infidels possessed, they need not be seen by a pilot to be in danger. Their very body heat would be enough to give them away to their enemy, who could shower them with missiles, bombs, and machine guns.

At first, no one spoke, waiting for the noise to pass, and then Muktar began again.

"As I was about to say, the Americans will be pressing us further. An increase in equipment has been seen in the valley. It is their Army Rangers with attack helicopters. Last week, a missile struck a camp in Dweli-Abas, killing several of our men. We believe this came from a ship or a submarine, since no helicopters or planes were spotted. They are bringing in more men as well. The infidel dogs will be walking in our valley before many more nights pass. We will not have enough Mujahidin fighters to resist them long here. I suggest we move farther north. There are passages we can use that will be difficult for the infidels to find. We can booby-trap them behind us in case we are followed by foot soldiers. When we are stronger in numbers, we can fight them in the place of our choosing. We have another month before the weather gets too bad for them to fly regularly. Until then we need to use great caution."

The others silently nodded their appreciation of his comments. After a moment, Ibrahiim spoke. "In this case, your caution is very wise. I have waited until now to speak for fear of too many ears connected to too many mouths, but I have news as well."

The others smiled and listened to every word. When Ibrahiim spoke like this, it meant death to the infidels.

"Our brothers in Al Qaeda have been busy preparing to strike at the Great Satan for a long time. The time is getting very close now. As important as striking them at home is this: Al Qaeda has managed to weave commitments from all of the faithful around the world to begin our work on a much broader scale. Just as Al Qaeda has helped to train our men and given us money and weapons, they have done the same for our brothers around the world. Hamas, Islamic Jihad, and many smaller groups in Sudan, Yemen, Saudi, Palestine, the Philippines and the Far East have all pledged to begin to work together under central leadership. This has never been so. We can never win a war against the infidels until we work together, and that has been impossible for many reasons.

"First, the Americans and the Jews are too good at intercepting our messages when we use radios and phones. We have to use couriers or encrypted, coded e-mail. Not all of our brothers have computers, and that makes this difficult. Message by courier works locally but not globally. Al Qaeda is trying to get computers and training to all of the smaller groups. Second, the chiefs and small group leaders have egos that make it impossible to organize everyone under central leadership. In the past, no one would listen to anyone else's plan. Since our great success in 2001, our brothers are impressed enough with Al Qaeda that they are willing to be part of the bigger plan. They have pledged their alliance to Fadi bin Hakim Wazeeri, blessed be his name."

The others sat quietly, devouring every word. They could already see the Western cities in flames, and leaned closer to their leader, awaiting every next word.

"A plan has begun. We will attack the Great Satan at home in such a way that they will run from our homeland. Their dead will leave a trail from our holy land all the way across the sea to their country. We will follow this trail of corpses and bring death to all of them. Only the true believers of the Koran will be left to guard this Earth as we wait for Paradise."

"God is great," mumbled the others quietly.

"Muktar has told us to head north. That is perfect. We

shall move around the infidel army and head northwest, to
Tajikistan. We have Sunni brothers there who are sympathetic to our mission and who will help us when we get
close.

We have been honored by Fadi Wazeeri to help in his
plans to attack the infidels. We will go northwest to Tajikistan, and meet our Sunni brothers. They will help us
acquire a nuclear warhead from the old Soviet Union
stockpiles—those same Soviets whose blood ran in rivers
in our native Afghanistan." He paused and looked into the
eyes of those around him. Many years of hate glowed in
the eyes of these warriors, who had fought so bravely
against the Soviet Army. Never mind that it was the American CIA who had supplied them with the weapons they
now used against the Americans themselves. It had been an
alliance of convenience, and now with the Soviets destroyed by the Mujahideen faithful, the American infidels
would be next.

Ibrahiim began again, slowly and deliberately, his audi-
ence hanging on his every word. "The Soviets had lots of
nuclear weapons. We will have as much money as we need
from Fadi Wazeeri. With such large sums of money, we
will buy a nuclear weapon for Fadi and transport it to Syria,
with God's will. We will rely on Muktar to get us through
the mountains. In another two months, these mountains will
be impassable even on foot. The infidel army will never be
able to follow us. In any case, they would not cross into
Tajikistan, anyway. It will be a long, difficult journey, but
we will make it, praise Allah."

"God is great," the others mumbled once again.

"I know none of us have ever been into Tajikistan. None
of us has any family there, either. But it is temporary. Once
we strike the blow to the American dogs in their home, they
will leave our land. When they are gone, we will return
home as rightful rulers of our holy lands. In any case, we
cannot stay here. The helicopters are getting closer every

day and night. Now Muktar tells us there are more troops coming. Our brave fighters are too outnumbered. We will wait for the right moment for martyrdom, and then we will strike the infidels."

One of the younger, more hotheaded chieftains spoke up, "Ibrahiim, you say you have heard of a great plan to attack the infidels. Can you share with us any details? We have heard these stories before, yet we wait and wait and no news comes. We must spill their blood now! Blessed be Allah."

"Ibin, you are a great warrior, and I know you are a brave man. There have been other attempts since our great victory in 2001. In fact, there were three large attacks that had been stopped by the Americans and the Jews in the past year. One attempt was through Canada, the other two through Mexico. It has become too difficult on land. That is why this new plan is different. I can only tell you that it will be undetectable to the infidels until it is too late. It is a different method of delivering death to them. When it is closer to the hour, you will have more details."

The sound of rotor blades brought silence to the cave again. It was so close this time that Muktar quickly doused the three lamps that were providing light. He placed his finger to his lips and stood still. After the chopper passed, he turned the lamp back up.

"That is the closest they have ever been. If they sense our lamps they will come here. I have help coming to aid in carrying our belongings. Mules will help us get through the passes to Tajikistan. I suggest we all eat now. As soon as they arrive, we should be leaving immediately."

Ibrahiim nodded his approval, and two other men moved to the supplies in the rear of the cave to serve bread and dried, spiced meats. It would be a very long journey indeed.

CHAPTER 4

Jerusalem

Major David Cohen of Israeli Army Intelligence had just begun his briefing to the assistant secretary of defense and his staff, which included, unbeknownst to them, a Mosad agent from the Collections Department.

"Gentlemen, as you are aware, we captured this man Sufah Zannad." He pressed the remote for the PowerPoint presentation, and the man's face appeared on the screen. "Sufah is a lieutenant for this man, Abu Hassam Obduri, a major Islamic Jihad figure believed to be in Egypt." The screen jumped to an older man with a large white beard. "Obduri, as you know, has been linked to scores of terrorist attacks here in Israel. His walking bombs have killed more than eight hundred men, women, and children. His favorite method had been bus bombings, but apparently he is aspiring to do more.

"Obviously, I didn't travel to Jerusalem to tell you what you already know. I have reason to believe, from the interview with Sufah Zannad, that the Islamic Jihad has now formally linked itself to Hezbollah and Hamas. And it gets worse." He pressed the remote, and a picture of several men appeared on the screen at once, including a picture of Ibrahiim bin Abdul bin al-Bustan.

"These men are not operating around Israel, and yet there is a connection between them and our man Sufah. Of particular concern is this man, Ibrahiim bin Abdul bin al-Bustan. Bustan has direct connection to Al Qaeda. He is currently believed to be in eastern Afghanistan or western Pakistan, possibly in the Northwest Frontier Province area. We know that the Americans are pressing hard in this area with Operation Winding Serpent. Elements of Army Rangers and Marines are working deeper into the Hindu Kush Mountains area looking for nine-eleven masterminds. Intelligence tells us they are pleased with their results so far. There has been no news of their success up in the mountains because reporters can't get up there with them. The terrain is simply too rough for civilians to embed with the troops. We do know, however, that their casualties are down and that they are killing scores of fighters in the mountains. Their method has been to use their Army Rangers to find them, and then call in gunships."

"Easier for them to do that in the moutains than here in Gaza, huh?" interrupted General Shlomo Hod sarcastically.

"No doubt. The only collateral damage might be a sheep," he said with a smile. "Now, as I was saying, we have some cause for alarm. Sufah didn't know details of their specific plan, only a name: "Crescent Fire." There are links, albeit we don't know how, among Hamas, Islamic Jihad, Hezbollah, Al Qaeda, and Harakat ul-Mujahidin. They are working together on something."

"That is ridiculous," grumbled the general.

"Impossible," added a colonel at the end of the table.

The assistant secretary of defense exhaled slowly. "Not impossible. It is unlikely to get these primitive murderers acting in concert, but we have seen it is not impossible. Al

Qaeda has funded all of the groups you mentioned. Al Qaeda has reached out to them in the past, calling for Jihad. Ibrahiim himself has appeared on Arab television calling for holy wars against Jews, Americans, and Christians. In the past, it would be unthinkable that they could act together on a project. That is no longer the case."

The assistant secretary's aide, who was the Mosad officer, added, "The Americans have been monitoring the flow of money between terror organizations since nine-eleven. There is definitive proof of cooperation between some of these groups—"

Assistant Secretary Ben-Zion interrupted: "What do you know about 'Crescent Fire'?"

"Not much, I am afraid," said Major Cohen. "We do know that it is related to a large-scale operation against the Americans. We don't know when, where, or how. Unfortunately, our prisoner died during interrogation, so that well has dried up. We know that it is somehow a coordinated effort among the men you see on the screen, and from what Sufah said—"

"Before you killed him," interrupted a lieutenant colonel at the other end of the table, obviously annoyed at that news.

"We did not kill him. He simply died during routine interrogation—"

Again he was interrupted, this time by Assistant Secretary Ben-Zion. "Gentlemen, please, you can argue later. What did you get out of him?"

"As I was saying," Cohen began again, annoyed at the interruption, "Sufah told us that Hamas and Jihad have been sharing information regularly. They have also been in and out of Syria, Sudan, Afghanistan, and—"

"Afghanistan? That is ridiculous! There are American troops everywhere. Why would they go there now to be surrounded by their enemy?" interrupted General Hod.

"Please, General, let him finish his briefing. Everyone,

please, let him finish without interruptions," said Ben-Zion.

"Thank you, Mr. Secretary," said the major, and he began again. "Afghanistan and even Iraq. The terrorist groups know that phone and radio traffic has been compromised, and they have gone to couriers carrying actual messages. We believe they are also using computers for e-mail; however, we have had no luck breaking any codes on laptops we have seized in the West Bank and Gaza. We believe that these couriers are not only carrying messages, but are also escorting members of their cells to and from other cells. In other words, they are acting as platoons in a company-size force under central command."

Cohen pressed the remote and showed Ibrahiim's face again, this time alone, and looking older. "This is a more recent photo. This is Ibrahiim again. We believe he is the man they are all reporting to; however, he is not in charge of the entire operation." He pressed the remote and showed a Saudi in bisht, kufiyyah, ghutra, and igaal, the traditional robes and headwear of Saudi men. "This serpent is Fadi bin Hakim Wazeeri. He has personally given millions to every Islamic fundamentalist organization in the world and is the current head of Al Qaeda. I know you all know his name. Look carefully at his face. Now look carefully at this man," he said, as he advanced to the next photo. It was a grainy picture of a man in combat fatigues holding an AK-47. He still wore his headdress, but it was the same man.

"This picture was taken in Afghanistan. The photographer said he had interviewed Wazeeri near the Khyber Pass." He pressed the button, and another slide appeared on the large screen. It was the same man, back in traditional robes, in a desert camp. "This photo shows Wazeeri in the western desert of Iraq, right before the Americans invaded." Another click, and the picture was Wazeeri yet again, this time with several armed men, apparently near water, but with no way to tell where. "In this picture, we believe he is in Sudan, perhaps Port Sudan. He had been seen back and forth in Sudan and Egypt over several months."

He turned off the projector and faced the men and women in the room. "Wazeeri has been all over the Middle East for more than a year. We and the Americans are apparently always a few steps behind him. It was difficult enough just getting these photos. Fortunately, someone at Al-Jazeera has good contacts and has had opportunities to film him. I would give my right arm to be that close to him. In any case, I believe Wazeeri is traveling around personally building a coalition of terror organizations to strike a major blow to the United States.

"Mr. Secretary, I advise you to contact the Americans and allow me to debrief them on our findings. A centrally organized army of terror networks planning a single large event is a very disturbing and very plausible concept at this time."

The assistant secretary took off his glasses and rubbed his eyes. "You are right, of course, Major. The Americans need to be notified at once. I am disturbed, however, that we have no additional information on 'Crescent Fire.' I am sure you have looked into this further. What are you hearing?"

"Sufah had no knowledge of the operation beyond the name, and the fact that it was something of very large scale planned against the Americans, not us. He also knew that it was linked through Al Qaeda and that Wazeeri was the central figure. Beyond that, he knew nothing, of that I am quite certain. He would have told me if he knew."

The lieutenant colonel at the end of the table couldn't help commenting, "We will never know because you killed him. How many prisoners have died during your interrogations, David? We are supposed to be different than these common murderers—"

General Hod cut him off. "That's enough, Gidon. Major

Cohen's interrogations have helped prevent more than a hundred attacks on our children. He is not the murderer here. While I encourage you, Major, to show restraint and not seriously injure your prisoners, I understand your difficult position. The lieutenant colonel is correct in that we must make sure we are always on the side of justice and righteousness, because the media love to make us the villains, but we also have a duty to defend our country from these animals. That is enough conversation on this topic."

Hod continued to the assistant secretary, "Mr. Secretary, I concur with the major about contacting the Americans. We must give them access to any information regarding this intelligence. It is unfortunate they didn't heed our warnings prior to nine-eleven, but I don't think they will fail to listen to us again."

Assistant Secretary Ben-Zion stood up. "Thank you all for your efforts. I have another meeting regarding last night's terror attack on the school bus and preschool. I tell you, I'm not sure how much longer we can dance around with these people. If I could convince the prime minister, we would carpet-bomb the lot of them. That is all for now."

The group said their good-byes and headed out of the office.

"Major, a moment alone please," said Ben-Zion. The major walked back in.

"Tell me what's in your gut," Ben-Zion asked.

The major pursed his lips and shook his head. "I have never seen this type of coordination among these animals. A lion is a dangerous foe. A pride of lions is exponentially worse. If they were to hit the United States with, God forbid, a nuclear weapon or chemical or biological agent, the cost in lives would be immense. Moreover, their economy is still weak from 2001; another attack of that magnitude would send them into a tailspin. The war in Iraq is costing billions, and no one other than the British will help them. It amazes me that their so-called allies stand back and do nothing, as if appeasing these people will free them from harm."

Ben-Zion answered him quickly, "Do not be so amazed. The French, the Germans, the Russians, they were making millions under the table from the UN food program. Then the Americans come in and screw everything up. Hell, the Americans actually want food money to go to *food*. The Frenchmen may have to sell their homes in Nice and Monaco. The Germans might not be able to buy the latest Porsche—"

"Yes, you are right, of course. No one talks about that scandal at all. It's like it never happened. I will keep working on 'Crescent Fire,' Mr. Secretary. Pray God I find out what it means before we see it on the evening news."

CHAPTER 5

CIA Headquarters, Langley, Virginia

Agents Still and Hollahan entered the large building and walked to the information desk. There, they were given badges and escorted to a nonpublic area, where they were checked in. Since they were carrying weapons, they had to have their IDs rechecked and then sign in before heading upstairs.

As they walked down the spotless hallway on new polished granite and marble, Still smiled and shook his head. "I still can't get over this place, man. We work out of that shithole in Jersey our whole careers, and these guys have fountains, priceless artwork, new everything. Damn, man, this place is nicer than my house."

"Yeah? Maybe you can move in," answered Hollahan. The CIA staffer who led them to the conference building ignored their conversation until they arrived at their destination.

"Mr. Weaver will see you now, gentlemen. Have a nice day." With that, he wheeled around and was gone.

"Walks like a Marine, don't ya think?" asked Still.

"Yeah, definitely a jarhead," answered Hollahan.

The young staffer was still in earshot. Without turning his head he simply yelled a "hoooo-aaaaa" and continued down the hall, making sure his heels struck the granite with each step as hard as possible.

They entered the office and found a secretary sitting in a small outer room.

"Welcome to Langley, gentlemen," she said. "Mr. Weaver is expecting you."

Still gave an exaggerated low bow and said, "And thank you so much, good lady."

He turned to Hollahan, "Just like being back in Jersey, except Angie usually says something like, 'Go *f* yourself.'"

The secretary smiled and went back to her work, and the two FBI agents walked into Weaver's room. It was a beautiful office with a large wooden desk and Persian rug on the floor. The Stars and Stripes stood in the corner, next to pictures of the president and vice president of the United States of America. The room even smelled new. A large double window had a view of the koi pond and gardens out front.

"Yup, just like our office in Jersey," mumbled Still.

Weaver stood and walked around his desk, extending his hand with a hardy "Hello."

"Welcome to Langley, gentlemen," he said.

"So I hear," said Still.

Weaver was puzzled but let it go. "I appreciate you men coming to see me," he began. "Have a seat and we'll chat awhile. I'd also like you to meet a few people while you're here." He yelled out to his secretary, "Margie, send Cicero in, please."

A quiet "Yes, sir" came back from her outer office.

"Can I get you guys some coffee or something?" he asked. They both said no and sat down in large leather chairs. "Okay, I'll cut to the chase, gentlemen. First of all, call me Roy or 'Red' if you want, but no titles or 'Mr.'s' among working crews. When you are out working, get in the habit of using first names only."

Still shook his head. "This is like spy school already. I knew it—"

"Hardly, Bob. Or is it Robert?"

"Bob is fine."

Hollahan answered when Roy looked at him. "William or Will, not Bill."

"Fair enough. Bob and William, meet Anthony Cicero."

They turned in their seats as the door opened and a very large Caucasian man walked into the room. He was one of very few people who dwarfed Still. Anthony—"Tee" to his friends—was six-eight and must have weighed at least two-fifty. He shook hands with both agents and flashed a big, toothy grin.

Hollahan laughed. "Ya know, Bob, he looks like a young white version of *you*!"

Still laughed. "You a 'baller?"

"Played linebacker for four years at Purdue," he answered with a smile.

"If he wasn't such a lard ass, he'd have made the pros, too," said Weaver.

"Too slow for linebacker, too small for line. Story of my life," said Tee.

Anthony Cicero walked around to the vacant chair and sat after shaking hands with Weaver. "You just starting?" he asked.

"Yeah, you're right on time. Fellas, I am going to lay out some information that is all highly classified. We are going to have a theoretical discussion about philosophy and politics and war and the like. We are going to see if we like each other and would be comfortable working on a project together. When we are finished, you will decide if you would like to be a part of something much different than you are used to. If you say no, that's fine and you go back to Jersey, no hard feelings. We'll even buy you dinner for driving down and put you up in a nice hotel. If you say yes, you will still go home, but that will be for one week to take care of personal business, and to explain to your family and friends that you won't be around much for the next six months to a year."

The two men looked at each other and grimaced.

"I know it's a big commitment, but we simply cannot rotate personnel on something as big as this. Frankly, this whole thing may be over in a month, which would mean very bad news because we won't figure this out in a month, and if we don't, lots of Americans will be dead. If you do decide to work with our people, you will be undertaking a project that will have you doing things in different ways than you are used to, to put it mildly—"

Hollahan interrupted, "Excuse me, sir, but I have to ask you: Why us? I'm approaching retirement age. I'm a little old to be running around in the desert."

"With all due respect, I agree with you, Will. You and Bob would not be running around. You are not spies; you are not combat soldiers anymore, although I am very aware of your combat records. You would be doing analysis work, running interference as necessary—more on that in a moment—and collecting data and coordinating some operations. While you have not been specifically trained for this type of thing, you wouldn't be doing this alone. You would be surrounded by top-notch people, and they will help you every step of the way."

"Will you be there as well?"

"Actually, no. I will have no idea what you are doing. When you are finished, you will come home and retire with major improvements to your pension and grade promotions. What happens while you are working stays out there where you are working. The information will not be connected directly to this office, nor any other office in the United States. You will have United Nations credentials, should you need them for access to foreign ports, etc., but most likely you will not. The United Nations will not actually find you on their payroll, either."

Still and Hollahan sat back and looked at each other. "Sounds like a setup to make us scapegoats if something goes wrong," Hollahan said.

"Actually, the reason for the offshore setup is because this operation will be handled differently than those in the past. POTUS is in a difficult position. With the exception of the Brits, who have proven themselves to us yet again, and the Israelis, most of our allies have turned tail and run. They all have their reasons; mostly it's all about money."

"Like that's a big shocker," said Still.

"Yeah, well, the Frogs and the Krauts have been making big bucks with the U.N. money going to Iraq. Payoffs up the wazoo. That investigation is continuing, but won't be your task. Your task would be more hands-on. Let me put it this way: Let's say that an organization was set up that operated outside of the United States but had no official connection to the United States. Such an organization would not be under the restrictions of the United States Constitution."

"Sounds like we are all going to jail," said Hollahan.

"We're just talking theory, of course. An organization like this would be set up carefully and would use places that are safe, very safe—like maybe a battleship, or a jail in Guantánamo Bay. This group would have the best equipment and a highly trained group of operatives from various specialty backgrounds. Some might be boots-on-the-ground types, some might be Intel, maybe some organizational and analytical types, like yourselves. You getting the picture?"

"Like I said, sounds like jail time," said Hollahan.

"Well, as I stated at the beginning of our conversation, this is all theoretical, and you can simply tell me you aren't interested and go back to New Jersey, no hard feelings."

Still looked at Cicero, who hadn't said a word. "You goin'?" he asked.

"Wouldn't miss it for the world," he said and smiled.

Weaver sat back in his chair and said, "Tee here would be working with you daily. He is a trained field agent, and he has combat experience from Desert Storm One. He is a former airborne Ranger, a demolitions expert, and speaks some Arabic. He would be coordinating the special unit we have been discussing. We refer to it simply as Counter Operations."

"Counter to what?" asked Hollahan.

"Counter to the clear and present danger facing us from the Middle East," said Weaver. "You two were asked to join because of your success with the Bulovski case. You made a lot of people happy with your work on that one. You did a lot more to save the world than you give yourselves credit for. That's what we need now—quick-thinking people like yourselves who will aggressively pursue all leads and won't miss details. There will be men and women on the ground to gather intelligence and do the legwork. You won't actually be doing that part of the mission. But make no mistake: If you sign on to work with us, your work will be critical to the safety of the United States."

"It sounds like you have something specific going on. Why not use the usual means to gather intel and deal with it that way?" asked Hollahan.

"You are correct; we do have something specific. I won't go into that until you have signed on. Suffice it to say it is scary shit. The usual means aren't turning up intel fast enough, and with the lousy press POTUS has been getting for our operations in Iraq and Afghanistan, he can't afford to have some guy pop up with an ACLU lawyer saying how he was harassed and abused by the FBI, CIA, or whatever other initials you can think of."

"So this is pressing?" asked Hollahan.

"Very. Unfortunately, we don't know *how* pressing. As I said before, if this 'incident' were to occur now or a month from now, I think we're screwed. We don't have anything solid enough to act on yet. That's why the special unit.

Quite frankly, *if* a special unit were to be formed outside the U.S. it would be to work outside the laws of the U.S. for the purposes of protecting the U.S. Sounds ridiculous, but with tens of thousands of lives potentially at stake, we simply cannot afford to go by the book and lose."

"Let me ask you something, Red: If everyone knows the system is so screwed up, why isn't anyone doing anything about it? This is the kind of shit that happens and gets people like us arrested and put in jail. The press would kill everyone, and POTUS would find himself impeached. You really ready to take a risk like that?" asked Still.

"Word is, the director had a private meeting with the president to discuss the intel that brought us here. After a two-hour meeting, POTUS said, 'Do what you have to do, regardless of what happens to me.' He doesn't want to know how it happens, but he wants to make sure we have results. Don't misunderstand me now; all of our normal resources are being used as we speak. The problem is, we are grasping at straws. Using a new team doesn't mean we stop using traditional methods. We just need additional resources, and we need them fast. All the field agents and dark resources we lost in the past twenty years have caught up to us, and now we are behind the eight ball.

"The Israelis tried to help us by attempting to capture a Hamas leader who may have had information useful to us. This Hamas figure just happened to have a bomb-making factory downstairs in a medical building. The Israelis storm the place and he blows himself up, killing half a dozen commandos and wiping out half of a children's ward. The Palestinians blame the Israelis for massacring their children, never mind that the Israelis didn't pull the detonator. So now, any chance of getting good intel out of Gaza or the West Bank is almost impossible, with another war going on over there."

"The Israelis should have carpet-bombed them a year ago," mumbled Still.

"Yeah, well, people make comments like that, but no one would do it. But what if they had? World opinion couldn't get any lower of the Israelis anyway, so why not? If they had carpet-bombed the Palestinians, they would have been sanctioned, attacked in the world press, and on and on, and in the end, the terrorists would have stopped blowing up school buses out of fear of being annihilated. The world can't pussyfoot around with these people. When the Russians were the world's 'bad guy,' everybody looked at them as the evil empire, but nobody ever fucked with them. Ever. If they did, they wound up very dead. We're the world's 'good guy,' and everybody hates us. Even the countries that get our foreign aid hate us. What if we started acting like the bad guy for a while? Do we care if everybody hates us more than they do already if we have rid the world of terror?"

"That's a slippery slope, man. Whatcha gonna do? Start having death squads without trials for people who disagree with us?" asked Still. "Gonna start lynching us colored folk again?"

"No death squads for people who disagree with us. But for people who blow us up? Yeah. I have no problem with that. Let me ask you something: If we captured the guys responsible for nine-eleven and some tricky ACLU lawyer got him off, but you knew he was guilty, you were a hundred percent sure, if you had the chance, would you whack the guy?"

Still and Hollahan exchanged glances. "That's a lot of 'ifs,' but you know the answer to that. I had friends in those buildings, too."

"Okay, so hear what I'm saying. Look, we're not looking to start running a secret government; this is mission-specific. When this mission is over, everyone retires."

"Until the next mission," said Hollahan.

"No. You have my word on that. This is not a new agency; this is a unit for a specific purpose. When the threat is gone, the unit goes away."

Still looked at Hollahan. "What do you think?"

"I don't know. I want to think about it. Six months to a year out of the U.S.? That's a long time. I been there, done that, remember?"

"Yeah, I hear ya. Who's gonna water my plants?" Still said and smiled.

Hollahan looked back at Weaver. "Give me something more. Give me something about the mission. This is a big decision, Red."

"Crescent Fire," said Weaver.

"What's that?" he asked.

Weaver folded his arms. "I have no idea, but we're going to find out."

CHAPTER 6

Port Sudan

Port Sudan was a loud, dirty place. While there was some tourist activity, mostly people heading across the Red Sea to Saudi Arabia, for the most part Port Sudan was an industrial, crowded mess. With some offshore oil production, it was common to see large tankers all over the port. Most of these were older hulks, as the larger, newer ships typically were headed farther north, toward Egypt and larger, oil-producing nations. Port Sudan was more of a relic of the world's oil ports. It was an old port, established by the British near the turn of the twentieth century, and looked like not much had been done to improve it since.

People and animals mixed in the crowded, narrow streets, the smells from both filling the markets and small cafés. Tiny cars, honking and their drivers cursing as if that would move traffic along, tried to move through the throngs of beggars and merchants. The cars were old and belched black, choking smoke on the goats and mules and that dirtied the cobblestone streets and alleys. Arab sheiks in traditional dress pushed through men in business suits on oil business, who pushed away children wearing rags and begging for coins.

With the country in chaos or civil war for most of the past hundred years, Sudan remained a dangerous place for Westerners. There was little to no regulation of what came and left the port, which is what made it so desirable for the likes of Fadi Wazeeri. Wazeeri had been in and out of Sudan more times in the past three months than he had in the previous twenty years. His project was coming along fairly well, although securing all the necessary materials was getting frustrating.

The first item on his shopping list was a medium-size oil tanker, preferably an older one. The single-hulled tankers were cheaper to buy, since they would be obsolete in another decade or so due to world ecological regulations, but it really wasn't about the money. Wazeeri had plenty of money. The older oil tankers were simply easier to convert for his uses. With less pipes to wrestle with, his engineers and construction crews would have less work than on a more modern ship.

The plan was simple enough: Acquire a Scud-B mobile missile launcher. For the right amount of money, this was not undoable. There were still a few hundred of those floating around Syria, sent over from Iraq before the second Iraq war broke out. Saddam knew they would be destroyed before they could be used, so he simply buried them in the desert, or sent them out of Iraq to friendly neighbors. A Scud-B could handle a fifteen-kiloton nuclear warhead. If a nuclear warhead was unobtainable, high explosives, chemicals, or biological agents could be used in its place.

The Scud would be loaded into a specially constructed oil tanker, where it would lay belowdecks, invisible to any visual inspection. The tanker would head north through the Red Sea, out the Mediterranean, and across the Atlantic. While the Scud-B had a decent enough range of three hundred kilometers, it wouldn't really be tested. Rather, the oil tanker would get close enough to Washington, D.C., so that when the payload doors opened, which was actually the "deck" of the ship, and the Scud-B stood up and was fired, it could be "downtown" within a few moments. With so little time for American radar to light up, the damage would be unstoppable. The American military community wouldn't know of the attack much before they could see the White House melting on CNN.

The most difficult parts of the plan would be refitting the ship to construct a deck that could open with hydraulic doors, and then acquiring a nuclear warhead. Rather than build a hydraulic system for elevating the missile, they would merely load a truck-launched missile into the tanker. This would keep things much simpler, since the same truck would be used to haul the missile from its point of origin to the ship. The other little chore would be making a doorway and ramp system large enough for the missile-carrying truck to drive into the refitted tanker, where it would remain belowdecks.

The difficulty of acquiring the nuclear warhead was much more challenging. Feelers had been put out to North Korea, Iran, and even Pakistani radicals. There had been no luck communicating with the North Koreans, which was a shame, because if there *was* a way to nuke D.C. without getting blamed for it, they would probably jump right in. Iran, while sympathetic to the war against the Western Crusaders, was too afraid of the United States to permit any ties with a nuclear attack on the United States. They believed, and probably rightfully so, that a nuclear detonation in the United States just might lead to a nuclear holocaust in the entire Middle East. The Pakistani government was being very supportive of the United States, but its leadership was constantly challenged by radicals within their country.

Wazeeri had poured tons of money to the Pakistani

rebels to try to unseat the president. With the seizure of Pakistan's nuclear weapons, Wazeeri's problem would be over. So far, the Pakistani army had received help from the United States, and the rebels were constantly being knocked off before they could do much damage. If the time for the ship to sail came before a nuke could be obtained, then Wazeeri would settle for a chemical or biological attack instead. If that also proved undoable, then a conventional payload would at least strike terror into the hearts of the infidels, although it wouldn't be on the scale he was looking for.

Wazeeri stood at the dock, looking out into the harbor. There were several large tankers a few hundred yards offshore. Another man approached Wazeeri, also dressed in traditional Saudi garb.

"She is the one farthest to the south. She is smaller than the others, and old and rusty. But she is seaworthy, and no one would look at her twice. She is registered out of Turkey, so the Americans won't pay attention to her movements when we get close to our destination," said the dark-skinned man.

"The *Crescent King* will be renamed when we get out to sea, my friend. She will become the Crescent Fire. Fire from Allah, God be praised, that will be hurled from the heavens like a sword from Muhammad himself. The infidels will see what it is like to be attacked in their homes, in their beds. The Zionists will burn for a thousand years in a nuclear wasteland," spat Wazeeri.

"We have not been having much luck with our search for the weapon, Fadi," said the robed man. "The missile was easy; the payload is proving difficult."

"Yes, I know, my friend. But do not be worried. If it is God's will, we will get a nuclear warhead and kill them by the tens of thousands with one great fire, Allah be praised."

"I have spoken to our friends in Syria, Fadi. They are a little nervous about American satellites. They have moved the truck launcher underground to a temporary hiding place, but it is still two hundred kilometers from the coast. I have to tell them when we will be there with the ship to pick it up. Do we have a time frame yet? These are nervous people. They will hide the Scud for only so long before they panic. If we lose this one, it will be much more difficult to get another one. The Americans are watching very closely."

Wazeeri pondered that a moment. "The engineers are coming from Saudi in three days. Once they are here, we will have a better idea on time. We cannot have a thousand men working on this ship, my brother. We need a small crew who will not ask questions—preferably men who have worked on ships before. If they can refit the deck and make an interior deck within the hull in three months, we could be through the Suez Canal by the end of November. Allah be praised, we could be off the coast of Washington by December twenty-fifth. The infidel Christmas will be something they will never forget." Wazeeri smiled, his yellowed teeth making him look like a jackal circling prey.

CHAPTER 7

Washington, D.C.

Still and Hollahan had just walked out of the Vietnam Veterans Memorial and walked silently to a bench. They sat without speaking for almost ten minutes. Still, who usually couldn't go for more than five minutes without joking, wiped a tear with the back of his hand. A few minutes ago he had found the names of three good friends from a different lifetime, and it all came crashing down on him like it was yesterday.

Hollahan was the first to speak. "Ya know, Bob, it was a lot different for me. I spent most of my time flying around, taking pictures. Only had a couple of close calls the whole time I was there. The intelligence outfit I was in was small, and for the year I was there, we didn't lose one man. Had a few birds come back with some holes in them for sure, but no one ever was killed in combat."

Still cleared his throat. "I was in the jungle for almost two solid years, man. Khe Sanh, Quang Tri, Phu Bai . . . we were in the *shit*, man. I saw a few names back there sorta freaked me out, ya know? This one cat, Sanchez, a little dude, he was an engineer attached to our platoon. He was a tunnel rat. Made him a tunnel rat because he was only like, five foot. We used to joke about him not getting drafted 'cause he was too short. He told us he enlisted and asked for combat infantry. You believe that shit?"

"Yeah—and you volunteered for a second tour, remember?"

"Yeah, but I'm stupid. Sanchez, he was a smart kid. Anyway, one day he goes down into a tunnel complex and comes up after an hour, covered in blood. Tells us that he found a whole bunker complex. So we call in engineers and support units, but Sanchez won't wait, says he needs to get back in there and see what's what. We never saw him alive after that. The engineers found him in the tunnels. He had found a regimental headquarters. The bunker probably could have housed a few hundred men under where we were standing. Sanchez had killed a shitload of them with grenades and his forty-five before they got him. The gooks always took their dead when they could, but Sanchez had apparently killed almost all of them before they got him, so they were still down there with him. Engineers came up from the tunnels and asked who else had been down there with him. They couldn't believe it was just Sanchez by himself—there musta been a few dozen dinks down there with him. He got a Silver Star for that. Too bad he never saw it, 'cause he woulda thought it was cool, being so gung-ho and all. Anyway, I saw his name just now. Saw a couple other guys I knew, too . . . one of them is up there on the wall because he saved all of our asses."

Still wiped another tear from his eye and looked away from Hollahan, trying not to get caught crying. Still took a long, slow breath, trying to compose himself.

"So what are we going to do, Bob? We gonna reup? You think you want to be away from home another year? And I'm still not sure I buy this whole story about just doing one mission. I mean, I trust most of the guys we work for, but so did Ollie North. What if this whole thing is just a cover story for something else? You ready to be used as a scapegoat?" Hollahan said.

Still cleared his throat. "Man, I'm not sure about anything anymore. I don't know what to think, but I'll do it. Guys like Sanchez and Jensen would do it. How can I not do it? I've been divorced forever, no kids, no serious girlfriend. Who better than me? But if you don't want to go, that's cool, man. No shit, really. I understand you got other things going on here. If I leave, nobody other than you would even notice."

"Yeah, but if you go, I have to go. You'll go save the world and I'll have to listen to that shit for the rest of my life. I'd rather face Al Qaeda than listen to you dis me for the next twenty years."

Still smiled his famous toothy grin and slapped Hollahan on the thigh. "Let's go get a beer. Hell, I'll even buy you lunch. Then we'll call the spooks and tell them we want to be secret agent men, too. Maybe we'll get a little decoder ring and shit," said Still.

"Well, if you are buying, let's go someplace good. This only happened one other time that I can think of, and that was when I turned forty, so you *know* how long ago that was."

The two men stood and gave each other a hug, a sign of affection that almost never occurred, then walked out of the Mall, both of them stealing last glances at the black granite wall with the names of fifty-eight thousand of their brothers on it. It would be the last time either of them would come back to that painful monument.

CHAPTER 8

Washington, D.C.

Not far from where Still and Hollahan were deciding their futures, a member of the Israeli embassy was sitting with a young woman having an iced tea. They looked like every other young couple in an area of D.C. that was always crawling with tourists, except that they had each come directly from their offices for a face-to-face meeting.

Amy Lang was thirty-nine years old and very fit-looking. She was a runner, and it showed in her legs. The long skirt didn't cover her calves when she crossed her legs, and the young Israeli couldn't help sneaking peeks when she wasn't looking at him. From a country where most women were dark-haired and olive-skinned, Mitchell Weisel considered looking at the blond, blue-eyed woman a treat. He had worked in the embassy for four years. No one in the embassy, not even the ambassador himself, knew that Mitchell was a Mosad agent. Of course, the embassy knew that there would be at least one somewhere in the office, but no one asked or looked for anything unusual. Mitchell had used

Amy as his contact three times in the past six months, as things heated up in the Middle East.

Mitchell casually glanced around and sized up the crowd. Once satisfied that he wasn't being watched, he smiled and asked, "So to what do I owe the pleasure of your company, Amy? Usually I am the one who requests these meetings."

She looked around casually and then said, "We are getting very concerned about the last piece of news you gave us. We still only have a name and no details. While we appreciate the heads-up you gave us, we have no idea what we are looking for. We need more than you have given us. If you are holding anything back for a rainy day, it's pouring."

"Let's take a walk," he said. With that, he slid five dollars under his iced-tea glass and stood up. She followed him out of the small café and walked down the block, toward a park. When they were inside the park, she took his arm in hers and they slowed their pace, looking like another couple in love enjoying the day.

"We have lost four agents within three weeks," he began. "That has never happened to us before. They were all working independently, on different projects altogether. You know that our agency works differently than your CIA; we are much smaller and our operatives are given more latitude than yours. It is very unusual for us to hit a string of what you would call bad luck like this. It would be one thing if they were all on the same project and their cover was blown, but these were all good agents on separate assignments."

"Where were they working?" Amy asked.

"In the Middle East—in four different countries. They didn't even know each other. We are convinced that it is no one inside. Only the director himself knew what each agent was doing and where. We have reason to believe that many different terrorist organizations that never worked together before are starting to share information. I can't go into great detail, but we believe that Hamas, Hezbollah, Harakat ul-Mujahidin, and others are all working with Al Qaeda."

"Oh, please, Mitchell. That's quite a leap. I know it would be very convenient for Israel to be able to lump Hamas and Hezbollah into the same crew as Al Qaeda, but I don't think these groups would ever actually work together and share intel."

"Think what you want, but I am telling you, it is happening. We are working on getting you some hard evidence, but that is difficult at best," he said.

They turned down a path that led past a garden to a large water fountain. The rushing and splashing of the water were welcomed background noises in the otherwise quiet park.

Mitchell began again, "You know, your country makes war on terrorists on a much broader scale than we do. Why is it that Israel is criticized for surgical strikes when you are allowed to invade entire countries without the U.N. declaring it illegal? We erect a fence to keep out terrorists, and we get criticized. What about the fence between you and Mexico? Are the Mexicans getting ready to invade America?"

Amy smiled. "Some would say they already have. Just ask the congressmen from Texas and California."

"Yes, I read your papers. But you are making jokes. Dozens of countries all over the world have erected fences to protect their borders. Why can't we? How long would America sit back and watch their children murdered every day before you decided to clean house?"

"I didn't call you to talk politics, Mitchell," Amy said.

"Yes, I know. You called me because you need our help. Well, we need your help, too, is all I am saying. Perhaps the United States could be a bit more vocal in their support of Israel, and stop kissing and hugging the Palestinians. Now, as far as new information goes, there is none beyond what I told you. The animals of the world apparently are coagulating like a little cesspool. They have a common enemy that is uniting them, and for once, it isn't just us. They want to kill little shiksas as much as Jews these days."

Amy looked at him and asked, "Shiksas? Remind me to look it up."

"Shiksa, a cute non-Jewish girl," he said, smiling.

"Careful, Prince Charming, I'm not kosher," she warned. "Look, I understand the frustration of your government, but let's face it, the United States is your biggest ally. I'm not sure how much more we can do and still be able to put gas in our cars. I will relay your concerns up the chain of command."

He frowned at her sarcastically.

"Really, Mitch, I will explain things just as you have to me. In the meantime, I need you to stay in touch. We have a few things to work on, and we are going to try to shake the trees, but so far we haven't had any luck."

"Care to share?" he asked.

"Sorry, no can do. Just know that our government is taking the latest threats very seriously. We have nothing to go on other than the name you gave us, Crescent Fire, but so far it comes up zero. Rest assured we will share whatever we find, and we trust you will do the same."

"As always, you know we are your friends," he said. "Next time I think we should meet inside a building. No sense taking any chances."

"Getting jittery, Mitch? That's not like you," said Amy.

"Four agents, Amy. You bet I'm jittery. Something big is happening out there. And I'm starting to think 'out there' is over here, too. By the way," he said in a whisper, leaning to her ear, "I don't keep kosher, so you could easily be on the menu."

Amy's eyes gave away her surprise, and her smile gave

away her attraction to the young Mosad agent. She gently punched his arm and tried to casually laugh it off.

The two of them strolled out of the park and gave each other a quick hug and kiss like two good friends in case anyone was watching, then went in separate directions. Mitch went back to the Israeli embassy, Amy back to her little office in the basement of the FBI building.

CHAPTER 9

Port Sudan

Kareem Wazeeri stood on the rusty old deck of the oil tanker. He was a cousin of and trusted soldier for Fadi. A Saudi engineer was with him, having just finished inspecting the hulk from stem to stern. Wazeeri had explained what he wanted done, and had alluded to smuggling to avoid any questions from his new subcontractor.

A large door, at dock level, would need to be constructed into the side of the vessel, with internal ramps that would be directly below the deck. The deck itself would need some hydraulics and would need to be cut and refitted to become doors. It was all very basic work, all things considered.

"Cosmetics," Al-Ahmed explained. "How fast do you need this completed?"

"Three months tops," said Kareem.

Al-Ahmed dropped his jaw. "Three months? Kareem, this is not super-complicated work, but to get the materials we need and put a crew together this size will be difficult so quickly."

"The materials have been secured already, my friend. The decking material is here in Sudan already. It can be moved from the ship it is on whatever day you want it. The ramps will be constructed from corrugated steel decking. I have more than enough. I also have enough welding supplies to outfit fifty workers, although I would prefer twenty-five or thirty if that is enough to complete the job on time. A smaller, discreet crew is preferred."

"If you want this done in three months, I will need all fifty, Kareem. But not to worry—the workers in these parts know better than to ask questions. If you are willing to pay a little more than average, I can steal workers from the ship-yard. They know their way around ships and would save us much time and aggravation."

"Agreed. Tomorrow you will tell my associate Kufi exactly what you need. I will not speak to you again, my friend, but you will be paid a twenty-thousand-dollar bonus when you complete this on time. For every week you shave off of the schedule, I will add another twenty thousand as well. Kufi will be here on board ship until the work is finished. He has a captain to take the ship out when it is finished."

"You are most generous, Kareem Wazeeri. I wish I had more time—I could make the ship look brand-new for you."

"No, my friend, I don't want it to look brand-new. I want her to look exactly like she does right now—an old oil tanker that no one will ever look at twice."

"May she serve you well, my friend, as God wills," he said, and then bowed slightly.

The men said their good-byes, and Kareem walked quickly down the ramp to a small launch that skipped out of sight within moments, heading out of the bay and into the Red Sea. Al-Ahmed smiled as he looked at the ship he would convert. Of course, in his mind, he was curious as to what Kareem would be doing with the ship, but would never ask in a million years. Perhaps Kareem's cousin Fadi himself would be smuggling weapons to continue his jihad, he thought. Whatever he was up to, he always paid well, and Al-Ahmed didn't care what Fadi did as long as it made him rich.

Kareem continued out to sea to a small luxury yacht, where he would see his cousin face-to-face. It would be the first time in a year that he would see Fadi, who was constantly on the move. They would enjoy a few days in the Red Sea until everything was under way on board the ship that would become the *Crescent Fire*. After that, they would head north through the Suez and wait off the shore of Syria for their tanker. Once there, they would load the Scud-B and get into the Mediterranean, where they could disappear at sea until they procured either a nuke or some other weapon of mass destruction. That, unfortunately, was proving to be a frustrating part of their plan.

CHAPTER 10

The Hindu Kush Mountains

A small team of U.S. Army Rangers was working its way through the narrow mountain trails. It was slow going in extremely rough terrain, made tougher by the heavy pack each man carried. The eight-man team was irregular for Rangers, but they had been "thinking outside the box," as their colonel liked to say. Rather than travel in larger, stronger, platoon-size groups and risk being seen and ambushed, they had taken to working as long-range recon patrols, similar to LRRP teams used in Vietnam. The major difference between these small teams and the teams of the '60s and '70s was the major improvement to instant information and communication.

Using laptop-style computers, the team could link to satellite information for terrain mapping, instant location through GPS, and heat sensing and far-infrared searching. With a few keystrokes, a Ranger could search an area of a few hundred kilometers for heat signatures, for best possible terrain routing, or to see where his fellow Rangers were working. Air support was always within ten minutes or so, weather permitting, and cruise missiles were available for special cases. At five hundred miles per hour, a cruise missile was only a few minutes away from almost anywhere in their area of operation.

The squad had fanned out into a small perimeter facing in all directions and squatted down silently, watching the mountains around them as their sergeant sat in the center of the group with their captain. The sergeant was on a satellite phone speaking to air support.

"Tango Two to Spooky One, we are at waypoint four taking ten awaiting SatIn."

Tango Two was their team, which was at their fourth map reference point. Spooky One was the AC-130 gunship assigned as ground support and which had just refueled in the sky a few miles from their position. The AC-130U gunship, known as "Spooky" in the military, is one of the most advanced weapons systems in the world. With a crew of thirteen, the gunship is a modified heavy cargo plane fitted with a 25mm Gatling gun that fires eighteen hundred rounds per minute and has a 40mm Bofors cannon and a 105mm howitzer. All of the weapons are mounted on the same side of the aircraft, which circles its targets and rains destruction on those unfortunate enough to be called the enemy. With in-air refueling capabilities, this translates as a floating artillery barrage whenever called on. The results, for the soldiers who have seen it in action, are nothing short of spooky. With the ability to fire on multiple targets more than a kilometer away, there is simply nowhere to hide from Spooky.

"SatIn" was codespeak for satellite intelligence. The squad was taking a ten-minute break to review satellite pictures, and checking in with air support to see if they found anything with their own infrared sensors.

"Tango Two, this is Spooky One, confirm waypoint four. No contacts. We are topped off and standing by. Over."

"Roger Spooky One, we will advise ASAP. Over and out."

The squad quietly fanned out in a larger perimeter, moving silently through the rocky terrain. They wore the Ghillie suits usually reserved for snipers, but stealth being so important, the army actually spent the extra money outfitting the small Ranger squad. Ghillie suits weighed only about three pounds, but with hundreds of pieces of fabric resembling leaves and dirt, the squad became invisible even to a close-by trained eye.

One of the corporals was tapping away at his laptop, linking to a spy satellite hundreds of miles overhead.

"Sergeant, I have something," he said very quietly. "Looks weak, but it is definitely bigger than a bunny."

"Location?" asked the sergeant.

"Half a click due north . . . straight up," he said, pointing up to the very high climb ahead.

The sergeant moved to his corporal and looked over his shoulder at his small screen. A green contour map of their location was outlined on a black screen. There was a very small, very faint orange heat signature north of their position, which showed up as eight very bright orange dots, each labeled T2 for Tango Two. If the corporal were to expand his view to a larger map, he would be able to view the positions of Tango One and Tango Three, who were all within five kilometers of each other.

The sergeant motioned to his men, who followed his lead north up the steep side of the mountainous terrain in front of them. Half a kilometer on flat ground is no more than a few moments. Half a kilometer moving silently straight up a mountain with a sixty-pound pack and weapons, while keeping an eye out for booby traps and snipers, is a different story. After fifteen minutes, the lead Ranger pulled himself over a small ledge. Only his head, covered with his Kevlar and Ghillie suit, was over the ledge when he froze. He was looking at the mouth of a small cave.

His sudden stop did not go unnoticed by his squad-mates, who all froze. The lead Ranger silently dropped below the ledge and pressed his back against the rocky mountain face. He made eye contact with his sergeant, who was behind him, and using hand signals only, explained what was above. The team slowly moved down a few yards, and the lead three slipped their packs off and handed them to the Rangers behind them. These men found a spot to secure them and then removed their own. Feeling lighter and more mobile, the squad fanned out and moved below the ledge together.

Once in position, the captain and the Ranger medic who had stayed with him and the packs called back to Spooky One quietly.

The captain whispered into his satellite phone, "Spooky One, we have found a small cave with a heat signature. Be advised, we are entering at this location."

A quiet "Roger that" came back in his earpiece, and the captain and specialist moved their weapons off safety and took up positions behind rocks.

The first Ranger slipped silently over the ledge and belly-crawled to the mouth of the cave. Five others followed him over, fanned out along the ledge over a space of about twenty feet. All had their M16 assault rifles with the M203 grenade launchers at the ready. The grenade launchers were armed with tear gas, except for the sergeant's, which was loaded with high-explosive rounds. Not knowing who was in there, they didn't want to just go in blasting in the event it wasn't bad guys. That made their job much more dangerous, of course, since they had total surprise on their side, but they couldn't just fill the cave with explosive rounds.

The lead Ranger continued belly-crawling to the mouth of the cave. Once there, he pulled down his night vision to try to see better into the cave. It didn't help; he was still too far out of the cave in the light, so he crawled all the way into the small cave entrance. An average-size man could walk comfortably into the opening, but it was smaller than a doorway. Specialist White was halfway into the cave when all hell broke loose. The explosion was deafening, and in an instant, the young corporal was flying over the heads of his squadmates. Specialist White went right over the ledge and landed fifteen feet below, not far from the captain and medic with the gear.

The rest of the Rangers had gone prone instantly and covered their heads as dirt and rocks rained over them. The captain was screaming into his handset, "Be advised, Spooky One, we are under assault! We have casualties and are engaged at close quarters."

The sergeant fired a high-explosive round into the cave, and a white flash followed by a tremendous roar again sent rocks and dirt flying. Without thinking, all of the Rangers had opened fire on the mouth of the cave, before the sergeant was barking orders for a cease-fire. The medic had already run over to Specialist White, but one look was all it took to know he was already dead. Even with his Kevlar helmet, his head and face showed massive injuries. Most likely he was dead before he even heard the noise. The medic motioned to the captain to signal that White was dead, and then removed the man's dog tag.

Up above, the sergeant and one of his men scrambled to the mouth of the cave, which had crumbled somewhat. They squatted, and single file slipped into the cave with night vision on. It was a smoky, dark mess inside, and they both fought back coughing as they worked themselves into a small room. The other two Rangers followed them to the mouth of the cave but stopped outside, keeping an eye out for possible attacks from other positions.

The sergeant moved deeper into the cave and let his eyes adjust better. The place had been abandoned, but apparently a small fire had been left behind intentionally, along with a booby trap at the mouth of the cave. Most likely it was some type of rigged artillery shell or antitank missile. There was nothing of value inside the cave, so at the motion of the sergeant, the two men moved quickly outside. By the time they got there, they were both coughing and wiping their watering eyes.

"Where's White?" asked the sergeant.

"He went over, Sergeant," said Specialist Carter. "It blew up in his face." He was fighting back tears.

"Secure this area and keep your shit wired tight; I'll check with the captain. Eyes open, boys, they may still be around." With that, the sergeant moved quickly over the ledge to find the medic zipping up a black body bag on White.

"Goddamn it," the sergeant said as soon as he saw the body.

The captain moved back to the sergeant from his position scanning the area.

"What the hell happened up there?"

"Booby trap at the mouth of the cave. It was a setup. They made a fire inside to show up on our heat sensors. White must not have seen the trip wire. Goddamn it."

The mike on the captain squawked. "Tango Two, what is your sit-rep?"

The captain looked at the black bag. "We have one Ranger KIA. Negative contact. It was a booby trap."

"Roger Tango Two, hold your position, we will send a chopper. Jolly Green will take four-five. I will advise . . . hold." A few seconds passed, then, "Be advised, Tango Two, we have heat signatures. Possibly ten hostiles moving away from your position. Approximately one click from your position, headed north. We are en route to target."

The captain was up in an instant, looking for payback. He whistled once, which brought all of his men moving to him on the double. They all knelt by the body bag, placed their hands on it, and silently said a quick prayer. The captain gave them a few seconds, then switched into hyperdrive.

"Alverez and Doc, you carry White and keep up as best you can. Sweeney, Carter, and Dawson—you break up his pack and add it to yours. Leave nothing. Dawson, you're on SAW [M249 bipod mounted heavy machine gun]. Spooky is en route to making a call on the Hajis who popped Jared. They'll be on them in two minutes, and I want to be close enough to watch. Let's move!"

Everyone was instantly at work packing up, checking weapons, and reloading. Private Alverez and the doc ran climbing rope through the ends of the body bag that held Jared White, and each looped an end over their shoulders. They stood up so he hung between them, still warm, as he swung like a man in a hammock, relaxing. Jared White was twenty-two.

The captain and the sergeant were almost at a full run up the goat trail heading north to where they could hear the AC-130U roaring in, on station. Dawson was carrying the SAW and keeping up as best he could. Sweeney and Carter were slightly behind the sergeant, but off the trail by a few feet, watching the perimeter as they ran. Within a minute they could see the gunship make its slow descent into a banking turn. The thumping sounds began as soon as the gunship rolled on its side, its cannons firing at unseen targets on the ground.

The sound of the Gatling gun brought a cheer from Dawson, who began holding the SAW over his head as he ran, pumping it in the air as he cheered the Spooky to get payback for his friend Jared. When the howitzer began popping off rounds, the mountains began to echo and vibrate. The squad ignored the burning in their legs and continued toward the ground targets, which were getting pummeled. Spooky slowed even more and rolled higher, its tracers making pretty designs as it rained hell on earth at the enemy below.

The Rangers were close enough to see impacts on the

ground, and slowed down to begin looking around as they moved forward. They crouched and began slowing their breathing, finding cover and working through the rocks toward the explosions. Not more than 150 yards ahead, a man in tribal attire stood with an RPG. He aimed at the AC-130 as calmly as if he were on a picnic. He fired, sending a white whoosh skyward.

The captain yelled into his mike to Spooky One, "RPG inbound! Take countermeasures!" The gunship was out of range, and the pilot did not have to launch flares, as he would for a heat-seeking missile. His voice was calm as he responded to the captain.

"Roger on your RPG, Tango Two. Have your team hug some earth, please. That man made my gunners angry."

The captain yelled to hit the dirt as the gunship revved engines in a twisting turn to get itself in position for its run. The pilot slowed and banked hard, the crew firing everything available at the last known position of the man with the RPG. They fired enough ordnance to wipe out a tank column, but it was more a matter of pride and principle than actual combat necessity. How dare anyone shoot at their plane!

The Rangers on the ground held tight as the ground shook and rocks and hot metal sang through the air above their heads. The barrage lasted another three minutes before the gunship rolled level and began a large, slow turn to reassess their last run.

The captain called up to the gunship, "Tango Two moving into position. Hold your fire, Spooky One." With that, the captain had his men quietly move among the rocks until they entered the kill zone of the gunship. The ground that wasn't rock was burning. They could count five actual bodies, but there may easily have been more than that. The problem was the pieces were too small to identify. Sweeney yelled from the left flank, holding up a piece of what looked like an RPG launcher. He grinned for a second, then hopped back down off the rock to continue to secure the area.

The captain called back up to the gunship, "Tango Two to Spooky One, confirm five enemy KIA, RPG launcher recovered. Possibly more KIA, but unidentifiable. We need dust-off for friendly KIA. We will remain here until such time. Over."

"Roger that, Tango Two. Jolly Green should be on station in less than ten mics. I am advised that Jolly Green is bringing gifts. Good luck to you and your men, Tango Two. Spooky One is a phone call away. Over and out."

"Thanks, Spooky One. Over and out."

The Rangers moved about the field, collecting whatever they could find, then set up a quick perimeter around Corporal White and waited for the helicopter. The medic went through the robes and bags of the five bodies and returned to the captain with whatever documents they had, which were all in Arabic.

"They were pretty shot up, Cap. I'm not sure if any of this stuff is any good, but this is everything I could find." He handed the captain a plastic bag filled with bloody papers.

Thanks, Doc. We'll send this in with the Jolly Green to intel and see if we got anything worth a crap."

"Worth White, you mean, don't ya, Cap?" asked the medic sadly.

"Doc, I ain't seen nothin' in this whole country worth Jared White or anybody else here. All I know is I'd rather fight these fuckers here than at home. He was a good Ranger, but he should have known to be looking for booby traps. Check on the others and make sure they're okay. I think Carter and Alverez might have eaten a little shrapnel."

"Roger that, Cap," said the medic, and he was on his way. In the distance, the rotors of a HH-3E helicopter, known affectionately as the Jolly Green, could be heard heading toward the Rangers. It would take Jared White to their firebase for preparation for his trip home. It would also be bringing ammunition, MREs, and a CIA operative who spoke several local languages.

CHAPTER 11

CIA Headquarters, Langley, Virginia

Agents Still and Hollahan were expected at eight that morning, but unlike the last time, they were met in the lobby by their new friend Anthony "Tee" Cicero.

"Mornin', fellas," he said with his big, toothy grin. He extended his hand and shook firmly with Still and Hollahan. "Let's take a drive." With that, he passed them by and walked out the door they had just walked in through.

Hollahan and Still looked at each other, slightly baffled.

"We get thrown out already?" asked Bob.

Hollahan just shrugged, did an about-face, and followed Tee back through the door. Tee was a fast walker, and the two men struggled to keep up with him. He headed toward a parking area. He was still smiling.

"Glad you guys decided to join us. You're going to like the work. I'm taking you to our office. You have your gear in your car?"

"Yeah, suitcases are in the trunk," said Hollahan.

"Okay, hop in my truck and we'll swing by your car and pick up your stuff."

The three of them hopped into Tee's old GMC Jimmy and swung through the parking lot back to their sedan. When they got to Bob's car, Tee hopped out with him and helped throw the bags into the back of the truck.

"Leave the keys in the ignition, Bob. You want to have the car delivered to your brother, or you want it put in storage here?"

Still just laughed and shook his head. "My little brother, huh? You know everything else about me, too?"

"Up to and including how many times a week you go to the bathroom. And by the way, you should get more fiber," he said with a smile.

"I told ya," said Hollahan.

"My brother has a cool car. What would he want with this piece of shit?" said Still.

"My thoughts exactly," said Tee. "I'll have security throw it in storage. When you get out, you'll be able to get a new car anyway."

"Ya think?" said Still, laughing.

"Oh, yeah, baby. Uncle Sam is gonna take real good care of you boys. Just work hard and don't ask too many questions. Either one of you got a problem with flying?" asked Tee.

They both said no, which made Tee smile.

"This ain't gonna be like your last flight, trust me," he said with a laugh. With that, he spun out of the parking lot onto the highway and headed for a dirt road a few miles away on government property where there was an airstrip. They were stopped at metal double fences with razor wire tops. Between the two fences, German shepherds jogged about freely. A security officer dressed in a black battle dress uniform with no insignia except an American flag on the right shoulder checked Tee's ID and waved them in. They went through two more checkpoints before they got to a small building, where Tee parked.

Another guard approached them and greeted Tee informally, obviously knowing who he was. Tee threw his keys at the guard and said, "Take her, man . . . she's all yours. When I get back I'm getting a ragtop."

The guard laughed and said thanks, looking at his watch. He saw the time and pointed skyward, then walked away without saying a word. A moment later a small cargo plane, painted matte black, landed on the field and slowed to a stop.

Tee smiled as it wound down to a full stop.

"That, gentlemen, looks a lot like a De Havilland— from the outside, anyway. You guys are gonna love this shit." He laughed and started walking toward the aircraft. "I've flown on commercial planes that looked just like this one, except for the paint. But don't let her modest exterior fool ya."

Hollahan leaned over to Still. "NSA?"

Still shrugged and answered quietly, "No Such Agency."

"We don't get toys like this at home," mumbled Hollahan.

Still gave him a big smile. "We do now!"

The three men continued walking toward the dark aircraft. There wasn't a number, letter, or insignia anywhere on the plane. As they got closer, Still pointed at the unmarked plane and, pointing out its lack of markings, asked Tee sarcastically, "You sure it's ours?"

"Oh, yeah, baby. She's ours, all right. Ain't nobody else got one of these." His enthusiasm was obvious, and his smile was contagious.

Still looked at Hollahan and scowled. "What you laughin' at?"

Hollahan shook his head and laughed. "I swear to God, man, Tee is a white version of you. Maybe you two are brothers."

Tee heard him and laughed. "Ya know . . . the Moors invaded Sicily . . ." He kept walking toward the aircraft, which had opened a door at the bottom and lowered a set of stairs. A crewman, wearing a black jumpsuit, slid down the handrails and lightly hit the tarmac.

Like the plane, he had no insignia or markings. He wore a red baseball cap that looked about twenty years old, but whatever team logo had been on the front had been ripped off long ago. Hollahan noticed that immediately as the man approached and just shook his head. He leaned toward Still and whispered, "Jesus, these guys are whacked. Even his favorite baseball team is a matter of national security?"

The crewman, who turned out to be the pilot, greeted Tee with a big hug and a slap on the back.

"I guess they've met before," said Still to his old partner.

"You never hug me. Damn, you only bought me dinner twice in God knows how many years."

The men exchanged quick pleasantries and then turned toward Still and Hollahan. Tee put his hand on Hollahan's shoulder.

"This here is Will Hollahan. The big guy is Bob Still. They were with FBI for a long stretch, but opted for a more exciting career. Fellas, meet Chris Mackey, pilot extraordinaire."

The three men exchanged handshakes, and the pilot cocked his head at Still.

"Hey, don't take offense, but anybody tell you that you look like Tee over here?"

Still looked at Hollahan, who was holding his knees and laughing hysterically.

"Yeah, I think I heard that before, except that white boy ain't near as good-looking as me."

"Come on, guys, I'll show you the bird. She is something special. Either of you do any flying?" asked the pilot.

Still pointed to Hollahan, who answered, "Yeah, I did a little in 'Nam. Little birds, nothing like this."

"Well, I can promise you it was nothing like this. Come on up." With that, pilot Mackey scooted up the metal staircase into the plane. Hollahan and Still followed the pilot, with Tee bringing up the rear. The two Feds expected to find rows of seats. Instead, they were in the center galley of an aircraft crammed with electronic equipment. There were consoles lining both sides of the almost windowless aircraft. There was barely room to move inside without bumping into a swivel seat or a console. Their faces immediately showed their surprise.

Hollahan was the first to comment. "Jeez, you guys got your own version of a U-2 spy plane?"

"Actually, she's based loosely on a scaled-down EP-3 navy intel plane. But this baby has a little more umph and a lot more attitude. I'll brief you in detail later on. We usually carry ten crew, but we can handle up to eighteen."

"How do you get away with no markings?" asked Hollahan.

"Well, it's pretty rare that anyone ever gets to see us. We appear on radar with a transponder for a fictional commercial aircraft. When a tower contacts us, we just do a little fibbing. Hey, man, don't tell the FAA." He smiled. After a second, he added, "On second thought, you don't tell anybody anything. Ever." He gave a quick smile, patted him on the back, and scurried to the cockpit. He looked back and yelled to Tee and Still, "You two better sit on opposite sides so we don't flip over." He laughed loudly, obviously very entertaining to himself, and went to his seat.

A handful of crewmen walked up the narrow aisle from the rear of the aircraft and made quick intros. They all looked like very young poster boys for the Marine Corps. One of them showed Tee, Still, and Hollahan three vacant seats in the rear of the aircraft, and everyone buckled in. They were in the air in minutes and headed east, toward the Atlantic Ocean. Tee leaned over to Still and Hollahan from across the narrow aisle.

"Sorry, boys, no movie on this flight. All kidding aside, this is one of the most sophisticated aircraft in the world.

With a full crew, we can run a small war from up here. And while she isn't designed as an attack aircraft, she does have a few tricks up her sleeve. We're linked to several satellites, about a zillion computers, and direct access to our people all over the world. We have more radar, sonar, infrared, heat-sensing, and terrain-mapping capabilities than most fleets."

"How many people do 'we' have?" asked Hollahan.

"Can't say, but I know we just got two more." He smiled and winked. "Get comfy and try to sleep. We have a long flight, and you might not like the landing."

The two of them didn't like the sound of that.

"Hey, man, I ain't jumpin' out of no plane," said Still.

"Don't worry, nobody's jumpin'. You'll see. Get some shut-eye. Long days ahead." With that, Tee reclined in his seat and was sound asleep in less than three minutes.

Still and Hollahan tried to sleep, but were too busy watching the crewmen working their consoles, apparently with great skill, to really relax. The men seemed relaxed but busy. Most were smiling and chatting with each other as they typed away and did their work.

Still looked at Hollahan. "He tells us we might not like the landing, then says relax and go to sleep? When he wakes up I'm gonna kick his ass."

Hollahan looked over at Tee. "I don't know, man. He looks like he might give you a run for your money."

Still just made a face and mumbled, "Sheeeeit."

With that the two of them leaned back and tried to sleep.

CHAPTER 12

Atlantic Ocean, near the Mediterranean

Hollahan and Still were fast asleep when the De Havilland landed on the deck of the aircraft carrier. The tail hook snagged the arresting wire and snapped them to a stop, throwing both agents, who were the only ones sleeping, against their harnesses. The two of them woke up totally horrified, in a flash of light, instinctively reaching for their weapons, and looking all around them. This brought great laughter to the crewmen near them, who were awake and belted in tight, watching their faces when they hit the deck.

As Still yelled, "What the fuck?" the crew began applauding.

"Welcome to the team," said Tee with a smile from across the small aisle. Obviously he had given explicit instructions not to wake them before landing, although he had tightened their shoulder belts while they slept.

Hollahan and Still were obviously rattled and confused, and both looked around for a window to see what had happened.

"Where the hell are we? What happened?" asked Hollahan, obviously pissed.

"You are on board a United States aircraft carrier, allegedly, although I have no proof of that," said Tee with a smile.

"You landed this thing on an aircraft carrier? Are you out of your fucking mind?" screamed Hollahan.

"Yes, we did, and yes, I am. But we have done it before, so don't panic. There isn't much margin for error, but Mackey up there could land a B-52 on a carrier. He's as good as they get. Doolittle would be proud. Sorry not to wake you up, but that was priceless. Jefferson over there will give you the pictures when he has them printed. You shoulda seen your faces . . . it was beautiful."

"I told you I was gonna kick his ass," said Still to Hollahan.

Jefferson, the crewman next to them, handed them a picture off of his printer that he had taken with a digital camera. It was the two of them with eyes wide open and mouths agape at the second of impact, their bodies thrown into their belts.

"Remind me to show you the picture we took of Tee," he said. "I think he actually soiled his undies." He laughed and turned back around to secure his equipment for shutoff.

The plane moved forward to an elevator, where its wings folded up to allow it to fit. This was no ordinary De Havilland. The plane, with its entire crew, disappeared belowdecks into a small holding area. The holding area was empty except for them. The pilot came back from the cockpit and began giving casual instructions to the crew. One of them appeared with an M-16, in his unmarked black jumpsuit, and stood waiting for everyone to exit. He would stay on board until relieved. Even in the belly of the most feared weapons system on earth, this plane was guarded twenty-four hours a day, in six-hour shifts.

The rest of them followed the pilot and the copilot, whom they still had not met, down into a small hallway through waterproof doors until they got to a meeting room. When they opened the door, they were greeted by the executive officer of the ship and several other men who were all wearing black jumpsuits to match theirs. The men stood and offered the two newcomers seats. The exec, in proper navy uniform, spoke first.

"Gentlemen, I would say 'welcome aboard,' except you aren't here. I have been in the navy for twenty-four years, and I have no idea what the fuck you people are doing on my boat. Quite frankly, after the call I received from Washington, I don't want to know. You will have the full military and logistical support of this vessel and its crew; however, you will not fraternize with my sailors. You aren't here. You landed at night, and most of my men never saw you. We'll keep it that way."

Hearing that, Still looked at his watch, which read a little past 10:00 P.M. He had no idea where they were and piped up, "Excuse me, sir, but where are we and what time *is* it?"

"It is a little past oh-three hundred local time, and you aren't too far from the coast of Portugal. That's my time with you, gentlemen. I won't be seeing you again most likely, so good luck with whatever it is you are doing, and try not to get us into World War Three if you can help it. If you *can't* help yourselves, you have the finest carrier fleet in naval history behind you. Don't abuse the privilege. Good night, gentlemen. There will be food available in the conference room."

With that, the executive officer, whose name they didn't know, was up and out of the room. One of the other men in black who had been there prior to their arrival stood and addressed the small room.

"Good morning, gentlemen. I trust you had a pleasant flight. My name is Gary. That is all you need to know. You will use first names only, and there are no ranks. You will be briefed later on who answers to whom around here. While there are no ranks used, there is a formal chain of command, and you will all have specific jobs to perform. School starts this morning, gentlemen. I know you are all very capable men, and you have been hand-selected by the best of the best in every branch of the United States armed forces and intelligence communities.

"While you are all very capable, that was at your *old* job descriptions. The rules are different out here. You are sailing with a carrier group that doesn't know you exist. The XO and command of this ship know a little about us, and that is it. See that it stays that way. We will be based here for the time being, but we are fluid. We can, and will be, anywhere at any time. You have several roles here. Some of you are here to sort data, some to intercept and break codes, some to locate and destroy enemies of state. You are here on a specific mission, as you have already been briefed. At this time I will turn the briefing over to Dan."

The oldest man in the room stood up. He was in his late sixties and more than six feet tall. His white hair was cropped, and he had the look of a military career officer.

"Thank you, Gary. Welcome aboard. You are now part of a team, code-named Shadow because that is where we will live. The size of our group is unimportant, but as the XO said, we have some serious firepower behind us, and we have fire mission priority. That means when we find our target, we will destroy it without having to wait around for support."

He walked to the wall and pulled down a screen. There were a few photographs of Middle Eastern–looking men. "Gentlemen, the reason you are halfway around the world is because these lovely men want to kill you and your entire families. They want to kill your children and your children's children. Remember that if you feel any remorse about any part of our mission while we are here.

"Crescent Fire. A name. And that's it. That's all we have. A little name mobilized a new operations group operating outside the purview of the United States. You will not have dog tags; you will not be recognized publicly; nobody will ever know what we do. For some of you, that is not abnormal; for others, it is an 'adjustment.' But let me tell you this—not all heroes get parades. This isn't about getting a medal; this is about preventing an attack against our country . . . against your homes and families. We will do whatever it takes to prevent this attack. Whatever it takes, gentlemen. In a moment we will break for chow and sleep. You will awaken at oh-seven-hundred and begin learning. You will be working in teams of five or less depending on your job description, and you will not, in most cases, be sitting together again like this. Gary or I will give you your posts and instructions. You will answer to either of us unless instructed otherwise. Tee will handle intel; Mike will take care of insertion teams. That is all for now, gentlemen. Follow Gary to chow, and he will show you your quarters. Should you bump into a ship's crewman, you are efficiency experts from the Pentagon. That should send most of them running. Eat and sleep. Tomorrow is the beginning of lots of busy days."

With that, the man called Gary stood and walked out of the room. Everyone silently followed him down the narrow gray hallway to another room. This room was bigger than the first, and several platters of sandwiches, meats, and the like were waiting for them. Everyone piled food on their plates and found seats. Once they started eating, Gary walked around, handing each of them a key with a numbered tag on it. As he did so, he began to speak.

"Gentlemen, these are your room assignments. You are deep belowdecks, and some of you may not see the sun for a few days. You are two in a room, and some of you may know each other already. Those of you who don't, you have time to get to know each other; remember first names, and nicknames are fine. No ranks, and the less personal information the better.

"For some of you, after briefings and intelligence sessions, you will be going into Indian territory. There will be very few friendly faces. There will be a little black plane in the sky nearby most of the time, however, and this fleet backs a serious punch. Those of you working intel gathering and sorting, you will split time aboard *Thor*—that's the plane you came in on—and this vessel. We have several conference rooms assigned to us, and this part of the ship is off-limits to nonessential crew. Now eat up and hit the rack. We will hit the ground running tomorrow morning. Your rooms are down this hallway and are numbered. We will reassemble in this room at oh-seven-thirty. Showers and latrine are at the end of the hall to the left. That's all for this evening. Good night and good luck to all of us."

Gary left the room, and everyone continued eating. Most of them glanced around the room, sizing each other up, trying to figure out who was who, but no one spoke. Finally Still couldn't take the silence and stood up.

"Any of you bastards get a movie on your flight? I think I got screwed. They always messing with the black man."

Hollahan rolled his eyes and smiled, used to his friend's antics.

A Hispanic man, who looked to be not more than midtwenties, laughed and spoke up. "Yeah man, I didn't get no movie neither. If it hadn't been for the big, spacious seats and great-looking stewardesses, I would have filed a grievance with brass."

"There ain't no brass, remember? I don't know who salutes who around here!" joked a large, ruddy-faced man. His red face and blond crew cut were in stark contrast to his black jumpsuit.

"Hey, white boy, you get a movie?" asked the Hispanic man.

"Hell, yeah, three of them and popcorn and beer. You didn't get that on yours?"

"Damn, man . . . elitists even here. There is no escape from the power of the white man," joked the young man. "What's your name, white boy?" He was smiling when he said it, his brown eyes and dark hair gleaming.

"Whitey will work just fine. We have to use code names, bro. We're secret agents now."

That brought laughter from all over the room, except one older man sitting near a back corner. His silence was enough to tell the rest of them who watched him that he was definitely a hard-core player. Hollahan, who was closest to him, extended a hand and said, "Will—FBI, nice to meet ya."

The man, who was Hollahan's age but shorter, fatter, and balder, shook his hand and said, "Evenin'." That was the extent of his conversation, and with that, he finished his sandwich and stood up.

"Don't stay up late, giggling girls," he said. "Tomorrow is gonna be busy." He left the room.

Still looked at his watch, which he had reset and which read almost four. "Damn, fellas, we ain't getting a night's sleep, we're getting a nap. Let's hit it."

The rest of them finished the last few bites and shuffled down the hall to where they found their rooms. Still and Hollahan were relieved to see they were rooming together. The "room" was tiny—enough for a bunk, a small locker, and a metal desk. When Still stood in the center of the room, Hollahan couldn't get past him.

"Jesus, Will, I hope you ain't claustrophobic," said Still.

"No, but I call top bunk. The thought of that thing collapsing and your lard ass crushing me will have me awake all night."

Still opened the locker to put away his clothes and found four black jumpsuits like many of the rest of the unit were already wearing.

"Hey, we get matching jammies like everybody else. Last time I saw guys dressed all in black they were little and yellow and they were shooting at me. There're two extra-large suits in here. They must be yours."

"You're just jealous 'cause the chicks dig us big black men. Now shut up and go to sleep."

They both hit the rack and were fast asleep within a few minutes. It wouldn't be but a blink before Gary walked down the hallway beating a metal garbage can with a club for their gentle wake-up call.

CHAPTER 13

Port Sudan

Kufi sat on the bridge of the oil tanker, looking down at the open deck. Thirty feet below him, fifty local ship-builders hefted torches and gear, welding and cutting busily in the hot sun. Kufi dialed the number in his scrambler phone and called Kareem Wazeeri aboard the yacht some twenty nautical miles away. He had no idea where Kareem was, or that he was with his cousin Fadi. Neither of them used proper names on the phone, even though it was thought to be safe.

"My brother, I have good news," said Kufi when Kareem answered.

"Oh? Tell me, brother—how is the new house coming?" Kareem asked.

"Very well, and right on schedule. The door was specially made, but it is finished and makes a wonderful entranceway. We are still working on the roof. The large windows make it a little complicated, but we have skilled workers. We hope to be finishing within the month."

"That is excellent news, brother. Do tell my friend there

how happy I am with his progress on your house. I will be paying you both a visit soon, with a housewarming gift."

"Thank you, brother, you are most gracious. We will speak again soon."

With that, Kareem hung up and turned to his brother Fadi, who was getting a manicure and a pedicure simultaneously from two different young women.

"They finished the doorway and planking entrance for the truck. They are still working on the bay doors and decking, but are on schedule."

Fadi smiled, his crooked yellow teeth showing in the strong Mediterranean sun. With a motion of his hands, he sent the two women running away into the cabin. He stood and looked east to the holy lands.

"Kareem, this is going much better than I expected. The only thing we are missing is the proper payload for our missile. I have had no word from our people working in Pakistan, Russia, and North Korea. If we cannot get the nuclear warhead, we will have to find a worthy substitute. Knocking down a few buildings will not be sufficient this time. We need to break their back. As soon as the ship is finished, we will head immediately to the Syrian coast and pick up our launcher. We can stay at sea for a long time without worry, but I want to be off the coast of America before they celebrate the birth of Christ."

Kareem stroked his beard as he looked at the horizon in deep thought.

"We should check in with our friends in the Far East and in Russia. The Koreans and the Russians have nuclear warheads, and they need money. The infidels will be easier to get nuclear weapons from than the Pakistanis. The only way to get nuclear weapons from Pakistan is to overthrow the American puppet president."

"Yes, and we have spent a million dollars in weapons for the rebels. The Americans back their army with weapons. It is impossible. I will try to reach our friends in

Russia and the Far East. We had some contacts in Iraq, and they spoke of weapons-grade uranium, but no warhead. If we can reestablish contact there, that might be a possibility. Even if we can't detonate it, the bomb would cause a disaster for the Americans."

The Iraqis have chemical weapons also. But the problem there is getting them out. The American army is crawling all over that country," said Kareem.

"Yes," said Fadi, "but their chemical weapons are buried in the desert not far from our Scud. If we can't get the bomb, we will use sarin. They have drums of the stuff safely hidden from the Americans. They are pulling their troops farther away from the western border every day. The Americans are weak. They are folding under our great martyrs. We will find a way to get the drums to the ship if we cannot get the bomb, Kareem. It is Allah's will."

Kareem mumbled a quiet prayer and smiled at the thought of lethal gas raining all over Washington, D.C. With the right wind, they could kill hundreds of thousands of the infidels and strike terror into their hearts.

Servants brought the men a platter of dates and fruit, and Fadi and Kareem snacked quietly while dreaming of a massacre.

CHAPTER 14

Hebron, West Bank

Abdul-Bari had been at home sleeping when the phone rang so early in the morning. It was still dark outside, and the city was just waking up to its usual cacophony of merchants and the like. The voice on the phone told Abdul to be at the market at noon and hung up. The market was a busy place, and it was typically where Abdul met his contacts and passed information. It was easy to get lost in the crowd, or if need be, to duck into a building or an alleyway.

Abdul was excited. He stood and stretched; his body always stiff these days from the time he had spent in the Israeli prison. He was only forty years old, but he felt like an old man. The Israelis still watched him, he was sure, but he was careful and they wouldn't get him a second time. The beatings and interrogations yielded almost nothing, for truth be known, he didn't know much. He eventually told them what he knew, but he was sure it hadn't helped them anyway. He had been a small player at the time. Now was his time to strike back.

Abdul called Imad and told him to meet him at the market at eleven. They would have coffee and contemplate the upcoming meeting. Imad had been his friend since his days in the prison. He, too, had been beaten and held by the Israeli occupiers, and the two of them had sworn revenge when they were free. They had networked themselves with others in Hamas, and now their time was coming. Imad agreed to meet him at eleven and hung up. Imad made a quick phone call on a secure cell phone and showered.

They met a few hours later at their usual spot and walked until they got to a small outdoor café. There were only a few small tables with old rickety chairs, but the coffee was good, and the area was very busy. When the waiter brought them coffee and disappeared, Abdul spoke.

"Imad, something big is about to happen. I haven't heard any details other than the size of the operation. The rumors are true. Al Qaeda is working with Hamas, Islamic Jihad, and Hezbollah. They even have a few other groups working with them now. We are an army now, Imad, an army! What chance did we ever have before against the Jews or the Americans? But together, freedom fighters and the faithful working together against our common enemies, we cannot be stopped. We will destroy Israel to the last man, and we will leave America in ruins so they never cross the ocean again."

Imad leaned closer. "Abdul, with all respect, we have both heard about unifying our small groups of fighters before. It has never worked. What makes you think it can happen now?"

"Crescent Fire," he whispered.

"What is that?" Imad asked.

"To tell you the truth, I don't know. But I do know this. It will strike deep into the hearts of the Americans on their own soil. Whatever it is, it is bigger than nine-eleven."

Imad's eyebrows went up at that. "You believe this?"

Abdul leaned closer and spoke quieter. "We are going

to meet Hassam himself. He will know everything. And you and I will be given a chance to pay back the Americans and the Jews for our days in prison. To tell you the truth, I am a little nervous about seeing Hassam. He is a powerful man."

It was, of course, the truth. Hassam Abu Mustafa was head of Hamas and had participated in planning more than two thousand deaths over the past three years. He was rarely seen, and when he was, he was surrounded by an entourage of his bodyguards. The Israelis had tried once to kill him with a rocket attack from a helicopter, but unfortunately for them, the building he was using for his bomb-making factory was in the basement of a childcare center. The Israelis knew this, so they were forced to attack at night, when they thought the building would be free of children. The plan didn't go as they hoped. They ended up killing several custodians and teachers who slept over in the building. Although they had managed to wound one of the bodyguards and disrupt their activities for a few days, it didn't amount to much. Within a week, Hamas was retaliating all over Israel, including blowing up a disco, a bus stop, and two school buses filled with children.

To be invited to meet with Hassam was a great honor for any member of Hamas. Perhaps they would be asked to become martyrs, which Abdul quietly prayed wouldn't happen. He liked his life, such that it was, and was in no hurry to blow himself up. Of course, it would be difficult to say no to Hassam, but he still hadn't made up his mind about what he would do if coerced into wearing a vest.

"We will see what he has to say, Abdul," said Imad. "Perhaps he will tell us about Crescent Fire."

"Perhaps, but do not ask," said Abdul. "That man, he scares me as much as the Mosad."

Imad smiled. "Don't worry about the Israelis. We have seen the last of their prisons, my friend."

They finished their coffee and walked through the market.

As the streets grew more crowded and the cobblestone streets narrowed, they wound through Hebron until they got closer to Hassam's neighborhood. It was difficult to tell when they were getting closer. The streets began to fill with men in scarves and masks, all of whom carried AK-47 assault rifles. When they neared the building where they had been told to meet Hassam, they were stopped by a group of hooded men. They gave their names and waited while a boy ran down the block to announce their arrival. With a few minutes, the boy returned and showed them the way.

They wandered quietly through the dusty alleyways, the sun already starting to get hot. After a moment they arrived at a heavy wooden door, and the boy knocked a coded pattern. The door opened and several men came out and patted the two of them down outside the small stone building. They pulled out a very sophisticated phone from Imad's pocket, and the two of them studied it for several seconds. They argued quietly about it for a moment, and then one of them kept it and walked them in.

They went down a flight of stairs to a large basement. The furnishings were much nicer than the outside of the building would have you believe. Obviously, Hassam was not one to deny himself creature comforts, regardless of what he told his followers.

The bodyguards walked in first and greeted Hassam with bows and announced their guests. The one guard with Imad's phone mumbled something quietly and gave the phone to Hassam, who admired it and motioned for his guests to sit. A quick clap of his hands brought several young women scurrying in with plates of small appetizers and flat bread.

Hassam dismissed his guards and faced his guests.

"Abdul-Bari, you have been a faithful servant of Hamas for many years. You have languished in the Jew prisons for your efforts. You are a worthy soldier of Muhammad, praised be his name. You have earned an opportunity to be a part of something much bigger than anything you have ever seen."

He turned and looked at Imad. "And you, Imad, while I do not know you well, Abdul has always spoken of your bravery in their prison and your loyalty to Hamas and to me. You will work with Abdul on this project. Your family will sing your name long after you are in Paradise, and you will watch the Americans burn in their homes." He looked at Imad's phone. It was unlike anything he had ever seen.

"Tell me about this?" he asked. "It is a phone, yes?"

"Yes, Hassam. But it is no ordinary phone. It is the latest in Israeli technology. It has scramblers and shielding devices built into it such that the Israelis cannot even trace their own phone. I took that phone off of a Mosad agent after I slit his throat with my bare hands."

Hassam sat back, doubting him a bit, but still impressed by the claim. "You killed a Mosad agent? When was this?"

"Two weeks ago, outside of Bethlehem. He had been someone I trusted for a time, and would help me in and out of Israel. I suspected him after we were stopped one time and questioned. His story didn't match mine when we spoke about the interrogation, and I started following him closer. When I was sure he was double-crossing me, I killed him. I got this phone and charger, an automatic pistol, and thirty rounds from his pack. The phone is priceless."

Hassam looked at it more closely. "And you are sure this is one hundred percent secure? How do you know?"

"After I got it, I asked around a bit. I know a man who is good with computers and such things. He told me it is generations ahead of anything he had ever seen. We even made long-distance phone calls with it from rooftops and waited for helicopters to come. Nothing. They have no idea that I have it." Imad looked at his phone, which Hassam placed back in his hand. Imad pressed a few keys and explained.

"I just unlocked the phone so you can use it. It is my gift to you, Hassam. May it serve Hamas well."

Hassam smiled very broadly, having been very obvious that he wanted the fancy phone. He stood and walked to a cabinet, where he took out a very ornate gold dagger and scabbard.

"Take this as my gift. The phone is quite a useful instrument against the Jews. The knife is yours for another Mosad throat." They smiled and bowed slightly to each other.

"Now," Hassam said, getting serious, "it is time to discuss why you are here. I am sending you through Jordan to Syria. You have been chosen to be soldiers from Hamas in the war against the Americans and the Jews. You are to represent Hamas and go on to fight with our brothers from Al Qaeda and other freedom fighters."

The two men smiled. Abdul asked, "So it is true? The believers around the world are finally coming together to fight the infidels?"

"Yes. After three years of talking and planning, we are finally working together. It has been very difficult to plan from so far away, but finally a plan is beginning to take shape. You have been given a great honor, and I know you will not let us down. Tomorrow morning, one of my men will get you to Jordan, where you will be met by other freedom fighters. They will get you to Syria, where you will be taken to something special. It will be your job to transport this package to the coast, where you will be met by soldiers of Fadi Wazeeri himself. Once there, you will be a soldier to him like you have been to me. Representatives from Hezbollah and Harakat ul-Mujahidin will be there as well. We will combine our forces to create a new army of believers who, together, will crush the infidels once and for all."

Abdul was beaming. He was finally being recognized as a great warrior against Israel. Perhaps his family would be given money for his service, and his name would be remembered as being an important Hamas figure.

"We are honored, Hassam. Rest assured, we will represent Hamas well. The Americans will learn to fear the name Hamas just as the Israelis do."

Hassam stood, signaling the meeting was over.

"Get your things together and be in the market at dawn. My man will find you—he knows who you are. He will take you to Jordan. Allah go with you. Allah akbar!"

The two men left the basement, excited to begin their new mission against the Zionists and the infidels. Abdul and Imad went their separate ways, Abdul back to his house, and Imad to the nearest checkpoint crossing into Israel, to report back to his Mosad Metsada officer. The Metsada, or Special Operations Division, was the Mosad branch that handled high-level assassinations, sabotage, and psychological warfare. It was important that he be back in Israel before Hassam placed his third phone call.

CHAPTER 15

Mediterranean Sea,
U.S. Carrier Fleet

The "men in black," as they jokingly called themselves after the movie with Will Smith, woke at 0700 to a metal trash can being beaten on with a billy club. It was Gary, who was looking showered and fresh, like he had slept for ten hours. Still moaned from the bottom bunk.

"No way, man, no way. I ain't getting out of this bed. This guy must think we're at Parris Island or something. I saw *Full Metal Jacket*, too. This is bullshit." With that, Still rolled over and tried to close his eyes, but Gary returned down the hallway, still banging away on the trash can.

"Drop your cocks and grab your socks," he was barking, with a big smile on his face. "Chow in ten minutes *for* ten minutes, then right to work, boys. Let's move it!"

Hollahan sat up carefully so as not to hit his head on the ceiling, and dropped off the top bunk to the floor. He was in his underwear, and stood and stretched, with his ass in Still's face on the bottom bunk.

"Ohhhh, shit, man. Can this day start any worse? Get your ass out of my face, man!" yelled Still.

The two of them stumbled out of their door down the hall to the shower and latrine. The narrow hallway was full of men in the same condition as they were, all tired and grumpy, jet-lagged and half out of it. Only Gary looked like a normal human being, cheerfully insulting them as they all took quick showers, shaved, and double-timed it back to their rooms to hop into their black jumpsuits.

Hollahan and Still looked at each other as they zipped up their suits.

"Don't even say it, man. I said you didn't have to come," said Still through red, bloodshot eyes.

"What? And miss feeling like a nineteen-year-old recruit? I'm sure breakfast will be out on the terrace with soft music and maybe a back rub around noontime before our nap."

Still and Hollahan walked quickly down the narrow, gray hall to where the men filed into a small mess area, the same place where they had eaten last night. Powdered eggs, Spam, lousy orange juice, cold toast, and very strong coffee awaited them.

"Oh, man, the hits just keep on coming," grumbled Still. A big smack on the back made him spin around. It was Tee, looking fairly fresh, all things considered.

"Have a nice nap, boys? Gonna be a busy day. Have a good breakfast, a good crap, and head back to your room. I'll pick you up there in twenty minutes." With that, Tee grabbed a coffee and headed out.

Still, his eyelids only half open, looked at Hollahan and shook his head. Hollahan laughed and filled his plate. Unlike last night, there was no clever banter, just a bunch of tired men eating as fast as they could, and heading back out to the latrine or their rooms.

CHAPTER 16

Hebron

It was six o'clock in the morning in Hebron, and Hassam had just woken. He headed to the roof of his building and looked out over the street as it started to fill with morning activities. He had his phone with him, the new toy from Imad. He had used it twice last night and was very impressed with its clarity, but moreover with its scrambling capabilities. To be able to keep a phone for more than a single use was something he would have never dared dream of before.

He dialed the number for his contact in Jordan to alert him to the arrival of his soldiers. As Hassam listened to the second ring, the phone exploded in his hand, removing his head from his shoulders and raining his brains all over the street below. The explosion sent his men running from downstairs, who found his headless body kneeling against the wall of the roof, blood still pumping out of what used to be his neck. A pool of dark blood was sticky and thick as they ran over to their dead leader.

They were all screaming and running around the roof,

trying to see from where the assassin had fired. When one of his bodyguards looked closer at his boss, he saw that his right arm was also missing at the shoulder. He was the same guard who had taken the phone from Imad the day before. He began screaming to his fellow guards to get to the courtyard. He knew about the meeting in the market that would get the two men to Jordan.

Within seconds, half a dozen of them were racing down the street, brandishing AK-47s and trampling anyone who got in their way. Upstairs, two men wrapped their leader in some sheets and started cleaning up the large pools of blood. The bodyguards reached the market meeting place within a few moments and found Abdul and the contact person sent by Hassam. Imad was nowhere to be found.

Abdul and his guide were taken by surprise when the guards rushed them and seized them roughly by the arms.

"What are you doing? We are waiting for Imad! We are working for Hassam himself! Take your hands off of me before you answer to Hassam!" screamed Abdul.

The large guard who had taken the phone the night before grabbed Abdul by the throat.

"Your traitor friend has murdered Hassam! Where is he?" he screamed.

Abdul went white. "What are you talking about?" he screamed back into his face.

"Bring them back to the house," the large man said, and he shoved Abdul into the arms of his men. The crowd of guards pulled and pushed the frightened Abdul all the way back through the crowded streets to the house where their fallen leader lay wrapped in blood-soaked sheets and blankets. Word on the street was already spreading: Hassam Abu Mustafa, feared leader of Hamas, was dead. Women began their wailing, and the men began filling the streets, firing weapons into the air and screaming, "Death to Israel! Death to America!"

The guards pushed Abdul back to the house, with the

guide following them with the angry mob that was gathering. Abdul was pushed into the house and brought into the same room where he had sat with Hassam the day before.

The large guard who was the apparent leader of the group smacked Abdul across the face so hard he broke his nose.

"Where is your friend?" he demanded.

"I have no idea," he pleaded, spitting blood. "He didn't show up. Please! You must believe me! I had no idea about any of this!"

The guard grabbed him by his shirt and dragged him up the stairs to the roof, followed by his men who were pushing and grabbing at Abdul.

"Hassam's death will be avenged," he said with a sneer in Abdul's face. He dragged Abdul to the wall of the roof, where the pool of blood was still visible. He and another guard each held an arm as he screamed down at the crowd gathered below them.

"This man is responsible for Hassam's death!" he bellowed.

"No! Please! I tell you I didn't know! It was Imad, not me!" he begged.

The guard pulled a long knife from his belt and grabbed Abdul by his hair, pulling his chin up. With a quick movement, he opened Abdul's throat and sprayed blood all over the roof. He kept cutting until he had ripped the head from the body and held the head up to the crowd, who were now screaming wildly. It was beginning to look like nothing short of a riot in the narrow street below as men and women alike were beating themselves and screaming, mourning the death of their hero, and welcoming the punishment of the traitor. The guard threw the head into the street below, where it was kicked around like a soccer ball until someone picked it up and put a sword through the bottom, holding it up in the air and chanting, "Death! Death! Death!"

The men on the roof turned away from the mob and headed back into the house, where they would have to decide how to proceed without Hassam. Surely one of Hassam's number two men would contact them.

CHAPTER 17

Tel Aviv

Danny Herzog, also known as "Imad" when working in Gaza or the West Bank, was in a small, nondescript office building in Tel Aviv with his control officer, Barry Kliner. Danny was obviously exhausted. He had just finished his briefing on the successful assassination of Hassam Abu Mustafa.

"Honestly, sir, I believe if I had kept him alive and stayed with him on their mission to Syria, I could have found out everything about Crescent Fire. That name has been stirring around for months now, and we know it is something of immense magnitude. Now we have nothing to go on."

"Yes, yes, I understand your angst, Danny, but that was not your mission. You have been networking yourself to get to Hassam for more than a year, including four months in that shithole prison, making friends with Abdul. You carried out your orders and are to be commended. While you are correct that Crescent Fire is something we are trying to crack, it was not your mission. Hassam Abu Mustafa was personally responsible for hundreds, maybe thousands of

Israeli deaths. His people have killed more children than they have soldiers. You have done a service to your country that you can be proud of, Danny. Your mission was never about Crescent Fire."

"I know that, sir, but still, I was so close. I should have gone on with Abdul to Syria."

"Abdul is dead, Daniel. He was dead a few minutes after the phone exploded. If you had tried to make it on to Syria you would be dead also, and we have already lost four agents in the past few months. We need you alive and working. There will be other opportunities at Crescent Fire. At least we know that Syria is part of the picture and they are transporting whatever it is by ship. We will tell our friends in Washington and see what luck they have. Perhaps their satellites can search the desert for anomalies. In any case, you deserve some time off. Take a shower, shave, get a haircut, go to Elat, and get laid. Get out of here for a while and relax. You deserve it."

Danny stood and shook hands with Barry.

"Thank you, sir. I will be back to see you in a month or so."

After he left, Kliner picked up his secure phone and asked to speak to the American embassy in Washington. He left word for Mitchell Weisel to call him back from a secure phone. A few minutes later, his secure phone rang.

"Hey, Barry. You know what time it is here?" he asked, sounding a bit groggy.

"Sorry to interrupt your beauty sleep, but this is newsworthy. One of our men working undercover with Hamas was successful in dealing with Hassam Abu Mustafa."

"Hassam is dead?"

"Affirmative. It is confirmed."

"That is wonderful news, Barry. Even the Americans will be happy about that."

"Yes, but that is not why I am calling. Hassam was somehow involved with Crescent Fire."

There was silence on the other end of the line for a moment. "Crescent Fire? Jesus, Barry. The stories we are hearing are confirmed, then. These animals are all working together."

"Yes, it would appear so. Our man here was a day away from joining with a few others and heading through Jordan to Syria. We believe they were picking something up in the western desert and transporting it to the sea. Whatever it is, they are apparently putting it aboard a ship."

"This is good information. It will greatly narrow our search. We've had nothing but a name for months. Do we know what they are to have transported?"

"Unfortunately, no. Our man had to get out after the hit on Hassam. His cover was toast, and his contact man inside Hamas was killed, which is no sin. He was another thug."

"Do we have any other information on places or dates?"

Barry frowned. "No, Mitch. I'm afraid what I just told you is everything. We do know that they were going to get help in Jordan and Syria, but we don't know by whom."

"Okay. I can take this to the Americans, correct?"

"That is correct. Tell them we will continue to work from our end."

Mitch hung up and called Amy Lang.

She answered after the fifth ring, obviously from a sound sleep. It was after one in the morning. She grumbled a "hello."

"Good morning, my beautiful American friend. The coffee at Starbucks over on Sixth is delicious at six-thirty in the morning. It will be just brewed. See you then."

Amy had never gotten a call from Mitch in the middle of the night before. Whatever it was, it had to be good. He had already hung up, so she was left hanging until the sun would come up. She tossed and turned the rest of the night.

CHAPTER 18

Port Sudan

Fadi Wazeeri was very angry. He had just been watching the Al Jazeera news and heard about the death of Hassam Abu Mustafa. This could only be the work of the Israelis. He was counting on help from Hamas to move the Scud across the desert near the port city of Lattakia. While it would be impossible to drive a Scud launcher through downtown Lattakia, they could drive it via desert highway to a small port near Jabla. Here it would be loaded onto a barge and ferried to the oil tanker, where it would simply drive up the ramp into the hold of the ship, where it would sit until they were off the coast of the United States. The doors would open on the deck, and the missile could be launched within minutes.

Wazeeri also was concerned about the missile payload. He still had no luck in getting a nuclear warhead, and he had been spreading money around like hummus on a pita. He did have news of sarin being available, if he could get it from the Iraqi border near eastern Syria, where he had gotten the Scud, but that could take some time. He wasn't 100 percent sure how reliable the information was on who actually possessed the deadly chemical. In the worst-case scenario, they would just fire what they had, which would only do major damage to a small area, but if they hit the White House with the president at his desk, it would be enough. It would have great psychological impact on the cocky Americans far beyond the death of the cowboy president.

He was watching the news when his cousin entered the cabin.

"Fadi, have you heard?" asked Kareem. "They have killed Hassam Abu Mustafa."

"Yes, Kareem, just now. We will have to make other arrangements for our shipment. When did you last speak to Kufi?"

"Yesterday. They are getting very close. The doors are finished; they are just working on the hydraulics. The entrance door, gangways, and internal decking systems are completed ahead of schedule. Our shipbuilder friend is tasting his bonus money already, and his crew is good. He wasn't lying about stealing them from the shipyards. These men have been working on boats their entire lives. They work eighteen hours a day and are perfectionists. The outside of that ship is a mess, but the ramping systems are a work of art."

"Yes, Kareem, it will be a modern Trojan horse." Fadi smiled and said a quiet prayer to help destroy the infidels. "How long would you guess?"

"Another week—perhaps ten days."

"Push them. Go see Kufi yourself if you have to, but get them finished before the week is out. I want that ship under way. If the Americans or the Israelis have any idea about the location of our missile, it will present many problems. I want this boat loaded with that missile quickly, even if we have to wait at sea for a chemical or nuclear warhead. Once we are at sea, they will never find us, but we must get that missile loaded before it is found. Understand?"

Kareem nodded and left the cabin to make arrangements for the launch that would bring him back to the tanker and Kufi.

Inside the cabin, Fadi cursed and paced like a caged animal, wanting to be loaded up and on his way to America already. The waiting was killing him, knowing that every day they were delayed, the Americans were another closer.

CHAPTER 19

Mediterranean Sea,
U.S. Carrier Fleet

Tee had come by the small room and knocked on the door before he opened it. Both Still and Hollahan were sitting on the bottom bunk, leaning against the wall and looking like death warmed over. They both turned their heads to the door without moving any other part of their bodies; neither had the energy.

"You boys look like crap, if you don't mind me saying so. You better close your eyes before you bleed to death."

They both told him to "go *f*" himself simultaneously.

"Very nice. Now get up and follow me. Unlike the rest of these poor bastards who are gonna spend the next few weeks down here with the rats, you boys get to take a ride in the sky."

Still and Hollahan helped each other up and shuffled after Tee, who was peppy as ever, leading them back to the hangar where their plane awaited them. One of the crewmen was still standing guard with his M-16 and just "chinned" a hello at them as they approached. The men in black knew each other by sight, and Hollahan and Still were starting to get the hang of the way things worked with these guys. No ranks, no last names, no b.s.—just an attitude of getting the job done without interference.

Will and Bob followed Tee up the metal ladder, and Tee showed them into two seats next to each other in front of a bank of computers and screens. He sat behind them in a seat facing the other side of the aircraft. There were four other crewmen on board at their consoles, plus the pilot and copilot up front. The guard hopped in last after them and sealed the door closed. He secured his weapon and took a seat in the back of the aircraft at a different console. Within a minute, the plane began moving up the elevator until they were on the deck, at which point the wings began to unfold and lock into place. The pilot taxied to his proper place at the catapult, and deck crewmen began locking the launch blocks into place on the wheels.

Inside, Tee leaned over and whispered, "This is when you are glad you don't have a window seat, man."

Still and Hollahan just looked at each other.

"De Havillands weren't made to land on a carrier, and they sure as *shit* weren't made to take off of one," Tee said with a smile.

The carrier turned into the wind as the pilot maxed the throttle on his aircraft. The engine strained and then there was a sudden crushing force against their bodies as the plane was flung down the carrier deck. As they cleared the deck, the plane dipped and fought off plunging into the ocean. The pilot kept the engine at full throttle as they skimmed only a few yards above the water and picked up speed. They slowly began gaining altitude and started a banking turn starboard into the sun.

After a few minutes, Tee unfastened his belt and came over to Still's and Hollahan's seats. He knelt between the two and began flipping switches and turning on their computers.

"Okay, fellas, playtime is over. We are going to teach

you in the next few days what usually takes months to learn. Don't worry; there is nothing you can do that will cause any major screwups. For now, you are going to be an extra two pairs of eyes and ears. I am going to show you a classified piece of equipment that is going to help us catch bad guys. I know neither one of you guys is a computer head, so I will keep this in laymen's terms."

He switched a button, and the screen in front of them lit up with every color of the rainbow in blobs of Lava lamp colors.

"Imagine that you had a stereo system with great speakers and a volume controller that could go up to ten. Now imagine that same system, but it could go up to ten million. The problem is, your ears can handle only ten, and even that for only a couple of minutes. So instead of listening to your speakers at ten million, you are going to 'look' at them. This machine is like a giant boom microphone that we can aim at a geographic area. It 'listens' to an area, so amplified that it can hear a bee buzzing, no shit. If a bunny jumps, we can see it land. Every color represents a level of sound, and your screen represents an area map that can be zoomed in and out. Bob, you are 'Ears' now. That is your job today—to be Ears. That is your name for the rest of the day. I yell 'Ears—what you got?' and you are going to tell me what you are looking at."

Tee pressed a few buttons and dials, and an overlay grid appeared over the colors.

"Okay, now you have coordinates. We can plug in map references that appear on your X and Y axes. If you see bright colors popping up, you yell back coordinates and we will eyeball those locations. That's you, Will—you are 'Eyes.'"

Tee flipped some controls on Will's screen, and a live picture appeared.

"Your picture can be adjusted via touch screen. The picture you are looking at is not being shot from this aircraft;

it is being downloaded live via satellite. The resolution is pretty high, so when Still gives you a coordinate, you touch that part of your screen and hit the zoom button. You can keep redefining your search as he gives you more info. The sounds are a lot easier to pinpoint than the heat signatures or visuals. Remember, though: I wasn't kidding about hearing bees buzzing. It takes a while to get used to all the interference you are going to hear."

Still started typing quickly, and the screen turned almost black other than a bright orangy-yellow oval shape in the center.

"Okay, fellas, that is your aircraft carrier. The ocean always looks black. Any body of water will do that because the sound is absorbed and not bounced like land—ya follow? It's just the way this computer system sees it, anyway. The yellow is the loudest. If a jet takes off, you'll see a yellow dot shoot out of the orangy-yellow. Let's pull back a bit more."

Tee backed out the zoom and they could see another fifteen orange shapes of various sizes.

"That, gentlemen, is our battle group. We find what we are looking for, and you are going to see lots of yellow. We have a couple of hours before we reach our destination, so we are going to use that time to practice until you hate that thing, but trust me, it is very effective, particularly in the mountains, where it is fairly quiet and where visuals are difficult. You two have worked together as a team for a long time, and you know how each other thinks before the other guy says anything. That's how you are going to work with Eyes and Ears after a little practice."

Still mumbled, "What am I thinking now?"

Tee patted him on the shoulder. "If I could do that, I'd save lots of money on dates."

"Damn, he reads minds, too," Still said as he started experimenting with the controls and learning where everything was.

Tee smiled. "Just relax and play with the machines. They were designed to be operated by a high school kid, so I think you guys can catch up. The hardest part is figuring out what are ambient sounds and what are bad guys creeping around quietly, so you have to constantly check via visual and heat sensor."

"Okay, so what happens if we find something?" asked Hollahan.

"Well, you notice there are a few more of us on this aircraft. We have lots of choices. We can call in an air strike that we can monitor live; we can control ground forces from up here—we have several companies on the ground nearby; or we can drop a little present of our own."

Still looked at Hollahan then back at Tee. "You mean this bird has bombs also? I figured we were just observation."

"Like I said," began Tee, "no one has a bird like this. We can jam radar, listen to half the world, watch anything we want, use satellites, run a war, and yes, we even have a few little surprises. This baby has a slightly smaller version of a daisy cutter in her tail. We release that puppy, and look out below. One punch takes out a whole village. That's one of the reasons it's so hard to take off of a carrier—this bird is heavy as hell even with the comforts pulled out of her. We also have countermeasures for incoming missiles as well as rocket pods under the wings and a Gatling gun in her nose."

Tee pulled out two headsets and handed them to Still and Hollahan.

"Your lip mikes are voice-activated. If anything happens, don't get excited and start yelling—we can all hear you loud and clear. The cockpit can hear you as well, so if we start getting busy, he can maneuver us to wherever we want to be. If you two are just speaking to each other, press the button on the ear and you will cut out the mike so we don't hear you. Got it?"

They both said "yes," and Tee started going over the controls with them again. They would continue drilling and training for the entire trip to Afghanistan. They paused only once, to watch the refueling operation as a KC-10 topped them off when they got into Afghani airspace.

CHAPTER 20

Amy sat drinking a double latte and wearing sunglasses to cover the dark circles under her eyes. She was reading the *Washington Post* and killing time waiting for Mitch, who was rarely late. By six forty-five she was getting nervous. When he walked in a few minutes before seven, she found herself breathing a sigh of relief. He walked in, ordered a cup of espresso, and sat down with her. He surprised her with a kiss, which was normal to try to appear as a "couple," but this time he kissed her full on the mouth and embraced her for a second longer than normal.

He plopped down on the seat in front of her at the small table for two.

"My," she exclaimed, "aren't we in a good mood this morning." She was trying to act like it was all business, but she really did have a thing for him.

Mitch had already glanced around the busy Starbucks and decided all was as it should be. He leaned closer to his pretty blond counterpart.

"Good news, Miss Lang," he said, smiling.

"*Ohh*," she exclaimed dramatically, "now it's Miss Lang, after you practically ravaged me."

He smiled. "You would know if I ravaged you, trust me. Amy, I have good news. We may have caught a small break. Let me finish my coffee and we'll take a walk."

They sat in silence, just sort of sizing each other up as they drank their coffees. When they were finished, they got up and walked outside. They walked down Sixth toward the National Gallery of Art. Arm in arm and at a slow pace like lovers, Mitch leaned toward his espionage partner.

"There have been developments since we last spoke."

"Yes, I heard about Hassam Abu Mustafa. We figured it was one of yours."

"Good news travels fast. As a matter of fact, it just might have been, although I wouldn't know for sure," he said.

She looked at him and made a sour face. "Please. Did you wake me up in the middle of the night and make me run down here first thing in the morning to tell me what I could see on Fox News?"

"Of course not. The Hassam hit was an operation that was almost a year old. He was personally responsible for hundreds if not thousands of civilian deaths."

"We know that, Mitch. No one in D.C. will grieve over him."

"There is more. The agent who worked that operation was in very deep. His cover is blown now, and we won't be able to get any more intel, but he did hear about Crescent Fire."

Amy stopped walking and faced Mitch.

"If you are bullshitting me to get U.S. support against Hamas, you are going to be very sorry, Mitch."

"Amy, we already have U.S. support against Hamas. This is what I know: Our agent had worked his way to Hassam through a low-level thug named Abdul, who was publicly decapitated after Hassam's death. Evidently Hassam's people blamed Abdul for our man's ability to get to Hassam."

"Evidently," Amy said sarcastically.

"Our man was supposed to be accompanying Abdul to Syria through Jordan on a mission for Hamas that Hassam had set up personally. The name 'Crescent Fire' was used."

Amy still had a sour expression on her face. "Just like that, huh? Hamas is going to tell some low-level thug about a top secret operation that spans the globe that we can't find any intel on?"

"As you would say, Amy, 'evidently.' "

"Go on," she said, still very much doubting what he was saying.

"Abdul and our man were supposed to be getting a package in Syria and delivering it for Hassam. Syria has been a safe house for half of Iraq's weapons since before the war, although apparently the United States doesn't seem to care." He waited for a reaction, but seeing none, continued. "We are of the opinion that Hamas was delivering a weapon of some type to Al Qaeda operatives for a terrorist attack on the United States."

Amy stopped walking again. "Jesus, Mitch. We talked about this before. Why do the Israelis insist on the international terrorist conspiracy theory? I know it makes it very convenient for your government to be able to tie in Al Qaeda with the groups working against Israel, but you don't have any credible evidence."

"Actually, I believe we do. We have been watching Ibrahiim bin Abdul bin al-Bustan carefully for a long time. He is tied into Al Qaeda as well as Hamas and Islamic Jihad. He has had contact with Fadi Wazeeri himself, as well as his cousin Kareem. Both Wazeeris have been in and out of Syria, Sudan, Egypt, Jordan, and Saudi Arabia. We believe Fadi is running Crescent Fire out of Syria, although he hasn't been seen in months. We have no idea where he is. He could be anywhere from Afghanistan to Zimbabwe by now."

They walked quietly for a moment while Amy digested what he had said.

"Syria, huh? This is based on your man who may have been going to get a package there for Hamas."

"Not for Hamas. Hamas was getting the package for Al Qaeda. Like I said, they are all working together. They are operating like divisions of a central organization, Al Qaeda being the largest and most well financed. Wazeeri is worth multimillions. He finances all of these little terror groups. 'My enemy's enemy is my friend' is still the rule in the Arab world. Any enemy of the United States or Israel is given money by Al Qaeda to make their jihads. After nine-eleven, Wazeeri was elevated in stature and can gather these groups together under his banner."

"So what are your people doing now?"

"The same thing yours are doing: looking for Crescent Fire, which so far is a ghost. At least we have narrowed down the places to look. We are thinking Syria is a good starting point."

"Do you have assets on the ground in Syria?"

"Do you?"

Amy smiled. There was a point, of course, where neither could go further with the other.

Amy looked at Mitch and realized he looked tired also. "So we will stay in touch and see what develops. I will see what there is to see about Syria and Wazeeri. I hope your assets in Syria are better than ours."

Mitch grunted. "Tough place to work," he said.

"I'm sure. Think I would blend?" She smiled, batting her eyelashes and big blue eyes.

"Oh, sure. There are lots of beautiful blond, blue-eyed women in Western dress running around Syria. They wouldn't even notice you."

She surprised him with a quick peck on the lips and then said a quick good-bye.

"Talk to you soon," she said with a smile as she hailed a cab to her office.

CHAPTER 21

Eastern Afghanistan

The crew in the small plane had been flying a grid pattern for five hours near the Hindu Kush Mountains when Still announced matter-of-factly that he had to pee. The copilot came back from the cockpit and laughed at him, tossing him a plastic bottle.

"Aw, come on, man. This bird doesn't even have a john?" groaned Still.

"Good thing you didn't have to crap," mumbled Hollahan.

"We have plastic litter boxes for that," said the copilot, smiling.

Still was shaking his head. "This bird probably cost ten million dollars and you couldn't put a john in here?"

"Ain't no time to be shy now, sonny," said the copilot, and with that he was gone.

Still was standing up holding the chair with one hand and the bottle with the other when the plane banked hard to port. Still dropped the bottle and was standing there with his privates waving in the breeze, trying to hang on to the chair next to him.

Hollahan was laughing as he tried to hang on to his chair, watching his friend almost falling over with his privates exposed to the whole plane.

"I'm gonna fuckin' kill that fly boy," began Still when the pilot's voice came over the headsets.

"Be advised, we intercepted traffic on hostile ground action and are heading to investigate. Still, put that thing away and belt yourself in," said the pilot, obviously laughing.

The plane speeded up considerably and dropped altitude as it changed direction due north. Tee was working his computer board and speaking off mike to the man on his left, who was also typing furiously. He popped his headset back on and yelled "Ears!"

Still was zipping up and sliding into his seat when Tee yelled "Ears!" the second time.

"Yeah, I gotcha," replied Still.

"Adjust your scanner to 'auto coordinates' and I'll plug the data in from here. You watch your screen and see if you get anything. We're looking at a mountain pass in the Kush. A Ranger team hit an ambush over there and took a KIA. They took out five enemy KIA, possibly part of a larger force. There is a Spooky on station," said Tee.

Still looked at Hollahan. "He just call me a spook?"

Holahan laughed. "Spooky, you idiot. AC-130 gunship."

"How the hell would you know that?" asked Still.

"Air Force, remember?" said Hollahan.

Tee was listening in. "Affirmative on the AC-130 gunship. It is a bad-ass weapons platform. We are radioing the Spooky now so they don't see us as hostiles. You'll be seeing it off the port in about five minutes."

Five minutes later, sure enough, there was the modified cargo plane returning to an assigned patrol area. The pilot of their plane waved their wings at the gunship and continued due north. The gunship crew could tell with one look at the unmarked black plane that the CIA was working the area, although in this case they were wrong. They didn't know about the "men in black."

After a few more minutes passed, Still got very excited. "Holy shit, man! I see stuff!"

Tee was speaking from his console. "Coordinates and objects?"

Still was very excited, like a kid with a new toy. "Man, this is so cool . . . uh, I count seven orange blobs. X: 12.44.05 and Y: 120.20.01."

"Okay, man, relax. Press the zoom key and in the future just give me the last three numbers in a row. So it's X405 and Y001. Got it?"

Still hit the zoom key and the screen size jumped, centered on the seven orange blobs that glowed and moved on a purple background. A grid overlaid the blobs with numbers that were easy to follow. Tee came back on the radio.

"Eyes, plug in those coordinates and press the enter key. Each time you hit enter, it will zoom closer. Got it?"

Hollahan typed the numbers from Still and hit enter. "I don't see anything other than mountains and rocks."

"Hit enter again," said Tee.

He did. He looked but saw nothing. Then again. And again. After the fourth time he saw what looked like seven little bumps in the rocky features of the landscape. The bumps matched the layout of the orange blobs on Still's screen.

"Hey, I think I got something," said Hollahan. He hit enter again after he recentered his screen on the bumps and watched his picture become clearer. It was seven men, apparently U.S. Rangers in camouflage, moving slowly among the rocks. He hit enter again and again until he could actually see the tops of their heads.

"Holy crap. This thing is amazing. I can see these guys . . . I mean, I can look right at them."

"I told ya this was no ordinary plane, boys," said Tee. "That's a Ranger team."

The pilot called back just as Still yelled, "I got something else!"

The pilot heard Still and confirmed what he was about to say. "We have an inbound chopper on station. We will be heading farther north to see where the bad guys are heading."

Still watched as the yellow blob streaked across his screen and stopped at the Rangers. Another orange blob joined the group huddled around the helicopter, and Hollahan watched his screen as well.

"Looks like the Rangers are loading their KIA and adding another man to their team."

"Roger that," said Tee. "Pull out your zooms and I'll plug in new coordinates for you both. We are heading into the mountains to bag us some bad guys."

"Uh, Tee?" asked Still.

"Yeah?"

"Can I pee now?"

CHAPTER 22

Hindu Kush Mountains near the Tajikistan Border

To the northeast lay the Pamir Mountains—a desolate, frozen mountainscape inhospitable to even the locals. To the north and east, the harsh mountains of the Kush softened slightly and the elevations dropped somewhat into slightly more fertile river valleys. Muktar walked ahead of his mule with two guides who lived along the northern border of Afghanistan and Tajikistan. Ibrahiim bin Abdul bin al-Bustan and his band of followers from the Harakat ul-Mujahidin walked along the narrow goat path in silence behind them, ever vigilant against planes or helicopters. While fairly confident that they were too far north to be followed, they had heard aircraft more than once and could take no chances.

The trip from their caves in the Hindu Kush had been brutal. Although real winter was still at least three months away, it was already well below freezing at night, with wicked winds blowing through the mountains so loudly that they made eerie noises all night long. The days were gray and cold, and several times in the higher elevations they found themselves walking in snow. The mules had been invaluable—without them the trip would have been impossible for even the toughest of tribesmen.

As it was, it had taken three weeks to travel what would have been a day's journey by horse or mule on a flat road. The narrow trail wound up and down through the mountains. Occasionally it was so steep they would have to beat their mules with whips to make them climb, and many times the tribesmen carried the loads to allow the animals to rest after riding on them for a few kilometers.

The nights were spent in caves when available, but mostly huddling under overhangs in tents that were barely able to stay up in the night winds. They didn't make fires in the open, which was when they needed them most, so they had shivered and been miserable almost nightly. Each morning, when they knelt on their prayer mats and praised Allah, they thanked him for sending the morning sun over the mountaintops to save them from the frozen nights.

Muktar, who was a hundred yards ahead, stopped walking and spoke to his guides, who pointed and spoke in their local language to him. Muktar smiled and patted them on their backs, then gave them each small bundles of money and sent them on their way. He walked back to Ibrahiim and smiled.

"Allah be praised, the mountains of Tajikistan stand right before us. We should make it by tomorrow afternoon. There is a road on the other side of the mountain that will take us west to the village. No one will bother us there, as long as we make a small offering to the village elder. Our guides are headed east, back home, but have told me the way. We will simply stay on this trail and follow it west around the mountain. There will be one long climb, and the rest is downhill to the village. It will be warmer there as well."

Ibrahiim smiled and looked at the gray sky. "God is great," he said. "He has seen us out of the hands of our enemies. He will see us destroy them as well. Did the guides tell you anything about our delivery?"

"No, Ibrahiim. And I would certainly not ask them. I did not think it wise to share the information with anyone other than you. The Mujahidin contacts will be at the village when we arrive. I am sure they will have what we need. The guides know only that we will have people to meet us at the village; they don't know anything about what they are bringing."

Ibrahiim smiled his yellow smile and looked to the heavens. At the top of his lungs he began screaming, "Allahu akbar! Death to the infidels!" The others in his company picked up the war cry and began screaming. Muktar smiled at the men in front of him, fearless warriors of Islam who would crush the American invaders. By tomorrow they would be among friends.

Miles away, high overhead in a black, unmarked aircraft, orange blobs were lighting up all over Bob Still's radar screen.

"Yo, man! I got something!" Still was yelling. He had been at the computer for hours with dozens of false alarms as he tried to get the hang of his new toy, but this time he had very obvious colors lighting up like fireworks on his screen.

Tee calmly replied, "Eyes, get coordinates on that."

Hollahan, who was now pretty familiar with his console, asked Still for the numbers and dialed them into his computer.

He was having a problem, so Tee left his seat and stood behind him to coach.

"Whoa, man, no wonder you can't get this. How far out are you zoomed, Bob?" he asked as he looked at Still's computer.

Still shrugged, looking a little embarrassed. "Uh, I'm not exactly sure."

Tee leaned over and started typing, and a grid and contour map appeared overlaid on Still's blobs of colors.

"Wow. Okay, we're about a hundred kilometers away from that location. You had this thing maxed out. It's okay; you actually got something that looks like a decent-size party in a weird spot. Those mountains are not inhabited. The only people up there would be folks sneaking in and out of Tajikistan. That's the border right there, but that's not a regular border crossing location," he said, pointing to a map reference. He leaned back over Hollahan and started typing on his computer as well.

"Damn," Tee mumbled.

"What's up, Tee?" asked Hollahan.

"We're either too far away, or our satellite isn't aimed that far north. Sit tight."

Tee hopped back into his console and pulled on a headset.

"Black Star to Whopper, come in," he began. He was speaking rapidly to their team on board the aircraft carrier, giving coordinates rapidly but clearly.

Still started smiling, and leaned over to Hollahan. "Two to one we see F-16s smoking that place in about five minutes."

Tee finished giving coordinates and called up to the pilot to head home.

"What? We don't get to watch the fireworks?" asked Still.

"No fireworks, boys. We're going to get a team in there and take a look before we just blow the shit out of it. Make sure it ain't a bunch of goat herders, and if it isn't, maybe we can gather some intel. Good work, Still. Let's get home, debrief, and take a hot shower. I might even buy you a beer."

Still was still perplexed. "How the hell are you going to get a team in there? Those Rangers are a hundred kilometers away, and there's no way you can drop helicopters in there. What gives?"

Tee smiled. "HALO drop," he said. Seeing no sign of understanding from Hollahan or Still, he explained further. "High altitude, low opening. Understand? We'll have special forces guys parachute in tonight."

"Are you shittin' me, man? Parachute into those mountains at night? It'll be pitch-black and freezing," grumbled Still.

"Let me tell ya something: When you jump out of the aircraft at twenty-five thousand feet, it's pretty damn cold anyway. The team will have cold-weather gear, oxygen, satellite uplinks, and plenty of hardware. The only real tricky part is the damn wind and lack of visual navigation. They'll drop in unnoticed, hump it down to the targets you guys acquired, and see who's who down there. One thing for sure: The chance of finding goat herders down there is pretty damn slim. Dollars to doughnuts the guys you picked up on the ground are related to the ambush on that Ranger team. There shouldn't be anybody walking around in the mountains down there. Maybe we caught a break for once. Let's go get that beer."

The plane had already changed course and picked up speed and altitude as it headed back to yet another interesting landing on board the aircraft carrier.

Still leaned over quietly to his friend, "I'll let you in on a little secret. They could put me in front of a firing squad before I'd jump out of an airplane into frozen blackness to land on a fucking mountain filled with bad guys. I did some crazy shit in 'Nam when I was a kid, but nothing like this. These boys are crazy."

CHAPTER 23

Port Sudan

Fadi Wazeeri couldn't help smiling. He was standing at the rail of his luxury yacht, watching through binoculars as the oil tanker left the Sudanese port and headed north, toward the Suez Canal. With almost forty ships a day entering the canal, the chances of an inspection team actually boarding and demanding to see the oil tanker's interior hull were slim to none. Wazeeri had hired a normal crew of sailors with a captain who had sailed oil tankers for twenty years. If they ran a background check on the captain, it would reveal only a long history of commercial transit.

The captain himself, of Saudi background, knew nothing of the ship's real mission. He had merely been told to bring the ship through the Suez Canal headed into the eastern Mediterranean and to await further instructions on where he would be headed to load his tanker with oil. All sensitive areas of the ship had been welded shut, and there was no reason for him to suspect anything unusual. The exterior of the ship looked exactly as it had before it had undergone its transformation into a weapons platform in Port Sudan.

The Sudanese workers had been paid well, and their foreman had received a very healthy bonus for finishing ahead of schedule. In a country torn apart by civil war and ravaged by violence, with janjaweed thugs killing the poor black population by the tens of thousands, no one looked at the activity at the port twice. The workmen would take their earnings and live very well, by their standards, for another year or two without having to work if they chose not to. The smart ones used their newfound wealth to find a way to get themselves and their families anywhere but Sudan.

Fadi watched with intensity as the *Crescent King* moved slowly into deeper water toward Syria, where he would load his Scud into her belly and turn her into the *Crescent Fire*. He was grinding his teeth and having a vision of his fire raining death into the heart of the Great Satan, when his cousin interrupted his thoughts.

"This is a great day, cousin," said Kareem with a huge smile. "How long until we can pick up our cargo?"

"It will be two or three days to get through the canal into the Med, depending on how long the wait is at the canal. We can be off the coast of Syria in four or five days at the most. We must get word to our people in Syria to be prepared to move our cargo. Have we replaced the men from Hamas yet?"

"I have had no word from anyone on what is happening in Gaza or the West Bank. The Israelis are watching everyone and making it very difficult to get in and out. We may have to use new people in Jordan or Syria."

Fadi stroked the little beard on his chin. Kareem could hear him grinding his teeth.

"Get the word out to Syria, Saudi, and Jordan that we are looking for volunteers. We will need to cause distractions elsewhere when we move our missile. Events will begin to happen very rapidly now, Kareem. We must keep a few steps ahead of the Americans and the Israelis in the coming days. That will mean targets inside Israel, as well as any targets in Saudi and Jordan. We will keep sending money into Iraq and Afghanistan to keep the Americans off-balance as well. Their newspapers tell of our victories every day, and support for their president is gone. They will be out of our lands within two years, Kareem, and then we will be able to finish the Israelis. Once the holy lands are ours again, we will finish the Great Satan in his home. They are weak. They do not understand the commitment of our warriors. Their cities will burn, their crusade will end, and Muhammad will smile from the heavens."

Kareem quietly praised God and eyed Fadi carefully. When Fadi began his preaching he often became violent, and Kareem did not want to be a target of his anger. He stood silently waiting for Fadi's instructions. Fadi stared at his ship and mumbled to himself, his hatred of the infidels coming out of his very pores as he envisioned Washington in a mushroom cloud. The vision made him more agitated as he reminded himself that he still had no luck in procuring a nuclear device.

He turned to Kareem, his face looking quiet but disturbed now. "What do our people say in Iran and Korea? The Koreans will do anything for money. Why do they not sell us what we need?"

Kareem stood silently, fearing any answer was the wrong one. Fadi began pacing about the deck and stormed into the cabin where his computers were located. He sat down and began typing, something he rarely did himself. He e-mailed his cousin in Saudi Arabia:

The party plans have begun. Make sure you send invitations to all of our friends at home as well. Send them out tomorrow.

He hit the send button so hard he almost knocked the computer off the table. The message, although seemingly innocuous, would begin a series of attacks all over the Eastern Hemisphere as Fadi prepared for the big attack in the home of the Great Satan. He wrote another message to one of his contacts from Harakat ul-Mujahidin, a man named Farooq whom he had never met, but had worked through intermediaries before when planning hits on targets in Afghanistan and Pakistan. Farooq moved around quite a bit and had plenty of supporters. His group was comprised of true, battle-tested warriors. They had fought Indian soldiers in the Kashmir region, killed and kidnapped Westerners regularly, and generally disrupted normal government activities wherever they went. Farooq himself had battled the Russians for years, ironically with the help of the American CIA. Farooq answered to Ibrahiim bin Abdul bin al-Bustan himself, the leader of the Harakat ul-Mujahidin, but planned and carried out most of his own activities. He could, however, be counted on if he were needed for a specific purpose.

In his e-mail to Farooq, he merely asked in code for his present location so he might know best how to use his help. Farooq, though a tribal man, was fairly state of the art in equipment and weapons, thanks largely to money supplied by Fadi Wazeeri. And while Fadi supplied him with plenty of money, he rarely asked for anything in return. Now he was about to call in his marker, and he was sure he could count on Farooq's aid.

His next e-mail went to a reporter from Al Jazeera who was working in Syria and Iraq. The reporter was a true believer, and Fadi had given him several interviews at times when no one knew where Fadi was, thus making him an important news figure. In the meantime, the reporter always gave more information to Fadi than Fadi ever gave to him. He had given Fadi American troop strengths and movements in Afghanistan as well as Iraq, the locations of

U.N. inspectors before the war, which were always relayed to the Iraqis, and he had provided courier service into hard-to-reach places. His press credentials got him in almost anywhere at times when Fadi's people couldn't get close to certain areas. He e-mailed the reporter and told him to cover stories in western Syria, being watchful of foreigners and spies. This asset could keep his eyes out for any American activities near the ports where his tanker was headed.

Fadi turned off his computer and smiled. It had been a productive ten minutes. With a few keystrokes, he had begun his jihad that would spill the blood of the nonbelievers all over the land that belonged to the people of Islam and the followers of the one true God. Fadi stood and checked the time. It was time for prayer, and he went up on the deck, where Kareem was already on his prayer rug. Fadi joined him and thanked Allah for allowing him such good fortune. He was on his way to Syria to pick up his missile, his fire from the heavens that would change the course of history.

CHAPTER 24

Mediterranean Sea, U.S. Carrier Fleet

Deep in the bowels of the aircraft carrier, a SEAL team prepared for a mission that would make most professional soldiers shake their heads in disbelief. The special twelve-man team had painted their faces black and brown for night mountain warfare and zipped up into heated black thermal jumpsuits over their thermal underwear. They were silent as they slipped on Kevlar vests, knee and elbow pads, and special thermal gloves. By the time they were finished dressing and picked up their battle packs, weapons, and parachutes, each man carried almost one hundred pounds. No one grimaced when he slipped the straps over his shoulders and made his way to the elevator that would take him to the helicopter on the deck. These men had trained for years for missions just like this one. More often than not, they would mentally and physically prepare, only to be told to stand down. Not this time. The mission was a "go," and everyone knew it.

The men silently boarded the Marine helicopter that would ferry them to Portugal. There they would transfer to a waiting C-140 cargo plane that would fly them over the airspace belonging to Tajikistan, where they would hurl themselves into black, frozen air, illegally entering a country with which we were not at war. None of them wore dog tags or any identification, but no one in the world of Islam would mistake them for anything other than an elite American fighting machine. Marines and sailors on deck saluted them as they pulled themselves into the helicopter, not because they had to because of rank, but because they wanted to out of immense respect for and awe of these elite fighters. The helicopter doors were left open to keep the men from sweating in their jumpsuits and risk freezing in them later. As the helicopter slowly left the deck of the carrier and headed east to the waiting plane, Tee cracked open his first beer in several weeks.

Still and Hollahan held theirs up, and the three of them clinked bottles.

"To your first successful mission," said Tee. The three of them were in a tiny conference room next to the small cafeteria where they ate every day. Still finished his beer in one long chug, followed by a loud belch. Hollahan wasn't far behind him. Tee finished his and looked at his comrades.

"Okay, victory party is over. Time to go watch the show."

Still burped again. "What show?" he asked.

"The one that's going to happen in about three hours. We have to prep a bit before they jump," said Tee.

The two men followed Tee back up to the hangar where their plane stood, still guarded by a man in black holding an M-16. The guard acknowledged Tee, and the three of them climbed up the ladder to the plane's consoles.

"We don't have to be flying to be working. We still have the coordinates from our last flyover, which was uplinked to our satellite. We can still use 'Eyes' on that point and scan around the area. 'Ears' won't work from here, but we

can do our best to pinpoint the location of the target for our
SEAL team before they jump. We don't want them ending
up on the wrong side of a ten-thousand-foot mountain, or
dropping into a hostile village."

"If we can work from here, why the hell do we have to
fly around for ten hours at a time?" grumbled Still.

"We can only work from here if we know where to look.
The only reason we know where to look is because we already found them by flying over them with Ears and Eyes
scanning them. Got it?"

"Makes sense," said Still, who wanted another beer.

"We'll scan grids over the last known location until we
find them again, then give those coordinates to the SEALs
right before they jump. I've had a few combat jumps
myself, but damn, I can't imagine doing a HALO jump at
night into those mountains. Those boys have balls."

"It could be worse," said Hollahan. They both looked
at him. He smiled and shrugged and said, "It could be us
jumping."

It took more than an hour to find their target by scanning a grid pattern over the last known location. Using the
"Ears" locating equipment would have been much easier
but would have required flying back out again. Once they
had located the targets, they began zooming in on the location, which was right across the Tajikistan border. They
found themselves looking at grainy black-and-white aeri-
als of what looked like very small huts. There were several
people moving about, with what appeared to be mules or
horses moving as well. Once they had located the tiny village, they zoomed out and scanned repeatedly in the area
to make sure they weren't zeroed in on the wrong target.
Finding nothing in any direction for up to twenty kilometers, they rezeroed on the village again.

"This has to be it," said Tee. "I count about twenty or so,
but it's hard to say. There might be a lot more in those
buildings."

"You sure you don't want to just drop a Daisy Cutter in there first and *then* interview these guys?" asked Still.

"No can do, Chief," said Tee. First of all, you are looking at Tajikistan. We have no authority to be *in* Tajikistan; therefore, we aren't. We can't drop a huge bomb on a neutral country we aren't operating in. Second, we might not be looking at terrorists, they might be civilians. And third, if they are bad guys, which we all think they are, they may have information we need that we couldn't get from a bunch of charred corpses."

"All right, I see your point," said Still, "but they outnumber our guys at least two to one. You think they are just going to surrender? They are all going to end up dead anyway. Why risk our guys? That's my only point."

"Because that's how we operate. It is part of the responsibility of being the good guys. It's always easier to be the bad guy with no rules, but we follow rules of engagement, and our SEAL team understands that. They signed up for this, they trained for this, and they are very, *very* good at this. Two-to-one odds don't worry these guys. Chances are this will be over before anyone on the ground knows what has happened. The tricky part of this mission is not getting in and doing the job; it is going to be getting *out*."

Still and Hollahan looked at each other, then at Tee. Hollahan spoke up. "Okay, so how do they get out?"

Tee grimaced. "Plan A is they walk back to Afghanistan, where we can pick them up legally."

"What's plan B?" asked Hollahan.

"Plan B is what we do if there is a major fuckin' problem with plan A, which we don't want to think about right now. Let's get our team in first without getting them killed. The terrain and weather are murderous enough in daylight. Doing this at night is, well, a nightmare."

The three of them continued to monitor the village in silence for more than an hour when their radio crackled with a message from the C-130 cargo plane that approached Tajik airspace.

"Rock one to base, come in. Over," said a calm voice.

"Base to Rock one, you are five by five, come back. Over," replied Tee.

"Read you five by five, base. We are approaching commuter zone. Do you have a sit-rep?" said the voice. The voice was Captain Bernard Boyce, U.S. Navy, known as BB or Skipper to his friends, who were all in the plane with him.

"Sit-rep as follows: Minimum twenty possible hostiles. Location at map grid Lima Zulu two-two-six. Repeat, Lima Zulu two-two-six. Appears to be a small village with eight structures. You will be approximately two clicks over red line."

The red line was the map line that separated Afghanistan from Tajikistan. The landing zone was clearly a violation of international law, hence the purpose of operating outside of the United States with a team that didn't exist and reported to no one inside the Pentagon or the FBI.

"We copy, base. Will check in after LZ green. Over and out," said the captain.

Tee smiled, looked over at Still and said with a chuckle, "Rock one. Those guys are hilarious. They're jumping out of a plane at twenty-five thousand feet and they're gonna fall like a rock. Everybody's a comedian around here."

"How long until they jump?" asked Hollahan.

"I'm not sure, but they'll radio us back when they land and regroup. Now might be a good time to start praying if you are so inclined."

On board the C-130 cargo plane, the team members were checking altimeters, weapons, chutes, and each other. The rear door was open, blowing frozen air into the cabin as an airman stood harnessed to the rear door watching the red light above his head. When it turned green, he gave the thumbs-up to Captain Boyce, who high-fived the SEAL next to him and took a running jump out of the back of the plane. The eleven other team members sprinted after him as best they could with a hundred pounds of gear and chutes on, and within a few seconds were all diving through frozen black space. The airman pressed a button that closed the rear door, and the plane banked to turn back to base.

In the air, the twelve-man team could see each other's luminous glow sticks that were attached to their oxygen tanks. It was pitch-black except for the tiny yellow dots that looked like stars hurtling toward earth. The men all looked identical with their black suits and black oxygen masks, and within a few seconds, had somehow found each other in the black sky. They clasped hands and made a circle like a skydiving team showing off for a crowd. In this case, it wasn't to show off, but rather to stay together in hostile, dangerous terrain. Normally, in a daytime jump, they would have visual clues to guide themselves into their target. In the black of frozen night, they had nothing but Captain Boyce's GIS wrist computer that merely showed arrows to keep them heading to the predetermined location. They all had voice-activated microphones, but remained silent awaiting instructions from BB.

The SEALs were all adrenaline addicts, so free-falling at night only made them happy. Most were smiling under their masks, although they were all razor sharp awaiting the word to pull their cords to open their chutes. Both BB and "Homer," Terrance Homeshund, a Special Forces transfer, wore altimeters. Their job was to announce ripcord time, and by both doing the same job, it was a redundant safety. At the appointed time, Homer quietly said "rip one," followed closely by BB calling "rip two," at which time all team members let go of each other and pulled their cords. Twelve chutes popped almost simultaneously, and the men felt their stomachs leave through their feet.

They hit the ground within a hundred yards of each other, which was nothing short of miraculous in the windy dark. As soon as they regained their feet, they were out of their chutes, rolling them up and ripping off their masks and oxygen tanks. They hustled toward each other as fast as they could, carrying all their gear with them. BB spoke quietly through his mike to the team.

"Alpha Team leader on the ground," he said quietly as his men moved toward him silently in the rocky terrain.

"Alpha two on the ground," called back another.

"Alpha three," and so on, until all six Alpha Team members had found each other.

"Bravo team leader on the ground," came back another voice. This was Jimmy "Apache" Ramirez's voice. He was an All-American football player in college, and could have played tight end for any team in the NFL. He chose the navy instead, on September 12, 2001. His mission—to be a navy SEAL. Mission accomplished. His number two man, Howard "Whiz" Anders, looked like a computer geek, not a navy SEAL. In fact, he was an engineer who had joined the Seabees. How he ended up in the SEALs was any-body's guess. At barely 5 foot 8 and 150 pounds, it was amazing that he could have finished SEAL school at all, but he did so with flying colors. Whiz was Bravo team's computer whiz kid who doubled as an explosives expert. He was the kind of kid who could design a bridge, build it, and then blow it up for you all in the same day.

"Bravo two, three, and four on the ground," said Whiz quietly. He had Bravo three and four with him already, tak-ing apart their packs and repacking gear with weapons at the ready. Bravo five and six checked in and found the rest of the crew. They all had ditched their chutes and oxygen equipment from the HALO jump, and had hid it under some large stones in a small crevice in the rocky ledge where they gathered. With their night-vision goggles on, the black mountains glowed an eerie green. The cold wasn't a factor at all, partly because of the special clothing, but mostly because of the adrenaline rushing through their veins. Once they had their chutes and tanks hidden, they all gathered on the small hillside angling down into a gently sloping rocky landscape.

Whiz was checking a Palm Pilot–size computer that gave him GIS information about the location of the tiny village they were seeking. They had landed within a few yards of their target, even at night with gusty winds. It was a testament to years of training and a little luck. The twelve quickly and quietly double-checked weapons, discussed the best route to their objective, and split into two teams. Alpha was lead scout team; Bravo was watching their back and the landscape for any sign of danger. While the six men of Alpha stayed together and moved in a straight line to the village, Bravo split into three teams of two and fanned out several hundred yards to their flanks and rear. Boyce called on his satellite radio back to the aircraft carrier, where the men in black sat on the plane in the hangar belowdecks.

"Rock one is on target. Will advise when mission completed. Over and out."

The village was less than two kilometers to the north, and they would all reassemble on the south side of the village on a little hill overlooking their target. While the terrain wasn't difficult in this area, it still took almost an hour to cover the distance. Stealth was of the utmost importance, and they simply couldn't risk being detected. They moved painfully slowly, stopping every few yards to wait and listen, lest a dog bark or an enemy sentry radio an alarm.

When the two teams finally did reassemble on the hilltop, Bravo set up a perimeter with each two-man team having a sniper to watch in every direction. The SEAL snipers were some of the best in the world, and on a calm day, no one was safe within a mile and a half of them. The men settled in to wait and watch, the cold breeze chilling them slightly after the nerve-racking walk through the hills and rocky outcroppings. Their team leader checked with his forwardmost scout, Alpha six.

A quiet voice spoke back to him. "BB, one hundred fifty yards east of the last hut, a diesel generator with cables running to that hut. Big dish on top, and they ain't watching Al Jazeera."

"Roger six, sit tight," said Captain Boyce. He turned to the men on his left, and using sign language, told them to work down to the generator. He tapped his throat mike twice to get the attention of Bravo, who looked in his direction. He signed for them to move around to the west side of the village, except for the third pair from Bravo, who had their best sniper and spotter. Those two moved into a better position to watch the buildings, and could cover the SEALs when they moved in.

Alpha six had frozen in his tracks when a large dog that had been sleeping stood up and stretched, looking in their direction. Fortunately, the wind was blowing toward the SEALs, and the dog hadn't smelled them yet. Alpha six fired one silenced round and dropped the dog where he stood, then continued moving forward. In the quiet valley where only the wind made noise this time of night, even the silenced shot sounded loud. Everyone froze at the ready, but nothing stirred in the huts below.

Muktar sat quietly drinking hot tea and watching Ibrahiim bin Abdul bin al-Bustan assembling a computer. Muktar was not completely ignorant, but he had never seen a computer actually being used. A man who had grown up in the mountains as a tribal leader and warrior, Muktar had very little knowledge about anything other than warfare and the Koran. Whatever he knew of the outside world was what he had been told by his father before

him, or what he had witnessed when he fought the Soviets.
The Soviets were the first infidels he had ever seen first-
hand. Prior to fighting them, all his battles had been against
other tribes over local issues. Not until the Soviets poured
into Afghanistan did the tribes unite temporarily to fight
their common enemy. One thing was for sure, the Soviets
had brought with them weapons unlike anything ever seen
in the ancient mountains before them. Their Hind helicopters had been something out of a nightmare, mowing down
his tribesmen by the hundreds as the Mujahidin fighters
fired antique Enfield rifles in vain. The Soviets also had
brought land mines, sometimes disguised as children's
toys, as well as heavy machine guns and missile systems
that totally outmatched the Mujahidin cavalry.

Men like Muktar had fought the Soviets for years with
weapons smuggled to them by the American CIA, but it had
been so secret that the Afghanis had never known where the
weapons had come from. As far as they knew, they had
been fortunate enough, by the grace of Allah, to have recovered Soviet weapons from dead infidels. In fact, the United
States had gone to great lengths to smuggle in only Russian
weapons systems, to keep total deniability about any in-
volvement in the Soviet war in Afghanistan. The weapons,
some made by the Chinese, who were all too happy to make
weapons to kill their Cold War enemy, had been AK-47s,
heavy machine guns, and eventually shoulder-fired missiles. All these had been smuggled through Pakistan as the
United States used these mountain fighters to wage war
against the Communists.

For years, the United States armed these cagey mountain warriors to use them in the Cold War against the Soviets. How ironic that these same hard-line fighters were now
using these same weapons against the United States, their
infidel enemy who was, in their view, waging another Crusade.

Muktar admired men like Ibrahiim al-Bustan, religious

fighters who were intelligent and schooled. Warriors like this could fight on a much more even playing field, and could even bring the fight to the enemy. Muktar had seen too many brave Mujahidin fighters blown off of their horses by Soviet helicopters not to understand that they needed better weapons and tactics. Bravery simply was not enough to fight their enemy invaders anymore, as it had been when his grandfathers had fought the British Empire.

Muktar almost jumped from his quiet concentration when Ibrahiim cursed and slammed his hand on the table.

"What is the matter, Ibrahiim?" he asked.

"I have no power. Go out and check the generator. It should be running with a full tank," Ibrahiim answered.

The village didn't use electricity for anything except the single generator that powered the computer and satellite uplink. The room was a time warp, gas lamps and wood-stoves next to a state-of-the-art laptop computer wired to a dish on the roof.

Muktar stood and pulled on his heavy sheepskin cape. He opened and closed the door quickly, lest the cold wind bother their leader. His feet crunched over the snow and gravel as he jogged toward the generator, which, strangely, sounded like it was still humming.

Whiz and Apache were lying on their bellies watching the small village for movement when a door opened and a small man began running toward the generator. The Bravo sniper team had shot the cable out that led to the house to see what kind of reaction they would get when the power went out. The SEALs had surrounded the village and were ready with night-vision goggles. Sniper teams were positioned at both ends of the village as four Alpha SEALs slowly snaked their way closer to the buildings.

Apache spoke quietly into his mike, "One tango heading to the generator. No other movement."

BB spoke quietly back to the teams. "Snipers ready, Alpha. Are you close enough for a quiet kill?"

Alpha team checked back. "Affirmative."

"Go," said BB.

Apache and Whiz watched from their position as one dark shadow moved quickly and silently toward the lone figure near the generator. Just as Muktar traced the power cable to where the cord had been shot in two, the shadow moved like lightning. Muktar was bending over, picking up the cable in confusion when Alpha team member Lonigan jumped him from behind, and with one quick movement opened his throat with a large, black K-Bar knife. They both went to the ground with a quiet thump. Lonigan scanned quickly in all directions, then dragged Muktar into some rocky vegetation a few dozen yards away. Lonigan's partner sprinted to where they had been and used a tree branch to sweep all over the area, covering all footprints and sign of a struggle. He joined Lonigan in the brush, and everyone hunkered down and waited in silence.

After five minutes had passed, the door opened again, and a robed figure began screaming out the door, apparently looking for his comrade.

"I have a shot," came a voice from the sniper team.

"Hold," replied BB.

The shouting continued down in the small village, and eventually a few other men appeared from other huts. A group of seven stood talking to the robed man, who was getting animated, apparently over the whereabouts of their missing man. Three more came out of another hut and approached the group. After a moment the three, one of whom was carrying a rifle, started walking in the direction of Apache and Whiz, calling out in Afghani a word that sounded like "Muktar" over and over.

BB quietly spoke to Bravo team, "When they are close enough, take them out quietly."

"Affirmative," came the reply, and the SEALs all sat motionless. BB watched as the remaining group of men went into the same building, which is what they had been hoping for. The other three walked into the brush, the man with the rifle in front. There were three very quiet pops, and the men went down simultaneously. Apache and Whiz quickly dragged the men into the brush after making sure they were dead.

"Scratch three," said Apache.

BB spoke to his Alpha team closest to the village, "There are a minimum of eight tangos in the last building. Start at the other end and try and work one at a time toward that building. Snipers have cover. Apache and Whiz, work back to my location; we will come in from the other end. The hut with the dish on top is weapons hold, I want prisoners. Out."

The Alpha team assembled at the opposite end of the village and worked to the front door, a wooden mess covered with a tarp of animal hides. The four men had silenced automatic weapons ready. The first SEAL pulled the door open and kept out of the way, while the other three sprinted into the one-room building. The fourth member jumped in behind them, and after what seemed an eternity, they radioed back, "Negative contact."

The team half crawled to the next building and repeated the procedure. A moment later they radioed back, "Two tangos KIA, moving to three."

When they assaulted building three, it was empty, like the first one. Alpha radioed back to BB, "Negative contact, Skipper, but I smell food coming out of four."

The words weren't out of his mouth when the door of hut four opened and a man walked out, apparently to relieve himself. He was standing to the side of the building loosening his trousers when a Bravo team sniper silently took him out with a single head shot. Alpha team moved quickly to the door, two on each side.

BB radioed to the team, "Hold; that may get loud. I want whoever is in that first hut with the radio taken alive. We are moving to building one. If cover gets blown, take them all down ASAP."

Bravo team came together fifty yards from the first building, the one with the satellite dish on top. BB could hear voices inside, apparently loud and agitated.

"Change of plans, Alpha. We go loud on three, prepare to assault," said Captain Boyce.

The Alpha team members took out grenades, while Bravo prepared "flash-bang" stun grenades. After a moment, BB came back on the radio. "Prepare Alpha and Bravo. Three, two, one, go!"

Both teams ripped the doors open on the two huts at the same time. Alpha threw white phosphorous grenades that exploded in blinding white fire, incinerating the dozen men who sat eating by the fire. Bravo team threw stun grenades that exploded with a flash and a deafening noise, and then assaulted the dazed occupants of the hut, which turned out to be three men. As soon as they had wristlocks on the semiconscious men, BB started yelling into his mike, "Secure in one, check two now! We are missing tangos!"

The Alpha team tumbled out of the fourth hut, where they had fired a few hundred rounds into the burning mess to finish the job, and found themselves facing Mujahidin fighters running out of the second hut. The two groups of men were almost on top of each other when the Alpha team opened fire and started running into the crowd coming out of the hut. A fat old man with a shotgun was the only one to get a round off, which blew Lonigan off his feet. Apache fired a three-round burst into the man's chest and then jumped into the hut firing at the last man, who was grabbing a rifle.

Whiz ripped open Lonigan's uniform to see how badly he was hit. His body armor had kept the slug from entering his body, but the shell had broken a rib and knocked the wind out of him. Keegan was their acting corpsman, and he grabbed Lonigan's belt, picking him up and down off of the ground a few inches to get some air into his lungs. He poured some water on his face, and Lonigan woke up coughing and spitting up. Lonigan instinctively was floundering around looking for a weapon, and Keegan laid on him and told him to relax. Lonigan's eyes rolled around for a moment, then came back into focus.

"What happened?" he asked with a groan.

"You're dead and you're in Heaven. I'm Jesus here to welcome you, my son," said Keegan, smiling.

Lonigan's eyes were blinking as he tried to focus on Keegan.

"Fuck you," he mumbled.

Keegan looked over at Apache, who was scanning the village for movement.

"He's fine," said Keegan, who helped Lonigan sit up.

BB appeared out of the first hut and jogged over to Bravo team. He saw Keegan helping Lonigan. Apache saw BB's concern.

"He's fine, Skipper. Whiz is counting bodies. You bag a bad guy?"

"Yeah," said BB. "We grabbed three of them. One of them was trying to get a laptop running. I'm guessing he's the boss. We might have scored on this one. We need to hump it back into the mountains ASAP. We've got two klicks to cross over the red line, unless they'll bend some rules and grab us closer to our present location. Not going to be an easy trip pushing these three along while we watch our back."

"Roger that, Skipper. There's no way to hide that we've been here. We used Willy-Peter on hut four. That sucker is gonna burn all night."

"Okay," said BB, "then let's get the hell out of here as soon as we have a body count and we know the area is secure."

Whiz jogged back to the two men.

"You got three, Skipper?"

BB nodded.

"Okay, then that makes twenty-six enemy accounted

for—twenty-three KIA and your three. We circled around two hundred meters, no sign of anyone else. Snipers are still looking."

"Good job, Whiz. As soon as we are secure, get everyone up and moving. We've got a brisk walk ahead of us. I want to get the hell out of here." Boyce used his satellite phone to call back to the aircraft carrier.

"Rock one heading to EZ one. Estimate arrival at oh-four-hundred hours Zulu time. Over."

Back on the carrier, Tee, Hollahan, and Still breathed a sigh of relief. Tee called back to their team.

"Roger, Rock one, will advise your taxi. Report back in one hour with progress to extraction zone. Confirm contact. Over."

"Affirmative. We have three packages for unwrapping. Twenty-three returned to sender. Over."

Tee smiled. Boyce was a cool customer. "Roger, Rock one. Out."

Tee sat back in his chair and looked at Hollahan and Still. "They're bringing in three men. I can't wait to see what our fishing expedition netted."

Back in Tajikistan, the small band of SEALs walked quickly in the mountains, pushing and pulling their three gagged captives as they hustled back to the border of Afghanistan.

CHAPTER 25

Mediterranean Sea, near Syrian Coast

Fadi Wazeeri was on the deck of his luxury yacht, watching the *Crescent King* moving at twenty knots north along the Syrian coast. His brother had used their private helicopter to leave the yacht the day before and landed in Syria to meet with their contacts from Islamic Jihad. They needed to make final arrangements for the transportation of their Scud onto the ship, as well as speak to someone about getting a better weapon than a conventional warhead. Kareem could be counted on to come through for him, but still, Fadi was worried. They were so close, they couldn't fail.

Abu Hassam Obduri was to be met in a small village near the port of El Haram. The worry was that one of Obduri's men, Sufah Zannad, had been captured and interrogated by the Israelis. He had died in captivity, presumably tortured to death by their intelligence officers. What had he told them before he died? Granted, he didn't know much about Crescent Fire, but he did know places and names that could hurt their operations. Kareem had picked the place

to meet Obduri, and then changed it twice at the last
minute to avoid an ambush. Fadi and Kareem could only
put their trust in Allah now and pray for the best.

As Fadi ate dates and figs on the deck of his yacht and
smiled at his *Crescent King* gliding through the water toward Syria, Kareem walked carefully through the streets of
El Haram. Obduri had arrived an hour earlier, and his men
had fanned out around the small mosque where they would
meet. His guards blended in with the crowd, although they
all carried automatic weapons under their robes. Kareem
removed his shoes and entered the mosque, which was
fairly empty, since prayers had ended an hour earlier. He
walked silently to the back of the mosque, where a door led
to another room.

The imam left as soon as he saw Kareem walk in. He
knew enough not to ask why he was here. The mystery men
had made a sizable donation to the mosque. And in Syria,
one did not ask too many questions about anything. After
the imam left, Kareem closed the door and greeted Abu
Hassam Obduri.

After they exchanged greetings, praised God and his
prophet Muhammad, and discussed local security briefly,
they got right down to business.

"Have you had any luck finding a better gift for the infidels?" asked Kareem. "Fadi is counting on you to come up
with something special."

Obduri smiled. "You know I would never let Fadi down.
Allah has smiled upon us, Kareem. While I had no more
luck than you in obtaining any leads on a nuclear weapon,
I have found a large store of sarin that can be used in the
warhead. With the blessing of Allah and the right weather,
we can kill hundreds of thousands of infidels. Tens of thousands would be the very least, even in bad weather conditions."

Kareem started a slow, evil smile that showed his
stained teeth, just like his cousin Fadi.

"We *had* followed some leads in the hopes of getting some nuclear material. It wasn't weapons-grade, but would have been catastrophic nonetheless. Unfortunately, we had no luck. Apparently the Iranians and the North Koreans are getting jumpy with this Christian president. They have stopped cooperating with us in our plans to acquire nuclear materials. They think it is too dangerous right now, and tell us to be patient. I am out of patience, and I know Fadi is as well. The Sarin will have to be good enough."

"Where is the nerve agent?" asked Kareem.

"Not far from where we have the Scud. It is in a bunker in the desert. The biggest problem will be getting the Scud from there to the port for loading. The sarin fits into a small truck that no one would look at twice. Driving a Scud launcher across the desert is a different story."

Kareem stroked his small chin beard. "Fadi and I have discussed this problem as well. The Scud will have to be moved at night with some type of camouflage over it so it looks more like a large truck. A satellite photo will take a few days to analyze, and by then, the ship will be at sea. With a thousand tankers on the ocean every day, they will never find the *Crescent Fire* before we have fired the weapon into their White House. I only hope their cowboy president is sitting at his desk when the warhead explodes over his head."

"God is great," said Obduri.

"We need to move quickly now, Abu. Our enemies are not too far behind us. We had been waiting for the last possible minute in the hope of obtaining a better weapon for the Scud, but we have to make our move now. We haven't heard back from our people in Afghanistan. They had moved north to Tajikistan and were going to try to obtain a nuclear device from the old Soviet Union. We had made contact with the Chechens in the hopes of acquiring a warhead, but they can't get one even for themselves. With the state of affairs in the western states of the old Soviet Union, we were hopeful that it was achievable, but we have heard nothing. We can wait no longer. The ship can be in port in a day or two at the most. I want the Scud on board the ship the same night. We can assemble the warhead after we are under way. For now, the priorities are loading the ship and getting out to sea. I won't be comfortable until we are out of the Mediterranean and into the Atlantic Ocean."

"I will get started at once. I will need some more money to take care of any officials who might get nosy when we move the Scud. There is a coast guard station nearby as well. They will have to be paid off. Also, I will need to hire a few more locals for security," said Obduri.

Kareem opened the leather case he carried and took out a large bundle of American money.

"One hundred thousand dollars, Abu—that will be more than what you need. The balance is a gift from Fadi."

Obduri smiled and bowed. "Fadi is too kind; I am but a humble servant." With that, he quickly picked up the cash and shoved it into his robe. "I will be at the port the day after tomorrow. Three in the morning will be a good time. We will be loaded and out to sea before the sun is up."

CHAPTER 26

U.S. Carrier Fleet

The executive officer of the carrier, the same officer they had met their first night on the ship, was back in the wardroom with a few other officers and the two other team leaders they had met that first night. Obviously something big was going down. Tee, Hollahan, Still, and three other members of "the men in black" were surprised when they entered the room to find the XO back belowdecks with them.

The six of them sat, and the XO began speaking.

"Nice to see you again, gentlemen. Apparently you have been busy little beavers here. I came down to tell you that you have guests arriving who will be seeing the inside of our brig until you make other arrangements. There are three helicopters en route to this location as we speak. The SEAL teams assigned to you have completed their assignment and are, I am happy to report, intact. The SEAL team will also be bringing in some computer equipment for your intel guys to take apart."

The six of them glanced over at their team leader from the men in black, who ignored their confused looks.

"I can see you are wondering why I know about any of your activities. I am not here to interfere with your operation; however, this is our boat. No hostiles may be brought aboard without the XO of the ship—that's me—signing off on it. Your team commanders had no choice but to update me on your recent operations.

"First of all, let me say, 'congratulations.' You have captured three terrorists and a computer that may shed some light on what is going on in the world. Second, as I told you before, this fleet packs a solid punch. If you find a larger force, we can help in conventional and nonconventional ways as well. And third, since you are bringing these scumbags aboard this vessel, we would appreciate it if you would find it in your hearts to update us on any pertinent intelligence. I spoke with your team leaders about having our naval intelligence officers present during interrogation. We concur that it may be in the best interests of national security if this interrogation is conducted entirely by your team.

"This entire operation is classified as top secret, and only a couple of command officers of this vessel have any idea about what is happening. As I said, we would appreciate any information you can share with us, but we will not interfere. The helicopters will be landing at night, and we will see that the immediate area is cleared of nonessential personnel. Your SEALS are returning with two terrorists who will immediately be brought to the brig. There was only one other sailor in there, and he has been released to give you full privacy. If that changes, I will personally let you know. The sooner you get these murderers off my boat, the better. That is all, gentlemen, unless you have any other questions."

Tee looked around, a bit uncomfortable to speak in front of the navy officers.

"I was told they had captured three terrorists. You just said they are bringing in two?"

The XO looked over at the team leaders and stood without speaking. He left the room, and all eyes went to Gary and Dan.

"Apparently one of the bad guys attempted a John Wayne on the chopper as they were cruising at a hundred and fifty knots in the chopper. He was handcuffed behind his back, but managed to get to his feet and go wild inside the aircraft. They were flying with the doors open a bit because they still had their winter gear on, and that stuff is hot as hell. The bad guy decided to jump rather than speak to us. I'm very flattered. Hopefully he wasn't the leader of the cell, 'cause only the fish are gonna get anything out of him now."

"Can we be sure he's dead?" asked Tee.

"Pretty sure; they were flying at over five hundred feet at a hundred and fifty knots."

"Yup, that'd pretty much do it," said Tee sarcastically.

"Okay, let's get topside and wait for the choppers to come in. There's no keeping this one quiet with the crew. They are all going to see the choppers unload, and our two fish don't exactly blend."

"Roger that," said Tee. With that, the group stood and headed for the stairs.

CHAPTER 27

Near El Haram, Syria

I t was nearing three in the morning, and the small village was asleep. More than forty men moved quickly through the main street of El Haram, taking positions at street corners and watching for anyone who might be awake at such an hour. It was cold this late at night, and a slight breeze made their robes flutter. This was the only road that went straight through town and led all the way to the sea. It was this road that would take their precious cargo to its destination aboard the *Crescent King*.

The first vehicle to pass through the street was a Syrian army truck. It had been borrowed for a small sum to the local base commander, who was all too happy to aid anyone who had ten thousand dollars. Inside the truck were four fifty-gallon drums. Each drum contained a specialized container inside, filled with sarin nerve agent, still in powder form. Second in the convoy was an old jeep, in which Abu Hassam Obduri rode with several bodyguards, armed to the teeth. Last, an extremely oversized truck draped with netting and camouflage rumbled through the street, making every building vibrate as it pushed its speed to the engine's limit. Two men sat on top of the netting, with AK-47s out, visibly at the ready. Most civilians would recognize a giant Scud missile lying on its side, with or without the camouflage. The mobile launchers had been seen in the area before, but always with Syrian Army escorts and many troops. It wouldn't take a rocket scientist to figure that something unusual was going on.

As the huge vehicle rumbled through the city, a few lights went on to see what could possibly cause such a ruckus at three in the morning. The men along the street swiftly responded to the lights by running to the windows and tapping on them with their rifles, telling the occupants to go back to sleep. The occupants always complied immediately.

It had taken more than two hours to drive the Scud launcher and truck full of sarin from the desert bunker to the village. They had been in wide-open desert, and it had been an extremely stressful trip. They kept the launcher at full throttle the entire time, stopping only once to refuel, lest they have to stop in a populated area. As they passed through the village and neared the wharf area, they began to get very excited.

Inside the launcher's cab, the driver and guard were singing and smiling. They would be the ones firing the missile into the White House, and could not have been prouder. Although both were Iraqi nationals, they were brothers to be welcomed and treated with great honor, since they had been trained to fire the Scud. They, along with almost another hundred Iraqis, were now living in Syria with their expatriate Scuds, waiting for the infidels to leave their land so they could return with their weapons. When they had been approached by Obduri, it didn't take much to convince them to take the ride to the American coast. Life in Iraq would never be the same for a Baathist, thanks to the American meddling. This was a chance to repay the infidels in a way that Saddam himself could not do successfully.

Ahead in the darkness, lights could be seen—the lights of El Haram's port. It wouldn't be totally unusual to find activity at this hour, as ships prepared to leave at first light, but this particular night, the local coast guard had come to port and shooed everyone away for the evening. It was very unusual for the coast guard to interfere with local shipping traffic, but no one was going to put up much of a fuss against the station's chief officer when he arrived with his entire force. The coast guard secured the area until they saw the lights of the small convoy approaching, right on time. When they got close, the chief gave the order, and the C.G. personnel all dispersed. They would all be able to say, "I didn't see a thing" if ever questioned. In the meantime, the chief was daydreaming of his retirement with fifty thousand dollars in cash.

The convoy pulled into the port area proper, and several men jumped out of Obduri's jeep. They ran ahead to the pier, where an old tanker sat tied to her moorings. Kareem Wazeeri himself was at the rail of the tanker, beaming with joy at the sight of the trucks. Obduri saw him and leaped from the truck. He ran to the ship's gangway and yelled to Kareem.

"I didn't think you were bringing her all the way in. I expected a ferry."

Kareem was still smiling his crooked, yellow-toothed smile. "The coast guard was very cooperative!" he yelled down. "This is a deep-water port. Wait a moment and we will open the rear door."

He began yelling orders to crewmen, who disappeared belowdecks. There was a slight groan of metal as the stern of the ship began to open. A huge rear door dropped open slowly, while inside, crewmen began pushing out giant ramps of corrugated steel. The steel rampworks bridged the gap between the pier and the ship, and none but Fadi

Wazeeri himself walked out from the belly of the beast. He crossed the steel ramps and stood on the pier, hands on his hips, with his evil grin matching his cousin's.

Obduri saw Fadi Wazeeri and rushed to him. Obduri took his hand, kissed it, and bestowed blessings on him and his family. After a few moments Wazeeri bade him to stand up.

"There is much to do, loyal servant. Get this gift from Allah into the ship as fast as possible, but with great care."

Obduri backed away, bowing and blessing him, and then ran back to the small convoy while barking orders. The first two trucks pulled to the side and allowed the Scud launcher to pull in first. When it got to the ramps, the men readjusted the width, the fit, the tire span, and held their breath as the huge truck launcher slowly crept aboard. The steel ramps groaned and bowed under the tremendous weight, but as promised by the engineers, held firm. The giant missile launcher slowly disappeared inside the oil tanker and crept along the ramping system until it was directly below the doors that were the main deck above. Once in position, it was secured with giant blocks, and the truck with the sarin was loaded. The rear door was closed, like a giant mouth swallowing the weapons of mass destruction. As it closed tight, the light disappeared from within the belly of the ship, and all that could be seen was the black stern of the ship that read in Arabic *Crescent King*.

A small cheer went up, and Fadi appeared on deck with Kareem and Obduri. They watched as their men prepared to cast off and the captain of the ship called for the tugboat to pull him out of the slip. The tugboat had been on call, but intentionally kept away from the pier to avoid an extra pair of eyes watching the activities. The tug was there within twenty minutes, and lines were thrown from the bow of the tanker to the stern of the tug. The lines were cast off from the tanker to the wooden pier, and the giant tanker slowly began to pull away.

Fadi left Kareem in charge in the wheelhouse with the captain, who watched the small tug bring him out to deeper open water, where he could get under way. Fadi went belowdecks where a few dozen men carefully went about unloading the four drums from the back of the truck. The inside of the tanker, which would normally be filled with thousands of gallons of crude, was instead a well-lit series of corrugated catwalks and decks. The giant Scud was a sight to behold, and several men had taken to chanting prayers of thanks to Allah.

Fadi found the man in charge, a weapons technician who would be responsible for loading the sarin into the warhead. The two Iraqis who would fire the weapon had already begun the process of opening the warhead to remove the payload and prepare to retrofit the sarin in its place. This would take several hours, but time was no longer an issue. They were safely aboard the ship and in a few minutes would be out to sea, where no one would ever find them. They could take their time, safely prepare their weapon, and follow the regular shipping lanes to the east coast of the Great Satan.

Fadi watched intently as the men worked to open the Sarin drums and reveal the precious cargo of death inside. As the men slowly removed the smaller sealed boxes from within the drums, Kareem appeared belowdecks.

"Cousin, the tugboat has left us. The captain is taking us out to sea. In a few days, we will leave the Mediterranean and be in the Atlantic Ocean. Nothing can stop us now, God willing," said Kareem with a smile.

Fadi stared at the steel drums being taken apart. He stroked his small chin beard and said quietly, "God is great."

CHAPTER 28

Washington, D.C.

The phone rang three times before Amy Lang heard it. She jumped up on the fourth ring, realizing she wasn't dreaming, and grabbed for it.

"Hello?" she mumbled, fumbling for her clock to see what time it was. The digital numbers glowed 3:30.

"My apologies, Amy." It was Mitch's voice. He sounded as tired as she did. "My phone rang a few minutes ago, and I think we should meet right now. I can come to you if you want."

"Romeo, if this is your idea of how to get into my apartment, you'd better think of something else."

"I'm serious, Amy. Give me your address and I'll be there as fast as I can. I have something."

Amy recited her address, questioned her sanity for allowing him to come to her apartment, which was probably against about a million rules, and then hung up the receiver. She fell back into her pillow and rubbed her eyes, exhaled slowly and stretched, and then jumped up to head for the shower.

Half an hour later, she was in a running suit and making coffee. The door buzzer made her jump. It was still pitch-black out. She pressed the intercom on the buzzer. "Is this my paperboy?" she asked the white plastic intercom box. Mitch's voice came back from the plastic, saying, "Yeah, and I have a big headline for you." She pressed the door buzzer to let him up. A moment later he was gently rapping on her door.

He entered looking much worse than she did. He hadn't shaved or showered, merely jumped into sweats and got to her as fast as possible. She, on the other hand, had managed to put on eye makeup, pull her long blond hair into a ponytail, and look fairly perky, all things considered.

"Geez, don't you ever look like crap?" he asked. She was quietly happy that he noticed her extra effort to look good on his behalf.

"Yeah, I'm sure I look great at four in the morning," she replied.

"I bet you'd look even better if I woke up next to you after letting you sleep in after a long night of—"

"Easy, big fella. Don't get yourself all worked up. What's got us up so early in the morning?"

"We had spoken once before about assets in Syria. We don't have any actual Mosad agents in Syria, but we do have some informants. One of them got a message out a few hours ago to his control in Israel. Our informant says there was a big buzz about sarin nerve agent being moved in Syria. One of the people we have been watching closely is a snake named Abu Hassam Obduri. He was the one reportedly looking to buy the sarin."

"We know who Obduri is. He's Islamic Jihad, not Al Qaeda. Are we back to your conspiracy theory again, Mitch?"

"This is no theory. Why are you Americans so opposed to the idea that these animals can work together?"

"Because they never have before," she answered.

"Yes, in fact they have. Why do we go in circles, Amy? Look at the 'insurgents' you are killing in Iraq. Half of them aren't Iraqis. But you can be sure some of them are Al Qaeda, Jihad, Hezbollah, and a dozen new terrorist organizations. There is a new one every day, and they *are* working together."

"All right, Mitch. I'll humor you." She poured them both a mug of coffee. "How do you take it?"

"Light and sweet," he said dramatically, blowing her a kiss.

"Oh, *pull-eeze*. It is way too early for you to be horny."

"I am Israeli. I'm eight hours ahead of you. We should already be naked by my estimation."

"Dream on," she said, smiling. She did her best to act uninterested, but his flirting was getting to her.

"Anyway, Obduri had put the word out that he was looking for sarin. Our contact says he had heard other talk, of nuclear weapons, but apparently they didn't have any luck. We know the Iraqis *did* have large stockpiles of sarin before the war. We had always maintained that they hid them in Syria, with Syria's full cooperation. We believe that Obduri has, in fact, obtained weapons-grade sarin from those Iraqi stockpiles for use against the United States."

"What else?" said Amy, sipping her coffee

"The name *Crescent Fire*."

She put her cup down. "Mitch, if you are bullshitting me on this—"

"Why would I, Amy? Israel wants nothing more than to be a good friend to the United States, as you have been to us. We are happy to share intelligence with you."

"Yes, but with your own spin on it," she said drily.

"Not our 'spin,' as you say. It is the best we have to go on right now. This contact has been useful twice before on operations. He actually prevented an attack early last year in Jerusalem."

"Why? What's in it for him?"

"Money. Same as usual. He isn't a radical. He's just a regular guy. But he has a family and he is poor. He'd like nothing better than to get out of Syria with some money in his pocket."

"So what did he tell you about *Crescent Fire*?"

"The word is, it is a ship. We don't know what kind, but we figure a container ship. They arrive in the States by the hundreds a month. Your port security isn't that great. Maybe they search the ship and they open a rigged container that detonates a sarin gas weapon. Maybe they blow it up in the port. There are a million scenarios. Bottom line is, they may have sarin, they are putting it on a ship called the *Crescent Fire*, and they want to kill Americans. How much more do you need me to tell you?"

"Where the ship is," she said with a smile.

"That, unfortunately, we don't know. I would guess a port in Syria. That would be easiest. But there is the possibility that they could truck it elsewhere and ship it from there."

"Mitch, we have been trying to trace the name *Crescent Fire* for weeks now, with no luck. We checked a dozen countries, and none are registered in that name. It's a wild-goose chase."

"Perhaps *Crescent Fire* is a code name for another ship."

"Very likely. Unfortunately, it's a needle in a haystack. There is simply too much shipping traffic to try to track this down. We need more intelligence to narrow our search. If your contact is as reliable as you say he is, see if you can get more out of him. In the meantime, we'll intensify our intel-gathering on Syria. It does mean we have to take it away from somewhere else, I'm afraid. Our resources are stretched thin these days."

"I understand. I will see what I can do from my end. I thought this was worth ruining your beauty sleep. Apparently you don't need it anyway."

"It's called makeup," she said, batting her eyelashes.

"Thanks for the coffee," Mitch said, standing up. "Are you calling this in now?"

"I don't think I'll wake up the boss for another hour or two. There isn't much we can do at this point anyway, until we start working Syrian intel."

"Well then, I'll buy you breakfast," he said, smiling. "Unless you prefer breakfast in bed?"

"There's a diner a block from here. And after waking me up this early, you bet your ass you're buying."

CHAPTER 29

U.S. Carrier Fleet

The executive officer, Tee, Hollahan, and Still were standing at the helicopter landing pad when the three choppers came in low over the water. They landed quickly, and the SEAL teams piled out, dragging two hooded and shackled men, along with a laptop computer. They quickly moved the men inside and took them belowdecks to the brig. Six Marine MPs escorted the group of SEALs and their two captives.

Captain Boyce ran over to the XO and saluted as his men went below. The XO returned the salute and introduced Captain "BB" Boyce to the three "men in black," and quickly explained that the captives were the sole responsibility of the men in black once they hit the brig. The XO excused himself, and left Boyce with the three agents.

"Excuse me, sirs, but this is a bit irregular," said the captain. "Shouldn't the S-2 take the POWs?"

Tee put his large arm around the captain's shoulders and began walking him toward the door of the tower. "Captain, ya see, the thing is, you were never here. In fact, we were never here either, which is why you and I never met. As far as any 'alleged' captured terrorists go, I wouldn't know anything about that. Your personnel file will reflect a search-and-rescue operation for which you and each of your men will receive a Bronze Star. You did great work out there, Captain, except that it never happened, you get my drift? No one ever knows anything about what you did out there. Ever. There is no statute of limitations on espionage or treason, so I would forget the entire episode if I were you."

Captain Boyce stopped walking and just stood there with his mouth open, speechless. Tee stopped walking and turned back to the captain. Tee stood at attention, snapped a salute at the captain, said, "Dismissed," and turned back around to follow the MPs to the brig. Boyce exhaled slowly and composed himself, then grabbed his gear and headed for his billet to shower and change.

Tee hustled down to the brig, where several Marines stood with Colt .45s drawn, but at their sides, as they watched the prisoners being strip-searched for weapons or explosives. Hollahan and Still sat on a metal table with their arms folded, watching the whole process in silence. When the Marine sergeant completed his body searches, he threw orange jumpsuits to the two captives and told them to dress. Neither spoke, but both took the clothes and began to dress.

The Marine sergeant took off his rubber gloves and stood back out of the way while four Marines stood with their Colts at the ready in firing stances, watching the men dress. As soon as the men zipped up their jumpsuits, the Marines were on them, shackling their wrists and ankles once again. They escorted them out of the small room into two separate holding cells and chained one ankle each to the bottom of a cot. They each had enough room to walk to the small toilet and sink, or lay down on the cot, but that was about it. A large three-quarter-inch-thick Lexan window was in each door, as well as hidden cameras so the men could be observed at all times.

The Marine sergeant approached Tee and snapped a salute. "Sir, as per the direct order of the executive officer of this vessel, I am turning over all responsibilities of these prisoners to you. I am instructed that there is no paperwork on these prisoners, and I have nothing for you to sign to accept them as your responsibility. However, I am following a direct order from the XO and at this time—"

Tee interrupted him with a pat on the arm and quietly whispered, "Don't get your skippies all up in a knot now, sonny. We're gonna take good care of these terrorist dirtbags. You have done your part to save the world, and you are duly relieved. Go take a walk."

The sergeant snapped a smart salute, spun on his heel and marched out of the brig, followed by his detachment of Marines. Only two remained, stationed outside the brig in the hallway, M-16s across their chests.

Tee took an encrypted cell phone off of his belt and dialed a long number. "We have the package and are waiting for you to open it." He hung up and sat down in a chair that looked too small for his large frame.

He eyed Hollahan and Still for a minute, then spoke. "Fellas, in a few moments, professional interrogators are going to arrive to speak to our guests. Now I'm just guessing, you understand, but I'm guessing that they are going to violate every accord of the Geneva Convention as well as every civil right these men would be allowed under U.S. law. These men aren't enemy combatants, they are terrorist murderers. Now would be a good time for you to decide if you wish to leave before the interrogators arrive. Once they get here, you are witnesses to things that aren't supposed to happen. If it is a problem for you, I understand."

Still and Hollahan looked at each other. Hollahan rubbed his chin thoughtfully and spoke quietly. "I don't know who you are bringing up here, but I'm going to go out on a limb and guess CIA. It doesn't matter. I don't want to know. I don't want to watch these two men tortured. You find me when you're done. Let's just hope they know something."

Still folded his arms and dropped his chin to his chest. "Will, I'm gonna stay. Not dissin' you, man, but I want to see for myself."

"No problem, Bob. Come find me when they're done." With that, he walked out, passing four men in the hallway, including the older, short, quiet man he had met in the galley his first night aboard the ship. Each carried a small black bag. They made brief eye contact, and Hollahan muttered to himself that he wasn't surprised to see him here. Then Hollahan headed to his tiny room to stretch out for a nap.

As the men entered the brig, the older man acknowledged Tee with his chin. They ignored Still and started opening their bags and placing various items on the small table. Finally, after unbearable silence, the short mystery man looked at Tee.

"Mr. Cicero, do we have any names on these men?"

Still raised his eyebrows. It was only the second time he had heard Tee called by his proper name since he met him.

"We have ID'ed one of them, and he was quite a catch. Ibrahiim bin Abdul bin al-Bustan—"

Before he could get the name out, the short man interrupted, obviously quite excited. "You have al-Bustan on this boat? Jesus Christ! How long have you known it was him?" He didn't wait for an answer, but just pushed past Tee like he wasn't there and headed for the cells. He looked into the first cell and glanced at the first man. He didn't recognize his face, but knew it wasn't Bustan. He immediately went to the next cell and flung the door open to find Ibrahiim bin Abdul bin al-Bustan sitting on the floor with his back against the wall.

This short bald man, who was apparently overweight and no spring chicken, crossed the small room like a lion and pulled the startled man to his feet from the floor like he was weightless. He slammed him against the metal wall so his head bounced off with a loud ring. The man began speaking quickly in Arabic to the prisoner, who was apparently surprised by his language skills. He threw al-Bustan to his small cot and hollered to his men to join him.

The other three men entered the small cell, filling it to capacity. They all began speaking at once in Arabic, with occasional head slaps and pushes. This continued for five minutes, and then the four of them walked out of the cell, closing it behind them.

"Do you know who you have in there, Mr. Cicero?" asked the man, who was very red in his face.

"Apparently not," said Tee.

"Robert Still, do you know who that man is? Please tell me the fucking FBI have a clue who that is," he said with a sneer

Still was surprised that the man knew who he was, as he had introduced himself, and had met him only once. Still wanted to handle him just right, and continued with caution.

"I have only learned his identity just now. I would need a moment to do some background. And you are?"

"I am Andrew Wyatt, former assistant director of none of your fucking business. That piece of crap in there is wanted in about a dozen countries for killing everything that moves that doesn't bow to Allah and his idea of what fundamental Islam is all about. I don't know how you guys found him, but he is a grand prize. We are going to spend the next hours or days taking his little pea brain apart until we find out what he knows. Then I am going to find out who his little buddy next door is, and what he knows. And then, my friend, I am going to feed the crabs with what is left of them. Remind me later to show you some pictures of villages after he and his little friends got finished with them."

The more he spoke, the more worked up he became. When he had just about turned purple, he stopped and took a long breath. "Now then, Mr. Still, I suggest you and Mr. Cicero take a walk. I would also appreciate knowing everything about their location and recovery. Where there is one, there are a dozen."

Still wasn't ready to be dismissed yet. "We grabbed them up in Tajikistan, across the Afghan border near the Kush."

Wyatt clucked his tongue. "Go on," he mumbled, obviously intrigued.

"They had a little base set up with a computer, which we have and are preparing to have our tech guys take a look at. They had a little generator and a satellite dish out in the middle of nowhere. Maybe you can ask your friend in there who he was talking to."

"As a matter of fact, that is exactly what I am going to do. What else can you tell me?"

"You said, 'Where there is one, there are a dozen.' Actually, there were more than a dozen of them. The rest of them are dead. So that's it in a nutshell."

"What led you to them in the first place?" asked Wyatt.

"Dumb luck. We found movement in an area that was pretty remote along the border, so we checked it out. We had no idea it was a big fish."

"Well, I'd rather be lucky than good," Wyatt said. "I might even buy you a beer later, if we can find one on this floating prison." With that he turned around and walked back to the cell. Apparently an offer of buying a beer was about as cordial as this guy was ever going to be, but evidently he was impressed enough with Still to acknowledge his efforts. Still looked over at Tee, who motioned to Still to follow him. The two left the four interrogators to their work. The sight of Wyatt snapping on rubber gloves gave Still the willies.

CHAPTER 30

Mediterranean Sea

The *Crescent King* chugged along in the warm, sunny afternoon, following the same shipping lanes that hundreds of other tankers and container ships used as they headed to the Americas. The weather was unseasonably warm—a gift from Allah to hasten them in their journey to bring death to the infidels. The old barge looked like dozens of other old tankers on the Med; ships that would be replaced in the coming years with newer, double-hulled vessels. Fadi was in a small office upstairs looking at a map of the eastern seaboard of the United States when Kareem entered, obviously agitated.

"What is it, cousin?" asked Fadi as he looked at his cousin's face.

"I have just gotten news that our Afghan friends were killed or captured in Tajikistan."

"Ibrahiim bin Abdul bin al-Bustan's men?" asked Fadi.

"Yes, and they captured or killed al-Bustan as well."

"Americans?" asked Fadi, knowing it had to be.

"No one can confirm anything except that their camp is

destroyed and all of the men were killed except al-Bustan and one of his chiefs, who are missing. There may be more missing, but those two for sure were supposed to be there."

"How did you find this out?" asked Fadi warily.

"Al-Bustan was supposed to meet Tajik rebels to try to acquire a Soviet warhead. The Harakut ul-Mujahidin had plenty of our money for that purpose, but weren't having any luck, so we went through the Syrians for the sarin. Al-Bustan never gave up, though, and was still trying to make contact when their camp was attacked."

"When did this happen?"

"Within the past two days for sure. One of our men is in Tajikistan and had just met with al-Bustan the night before. When he went back this morning, their were bodies everywhere and the base was destroyed. The shell casings were American and heavy-ordnance, but they left no other clues."

Fadi slammed his fist on the table. He looked at his cousin Fadi's eyes wild with rage. "Al-Bustan knows about this ship, Kareem. He was given details that the others were not so he could get the warhead to us. How could they have taken him alive?"

"He would die before he talked," said Kareem.

"They will make him talk, cousin. They will use drugs, they will torture him, and they will get information out of him. Al-Bustan also has an encrypted computer with dates, places, and names in it. If the Americans crack that code they will know almost everything. Once they have done that, they will be all over the Mediterranean. We must be in the Atlantic by then." He stood and grabbed the phone receiver for the wheelhouse. "Captain, what is our location? How long until we are out of the Mediterranean Sea?" He listened for a few moments, then screamed into the receiver, "As fast as you can go! Get us across the Atlantic *now*!" He slammed down the receiver and smiled at Kareem. "We are almost out of the Med already. By the time the Americans are looking for us, we will be sitting off the coast of Washington, D.C."

The old tanker steamed along heading east, unaware as it passed within three hundred nautical miles of an American naval task force off the coast of Portugal, which included an aircraft carrier housing their missing friends.

Fadi and Kareem entered the belly of the tanker, and several dozen men jumped to their feet at quasi-attention, except one man, who was painting Arabic words on the side of the missile. He looked up when the others jumped to their feet. Seeing Fadi and Kareem, he smiled and held up his paintbrush. He had almost finished writing "Death to the Great Satan, God is great" on the side of the missile. He puffed with pride when he saw Fadi smile at him.

The two Iraqi missile crewmen approached Fadi with a slight bow and traditional greeting.

"Tell me about our prize. Is she ready?" asked Fadi.

"Oh, yes, sir, she is fully loaded with sarin and fully fueled. She has a maximum range of five hundred kilometers and will be accurate to within a quarter mile."

"Five hundred kilometers? I understood the range to be only three hundred."

"Yes, sir. That was correct for many years, but the North Koreans assisted President Hussein in maximizing their fuel efficiency and speed. We do much better than the published specs now." He smiled and snapped a proud salute.

Fadi rubbed his hands in obvious glee. "Allah has blessed us yet again," he said. He looked at his cousin Kareem and said, "This saves us a day or two of travel. We will be so far away that after we fire our missile we can turn around and head home before they even know what happened. It had never occurred to me that this would be a round-trip journey, cousin, but with this kind of range, we can deliver death to the infidels and be sipping tea in Syria in a week and a half."

Kareem smiled. He was along on this trip because his cousin told him to be, but he had no death wish. Unlike his fanatical cousin, Kareem did not wish to hurry his trip to Paradise. His life in this world was very comfortable. He had many young beautiful wives from all over the Middle East, though most would consider themselves slaves rather than wives, and several beautiful palaces as well. The idea of making it home alive reinvigorated Kareem, and he walked about the men, praising them loudly. When the cousins left the hold, the men were cheering and in great spirits, prepared to rain death on the unsuspecting infidels.

Kareem's thoughts drifted back to al-Bustan and the interrogation he would endure. In Kareem's own mind, he questioned how long he would be able to hold out. He thought about the tortures he had inflicted on others over the years. Even the bravest warriors eventually begged for either mercy or death.

CHAPTER 31

U.S. Carrier Fleet, near Portugal

Andrew Wyatt had just finished his cigarette, and put out the stub in the palm of his hand as he eyeballed Ibrahiim bin Abdul bin al-Bustan. Al-Bustan sat up as straight and defiantly as he could, but he was exhausted. He wore only a pair of U.S. Navy boxer shorts, his orange jumpsuit having been taken away from him along with his turban. His grayish-black matted hair hung over his bony shoulders. He was a scrawny man, but sinewy with hard muscles from years of mountain living. His was missing several teeth, and the ones he had were yellow-brown from smoking his water pipe and drinking strong coffee.

Wyatt and his crew had been firing questions and head slaps for four hours, working in shifts to stay fresh themselves as they tired his mind with a thousand topics. This preliminary questioning wasn't expected to yield any hard intelligence, it was merely to set a fast tempo and keep his nerves stretched thin. Wyatt left the room and returned with all three men and a black medical bag.

Andrew Wyatt, who looked somewhat like a cranky

banker, was anything but. Twenty-one years in the field as
a CIA operative in the Middle East had hardened his heart
and honed his mind. His was methodical and focused.
Years of training as an interrogator had made him unemo-
tional and analytical, always watching his subjects carefully to work information out of them without breaking
them to the point of making them useless. This man would
be different, he knew. Al-Bustan would gladly die before di-
vulging anything to an infidel. Wyatt smiled as he thought
about that. In the past, most interrogations had been conducted in accordance with U.S. laws that protected the
accused. In this case, the accused was guilty, plain as day.
Moreover, there was no plan to ever bring al-Bustan to formal justice. He was a sponge that was to be squeezed dry
and discarded, appropriately, into the ocean.

Wyatt filled the hypodermic needle with the serum that
would get this animal talking, careful not to overdo it and
put him out completely. Al-Bustan watched him fill the needle, and his eyes grew wider. As wise as he was to the ways
of the West and espionage and terrorist training, he was un-
familiar with a needle. In his lifetime, he had never been
immunized, never been to a formal doctor, and certainly
never had a needle in his arm. The careful way that Wyatt
filled it with the quiet observation of his peers scared al-
Bustan like no Russian helicopter had ever done.

"We are going to have a little chat, Ibrahiim. I suggest
you be truthful and answer the questions I ask, because
when you try to lie, this medicine will eat your brain like a
wolf devours a sheep," he said quietly. "You are going to
tell us everything anyway, my little bag of bones, so why
not make it easier for yourself? Cooperate, and I promise a
painless trip to Paradise. Lie to us and I will wrap you with
a dead swine and cut out your eyes so you will never see
Paradise."

Andrew Wyatt jabbed the needle into al-Bustan's shoulder and pushed the clear liquid into his blood. Al-Bustan's

eye's fluttered for a moment, and he made a few high-pitched protests as his head bobbed about on his skinny neck before falling back against the metal wall.

Wyatt's partners took out video and audio recording equipment and set up in front of him. They also opened al-Bustan's laptop and set it on the table in front of him. One of Wyatt's men hooked electrodes to al-Bustan's fingertips and chest and began monitoring his heart rate, voice pattern, and body temperature. They would carefully analyze every utterance to measure the truthfulness of his words, and monitor him to prevent him from having a stroke.

Wyatt spoke somewhat quietly in Ibrahiim's dialect. "We need to contact them quickly, the Americans are close . . . use the computer."

He repeated it a few times to the semicatatonic man in front of him, then placed the laptop in his lap. Ibrahiim looked at the keyboard and squinted, obviously having trouble following what was happening around him. He muttered in his local language and pressed a few keys, but nothing happened.

"They are close, Ibrahiim. We must get off a message. You are injured from the helicopter attack, but don't worry, I will warn our friends. Tell me how to use this machine."

Ibrahiim leaned back and closed his eyes. It made more sense to him now. No wonder he couldn't move his arms so well or understand where he was. He was injured. He did remember the Americans attacking the base. One of his men must have rescued him. He must warn Fadi Wazeeri and the others—but he couldn't lift his arms.

"We must warn them!" he muttered, sounding drunk.

"Warn who? How can I do that? You are injured, and no one else knows how to use the machine. Everyone else is dead, Ibrahiim. You must tell me how to do it!" said Andrew, sounding so sincere.

"We can send a message from that machine, like a pigeon, Ammet. I will tell you how."

The others looked at each other. Perhaps Ammet was the man next door. They would find out soon enough.

"Press the keys I tell you," he said, still slurring, but intelligible.

Within minutes a screen opened that showed an e-mail server. An envelope was blinking, showing mail for Ibrahiim. Wyatt told Ibrahiim what he saw, and Ibrahiim told him how to open the flashing letter with the enter key. A picture opened in the mail. It was just a photograph of a village that could have been anywhere. At first Wyatt didn't understand, then realized the sophistication of the men he was dealing with.

Ibrahiim told him how to cut and paste the picture to another file, which turned the pixels into words. It wasn't a picture at all, it was a coded message hidden within the colors and shapes of an innocent-looking village. The message appeared, which Wyatt translated into English for the recording:

Hearing you have no luck with the Tajiks, we move forward without you. No matter, as Allah has bestowed other gifts. We will continue from Syria as planned within the week. Allah will guide us to hurl his fire into the Infidels. Your package would have been perfection, but we have enough sarin to kill more of them in a single day than all of the dead in both wars in our holy lands. Continue to try to acquire the warhead for the next operation. If you can no longer reach me, get the package to El Haram in Syria. You will find friends there. Use caution, as the American army is getting closer to you each day. Contact me only if you have success.

"Ibrahiim, the message says to get to El Haram in Syria. How could we get there? It is too far. And why would we go there, Ibrahiim? What is in El Haram?"

Ibrahiim was groggy, and his head was still bobbing. He repeatedly stared at Wyatt, looking for some recognition. Several times he tried to touch Wyatt's face, and he was obviously confused, but he kept talking to Ammet as he looked at Andrew.

"The ship is in El Haram, my brother. Fadi will get the missile to America."

When one of Wyatt's men said "holy shit" without thinking, everything stopped in the room and all eyes went to the man who had uttered the English words. Luckily, the words meant nothing to Ibrahiim, who spoke almost no English. Wyatt's eyes told the man to keep his mouth shut from now on.

"Fadi Wazeeri? Ibrahiim, is that who you mean? Is Fadi Wazeeri in Syria?" All of the Americans in the room could feel their hearts racing. Fadi Wazeeri was the single most wanted man in the world, and this little man who looked like a goat herder knew him personally.

"Ammet? How badly am I injured? I cannot see very well. Where are the Americans?" Ibrahiim mumbled. He was still convinced he was in a hut in the mountains where Ammet had saved him from the infidels.

"You will heal, my brother. Don't worry. Tell me, is it Fadi Wazeeri?"

"Yes, Fadi Wazeeri. And his cousin Kareem," he said quietly.

The agent who said "holy shit" earlier shot a hand to cover his mouth as he almost did it again. Even Wyatt was startled to hear them both in the same place at the same time. The e-mail was more than a week old. Evidently they had been grabbed when they were setting up the satellite dish to receive the message. The trip from Afghanistan to Tajikistan had taken them quite a while, and it was impossible for them to send or receive during the mountainous voyage.

Wyatt sat silently for a moment. Would Fadi know about the raid that grabbed up Ibrahiim? If not, he could send a message and pretend to be Ibrahiim himself. Of course, if word had reached Fadi about the raid, and he sent a message, it would let Fadi know they were getting closer. Too risky, Wyatt thought. Even so, there was more to get out of this man.

"Ibrahiim, how will we get a warhead? Who is our contact in Tajikistan? If you die, I will go in your place, my brother. Who should I ask for?"

Ibrahiim grew very agitated at that question. He began rocking back and forth and muttering incoherently. He looked like an autistic child having a tantrum.

"What is it, Andrew?" one of his men asked quietly in English. Ibrahiim's heart rate was up to 110 beats per minute from his resting 58.

"I must have asked a question I should have known. It isn't jiving in his head, and now he is fighting the serum. If he keeps it up, he'll have a friggin' stroke. A minute ago he was sure he was in the base camp. He must have just caught up inside his head to the helicopter ride and now he's having a meltdown. We'll take him all the way down and let him sleep it off for a few hours. He won't remember any of this," Wyatt said as he pushed another hypodermic needle into Ibrahiim's arm. Within two seconds, Ibrahiim was out cold. They laid him down and shackled him to the cot so he couldn't move.

"Jesus, Andy. You believe this shit? These fuckers got a missile loaded with sarin on a boat headed to the United States? And this piece of shit was trying to get a nuke from the old Soviet stockpile? We better get all of this packaged up and sent ASAP to the director himself. This is way over our pay grade, sir. That message was more than a week old. Those guys could be halfway to New York by now."

Andrew clucked his tongue a few times and said, "Let's go see who is next door first. You're right. This goes straight to the top, but let's give them as much as we can first. Let's go talk to Ammet."

The four of them went to the next cell, where a younger and stronger-looking man was shackled to a bench that folded out of the steel wall. He was in an orange jumpsuit. His large dark eyes looked wild, the whites of them standing out against his dark skin and black beard. The Afghan seated before them had never seen a helicopter up close, never mind ride in one, and the trip and landing on a ship the size of a mountain had freaked him out thoroughly.

The men entered, filling the small cell. Andrew began, with his perfect dialect, "Ammet, your friend Ibrahiim has been very cooperative. I hope you will be as well."

Ammet was startled to hear his own name. Ibrahiim would never speak to these infidels. He tried to stand and face his enemy like a true Mujahidin warrior but couldn't move in his shackles. He cursed them and spat at Andrew, who moved and let it hit the man behind him. The man responded by trying to push past Andrew to get at the offender, but Wyatt held him back with his arm.

"There will be plenty of time for that, Hank. Relax." Andrew smiled. "Really now, Ammet, there is no reason for such disrespect."

"You are barbarian invaders! Infidels!" he screamed. "You will burn in the fires—" He didn't finish before Andrew put his knee through the young man's nose. It popped like a balloon, sending blood flying across the cell and onto the stainless steel wall behind him.

"And you were telling me to relax?" said the man called Hank.

"You were acting out of anger. This is an interrogation technique." That said, he turned around and punched Ammet quickly two more times in the face. He spit in his bloody mess of a face and said with a sneer in his language, "Spit again and I will peel your skin off." His threat, sounding like dramatic bravado to a Westerner, was very real in Afghanistan. Many a Soviet captive was found skinned alive, decapitated, or dismembered by the Mujahidin during the Soviet war there.

"We know everything, Ammet. We know about the missile, the sarin, the boat, the port in Syria, everything. So what do I need you for? What use do you have other than as a punching bag, my friend?" Wyatt leaned closer. "Of course, if you do think of anything useful, I will promise you an easy trip to Paradise. If you refuse to talk, I will shove a pig up your ass, weigh you down with rocks, and feed you to the sharks. So tell me, Ammet, tell me about Syria."

Ammet's left eye was closed and his nose bled freely into his beard and orange jumpsuit. Ammet stared at Wyatt for a long moment, then spit a red gob of bloody mess at his face. It caught Wyatt on the cheek as he tried to turn his face.

Wyatt spoke calmly and quietly in his tribal language. "That was a big mistake. Huge. I am sending one of my men to the galley for a few pounds of raw bacon. Ask me what I'm going to do with it. Go ahead, ask me," he said with a sneer. He then punched Ammet a few more times in the face, this time knocking out two of Ammet's front teeth. "You should really see a dentist," he mocked, then punched him a few more times.

He walked out of the cell, leaving the man leaning against the wall as defiant as ever, as blood bubbled out of his face. Andrew turned to his men. "He didn't know shit anyway. The prize is next door. We'll concentrate on Ibrahiim. Wiley, go get a couple pounds of raw bacon."

"You serious?" he asked.

"You bet your ass I'm serious. It may not mean shit to you, but when I shove the bacon down his throat, he will know he fucked with the wrong infidel. And before you get all weepy, remember he was trying to nuke your fuckin' house. What do you know about the Afghans' war against the Soviets?"

The other men didn't answer.

"You know, the agency spent billions keeping the Mujahideen armed against the Soviets. The Soviets officially list their dead at thirteen thousand. We know it's more than thirty thousand, and they were losing a Hind helicopter a day to our Stingers by the end of the war. Little fuckers like Ammet in there were standing in the fields with shoulder-fired Stingers taking down the most sophisticated attack helicopters in the world. The Afghans lost more than a million people, and three million were displaced to Pakistan. The hatred between these people and non-Islamics is something you can't ever understand if you never saw the way these two armies fought each other."

He paused as he thought back to his days in the Khyber Pass during the eighties. "Neither side was really satisfied with just *killing* the other. They wanted to kill in so ugly a manner that the other side would be horrified into capitulation, and they were as barbaric as any Nazi or North Vietnamese soldier ever was. The Soviets annihilated entire villages, left exploding toys for children, mined civilian areas, killed prisoners by the thousands. It was unthinkable by U.S. standards.

"The Afghans, dubbed 'freedom fighters' by our people, were nothing more than barbaric tribesmen being used as cannon fodder to fight the Cold War. We armed them, trained them, and sent them off to die by the thousands a day. They vented their frustration against the Soviet Fortieth Army by killing every prisoner they took, but only after gang-raping them, peeling their skins off like animal hides while they were alive, cutting off arms and legs, and leaving them in mined roadways for their patrols to find, and worse."

The others didn't move a muscle as they listened.

"In the end, the Soviets left and we won the Cold War; but not before we had trained and armed hundreds of thousands of Stone Age barbarians and turned them into technowarriors. They were killing each other as soon as the Soviets left, same as they had for the past thousand years. Only difference is, now the warlords use rockets, mortars, and machine guns instead of muskets and swords. And guess what? They don't like us any more than the Soviets. Most of them don't even know that the weapons they used to fight for their freedom from the Soviets came from us. It was so secret an operation, and they are so backward, they actually believed all the weapons came from Allah. All we did was prove to these people that by being brave, they can take down a superpower. They weren't afraid of the Russkies, and they aren't afraid of us. But guess what? They are gonna *learn* to be afraid of me."

With that, Andrew went to the sink and washed the blood off of his swollen hands. "We'll give Ibrahiim two hours, then we'll start over. Get us some coffee and chow. And until you live in the mountains for a few years fighting with these people, don't ever question my methods."

CHAPTER 32

Washington, D.C.

Amy had worked for the agency for seven years. She had met the director in person only twice in that time. When her phone rang early Sunday morning and the voice said, "Please hold for the director," she nearly had a stroke. She would have thought it a joke had not the operator called on her secure phone with the typical sound of a headset and encryption muffling.

"Good morning, Ms. Lang. I trust I am not waking you?" said Wallace R. Holstrum, the director of the Central Intelligence Agency.

Amy was standing at attention, even though he couldn't see her. She was cute in her pajamas, standing at strict attention next to her rumpled bed at nine o'clock on a Sunday morning.

"No, sir, Mr. Director," she answered, sounding somewhat like a Marine.

"Glad to hear it; early bird gets the worm and all that. I need you in my office as soon as you can be here. In fact, by the time you put on some clothes, there will be a car downstairs waiting for you."

The phone went dead, and she just stood there for a moment, somewhat dumbfounded. She placed the receiver gently in the charger and sat on her bed. Her mind was racing. Mitch had been to her house that one time, which would not have gone over very well had he not been giving her information that she immediately reported to her boss that very morning. She grimaced. She couldn't be in trouble for that, so what then? The director himself doesn't call low-level field agents. Something must have panned out big-time with the intelligence she passed up from Mitch. She hopped up and ran for the shower, thinking about what she would wear as she washed her hair.

By the time she had semidried her long blond hair and put on a sharp black business suit, she could see the black sedan with government plates down at the curb. She froze for a second, trying to think of anything in particular she should bring with her. What *do* you bring to an unscheduled meeting with the most powerful spymaster in the United States? She grabbed her purse and cell phone and ran down to the car.

The driver hopped out when she approached and greeted her by name. He then politely asked her for all of her identification anyway. When he was satisfied, she hopped in the back and was whisked through the cold, quiet streets of a D.C. morning. The driver put on some smooth jazz, verified that it was an acceptable music choice, and then ignored her for the rest of the ride. He drove well over the speed limit and knew his way back to Langley blindfolded.

He pulled up in front of the glass and steel building and opened her door for her.

"They expect you on the sixth floor, Ms. Lang. Take the west elevator; there will be an agent to escort you up." He hopped back into his car and was gone. Although she was in the building almost five days a week, she felt like an outsider this cold November morning. She had never even been in a meeting with the director, never mind been called into a private meeting. And on a Sunday?

An agent was standing outside the west elevator and greeted her by name. He put in a key and took her to the director's floor, which was closed to most personnel. When the door opened, she stepped out, he said good-bye, and took it back downstairs.

She stepped through the glass entryway to where a secretary would normally be seated in the plush waiting area. The building was still fairly new, but this furniture was not like anything else in the building. Everything was mahogany and leather, and immaculately clean. As she walked in, another man walked out and greeted her.

"Good morning, Ms. Lang. The director will see you right away." She followed him in silence down the hall to the large office that overlooked the large garden behind the building.

They walked into the office, and Director Wallace R. Holstrum stood and extended his firm handshake. His size added to his intimidating credentials.

"Good morning, Ms. Lang. Have a seat. Thank you for coming on short notice. I was glad you were home this weekend. Lots of folks still with family from Thanksgiving. I trust you had your fill of turkey?"

"Yes, sir. It was a very nice holiday, thank you, sir."

"Relax, Amy. You aren't here to be grilled. We have a break on the Crescent Fire case and you may be able to help us out."

She was surprised and showed it.

"Your relationship with Mitch Weisel. How would you describe it?"

She felt herself blush. Even though she had never kissed him for real, there was a definite attraction there from both sides. Jesus, these guys knew everything.

"How do mean, sir?"

"You have used him for information in the past, we have used you to reach out to the Israelis before through him. Do you trust him?" Director Holstrum leaned back in his large leather chair.

"I have always found him to be pretty up front with me, sir. I am sure he has his own spin on things, in the best interests of his country, but his intel seems to shake out most of the time." She was a little nervous, and trying not to appear fidgety. She couldn't get arrested for having a crush on someone, even if he was a foreign agent.

"As you are well aware, we work under the assumption that Weisel is from the Mosad's collection unit. We need to work a little back-channel, and believe your relationship with him may help us."

"How do you mean my 'relationship,' sir? We have met a few dozen times to share information that is mutually beneficial when we can, but there is no relationship beyond that, really."

"Still, Amy, you are closer to him than anyone else, and we need the Mosad's help. I am not in a position to ask a formal favor of the Israeli government. You, however, might ask Mitchell for a personal favor. Maybe drop him a little hint. I will explain fully. Follow me." The director walked through a doorway into a neighboring room that resembled the Situation Room in the White House. There were banks of monitors on a wall, and a large conference table.

The director pressed a few buttons, and satellite images began appearing all over the wall. She watched in amazement as he worked a few keys and zoomed in on downtown Baghdad, Kabul, the American embassy in Moscow, and dozens of places around the globe.

"Amy, we have eyes all over the world. These are real-time satellite images you are looking at. Problem is, we can't see the whole world, and we can't see everything all the time. As I said earlier, we have had a break on the Crescent Fire case—"

Amy interrupted for the first time. "So this name actually means something?"

"I'm afraid so. Your reports were correct. The information you received from Weisel about terror agencies working together is accurate. Half of the passports we find in Iraq are out of Iran, Yemen, Saudi Arabia, Pakistan, Afghanistan, Sudan. Hell—everywhere someone reads the Koran and understands it to mean that everyone who isn't radically fundamentalist needs to die. Your report questioned the accuracy of Weisel's information, which I understand. After all, it is in Israel's best interest to lump them all together as we wage the war on terror. But—turns out, he's right. Islamic Jihad, Hezbollah, Harakut ul-Mujahidin, and dozens more are all working with Al Qaeda in organized, military fashion.

"They are a new army, spread out in battalion-size elements all over the globe. It is very difficult to fight a dozen men with ten thousand, as we have seen in Iraq and Afghanistan. These people are quite content to spread misery everywhere they go by killing children and civilians. We try to react with large-scale military units, but we are too slow and too lethal. We end up killing civilians ourselves. It's a mess, Amy. Quite frankly, I don't see things improving anytime soon. We need some new way to fight these people. These are people who don't fight by our set of rules. They don't have a code of conduct or rules of engagement. I am pretty sure the wake-up call we got on nine-eleven opened a lot of eyes in Washington to what we had been saying for years, but let's face it—the alarm went off, and a year later, the American public hits the snooze button. Americans don't want to see their young men and women dying on foreign battlefields. They forget that the other choice is watching civilians die here."

The director put his hand up, as if to stop himself.

"Look, I didn't ask you here to listen to a speech about foreign policy. The bottom line is this: We have turned to unorthodox methods of intelligence-gathering for the sake of time. These methods have turned up something big. *Crescent Fire*, Amy. It's a ship. Might be a container ship, an oil tanker, a barge, hell—a passenger liner, for all we know. What we do know is this vessel contains a Scud-B missile smuggled out of Iraq into Syria before the war. Various terror elements all had a hand in this operation."

Amy sat back in her chair, her mouth open as she listened to the briefing from the director himself. Her head was spinning as she tried to keep up, all the while trying to understand her role in all this.

"Harakut ul-Mujahidin used to be happy killing an occasional civilian in the Hindu Kush Mountains. What would you say if I told you they were dealing with Chechen rebels to try to acquire a nuclear warhead for Al Qaeda?" He paused and paced around the table in front of the monitors.

"This entire meeting is top secret and a matter of national security, Amy." He eyed her carefully. "You are a good agent, but underutilized. You are going to the next level. As of today you are a G-14, personally appointed by me, and will be given a bigger piece of the puzzle to work." Before she could respond, he held up his hand and continued. "Harakut ul-Mujahidin doesn't have the bankroll to buy a nuke. Money like that could only come from Al Qaeda. So it looks like he gave them a big bankroll and a shopping list and let them work their own contacts in the former Soviet Union. This might have turned into a major problem, but as I said, we have turned to unorthodox means of intel-gathering. A special team working out of the Med intercepted these men from Harakut ul-Mujahidin and grabbed Ibrahiim bin Abdul bin al-Bustan himself, along with another man, in a raid in Tajikistan. That, in and of itself, would be a major political problem if it ever be-

came public, which it won't. We don't have any business
crossing the Tajikistan border. Be that as it may, al-Bustan
was the number three most-wanted man by this office, and
a wealth of information. Interviewers are still working on
him as we speak, and have been getting quite amazing results."

Amy was still dumbfounded. What did this have to do
with her and Mitch? And why was she chosen for such a
promotion and high-level information?

"It turns out that Fadi Wazeeri and his cousin Kareem
have masterminded this operation with *Crescent Fire*.
Their intention was to detonate a nuclear warhead in the
United States. Our people have ended Harikut's ability to
operate. Their highest-level people are gone now, and it
would be very difficult to reorganize very quickly. The
problem is, according to Ibrahiim al-Bustan, Fadi had a
plan B to acquire sarin for his Scud if he couldn't get a
nuke. Apparently Fadi has been shopping the world market
for years, and so far no one will sell him one. Turns out
everyone else knows how crazy that son of a bitch is, too,
thank God."

He paused long enough for Amy to start asking questions. "Sir, if I may try to catch up, you are stating that Al
Qaeda, Harakut ul-Mujahidin, Hamas, Hezbollah, and others have formed some sort of army and have actually acquired a Scud-B missile to be fired in the United States?
And these groups have now acquired sarin for the warhead,
which is aboard a ship called the *Crescent Fire*?"

"Affirmative. You're a quick study—good. Now follow
along closely. The ship is believed to have left from Syria
from El Haram. The problem is, we didn't have any satellites over the Syrian coast. All of our spy satellites for that
region were realigned to get better intel for our operations
in Afghanistan and Iraq. Otherwise we would hit the old
rewind button and start looking at a month or two's worth
of pictures for a big missile being jammed onto a boat.

Now . . . *we* don't have any spy satellites over Syria. See what I'm getting at?"

"Sir, I am sure the Israeli government would share information with us if we merely asked for their help."

"You are right; if we asked, they certainly would. They would also pressure the president to publicly include Hamas and Islamic Jihad and Hezbollah in his war on terror. The peace process has been a disaster. The last thing the president needs is to throw this into the mix. Israel would demand a stronger U.S. stance against the Palestinians, and the whole mess would start all over again. No can do. I have that from the chief himself. What we need is someone with a contact they trust inside the Mosad to get us the intel from a satellite that they won't acknowledge they have." He leaned over and stared at Amy.

She exhaled slowly. "I will try, sir. What am I authorized to tell him?"

The director leaned back and stared at the ceiling for a moment. He sat up and again looked her in the eye. "Tell him everything. Tell him every damn detail. This is a war, Amy. We better know who our allies are out there, and they better know as well. But we need those satellite images yesterday. The intel we have is more than a week old. By now these people can be washing up on Coney Island. I want you to call him. Do whatever you have to do, but get us those photos—everything that has gone in and out of El Haram for the past two months. If he wants cash, you don't say no, you come back to me. Get us those pictures, Amy."

"Sir, one question: Are we sure the Israelis even have a satellite up there?"

The director laughed out loud. "Ms. Lang, the Israelis have so many damn satellites up there that we now have to confer with each other before we send new ones up there. This is after we had a forty-five-million-dollar collision two years ago, which, of course, never happened." He laughed again. "Yeah, they have satellites up there."

He stood, signaling the end of the meeting. He handed her a card with handwritten phone numbers on it. "You are to call me as soon as you have an answer."

She stood and shook his hand. "Thank you, sir," she said in her strongest voice, then walked directly to the elevator. When the doors closed she exhaled and was about to fall against the wall when she remembered there was probably a camera inside, watching her. She remained at attention in the elevator, trying to look as professional as possible, even though she wanted to start screaming or jumping up and down or *something*. The agent again met her downstairs and the car pulled up in front again to bring her home.

She sat in the backseat, thinking of the phone call she was about to make to her tall, dark, and handsome secret-agent man.

CHAPTER 33

Mediterranean Sea

Andrew Wyatt sat with Tee, Hollahan, and Still in silence, waiting for the boss. Wyatt had smoked two cigarettes during the wait, ignoring the dramatic coughing of Still. The four of them were exhausted. Wyatt had been questioning Ibrahiim on and off for forty hours with his crew. The drugs had worked remarkably well, and Ibrahiim had been quite convinced he was helping to strike the Americans from his deathbed in Tajikistan. He was kept half out of it, and the interviewers had eventually come up with the idea of covering his eyes. They had told him he was wounded in the American attack, but the infidels had been destroyed. After a while they started having fun with it. Ibrahiim never remembered from one session to the next, he was so doped up, so they had taken to making him a hero of the battle. He ate it up, and was determined to continue his mission.

Even under the most painful of tortures, Ibrahiim never would have divulged any information, but with the use of the drugs and clever interviewing, Ibrahiim gave them names, places, dates, philosophies, attack plans, and details of dozens of attacks, both past and future. The downside of keeping him so pumped with drugs was that after forty hours, his brain was literally developing lesions that wouldn't be saved by any brain surgery. He was a consumable good, made "to be used up and thrown away," and his shelf life was starting to get close to the end. Ultimately his memory would be totally shot, and he would end up catatonic, like an advanced Alzheimer's patient. When his condition came to that, he would be given to the sharks and crabs. That was a bone of contention between Hollahan and Wyatt.

Hollahan was FBI all the way. For his entire career, he had played by the rules, no matter how frustrating. He had never violated anyone's civil rights, or deviated from the rule of law. In his line of work, every facet of an investigation and arrest was in preparation for trial against very smart defense attorneys, and he had always been careful to assure that no criminal would walk because he had made a mistake in the due process of the law. Andrew Wyatt came from another planet. In his line of work, results were the only thing that mattered. He was every bit as professional and serious about his work as Hollahan was, but he operated in dark shadows where a defense attorney was rarely an issue. The CIA had been scrutinized much more heavily over the past decade, but that hadn't changed Wyatt's personal methods of operation. In his mind, he wasn't above the law, he *was* the law. He had only one goal—the protection of the United States of America—and no ACLU lawyer or liberal congressman was going to ruin an operation that dealt with national security because they didn't like how he ran his department.

Hollahan was very aware of the fact that he had signed up for a job that was different than what he had been trained for all his life. It was that awareness that kept him levelheaded around Wyatt, whom he would otherwise arrest for his treatment of prisoners. Instead, he just avoided Wyatt whenever possible. Bob Still, for his part in all this, was somewhere in the middle. He didn't sit in on the interrogations after that first one, but was constantly checking in for new information. He in turn would report back to Hollahan, and the two of them would churn out long reports documenting the results of the interviews and trying to put together the big picture. It was this report that eventually had landed on the desk of CIA director Holstrum, routed through Dan Archer from Andrew Wyatt. Archer was still in constant contact with Holstrum, even though the men in black didn't exist.

On a CIA table of organization—which, of course, didn't exist either—you would have found Andrew Wyatt directly reporting to the director himself. When this new task force had been formed, it had been done at the highest level, but with complete deniability by the director and the president. Holstrum had merely told Wyatt what needed to be done, made a few introductory phone calls, and was out of it after that. Wyatt then put together the team with the help of several other people from the agency, including Dan Archer, who would be known as "the boss," even though Wyatt didn't actually answer to him. Archer would be the direct connection to the agency, and for his part, Archer made sure he knew as little as possible about how anything had been conducted. He was merely briefed by the men in black, and forwarded all information to Director Holstrum. In the event of a congressional inquiry, it would fall to Archer to provide information—information he could provide in only limited quantities, by design.

Dan Archer was sixty-five years old, a retired Marine Corps colonel who had worked as an intelligence officer in Vietnam and ended up in the CIA. He still looked like a Marine, and was a widely respected man in the agency. There had been talk that he might one day be the next deputy director. Accepting this job had ensured that would never happen. This would be his last post, although men like him were occasionally used as consultants when something big was happening in the world. Archer, in Ollie North fashion, accepted a job he believed was in the best interests of his country, knowing full well that if the media ever found out about how the operation was conducted, he would be the one thrown under the bus. He never hesitated accepting the assignment.

When Archer walked into the room, Tee, Hollahan, Still, and Wyatt were sitting back in their chairs, looking wiped out. Archer smiled, something rare for the big Marine. He pulled a bottle of Scotch from behind his back, along with some plastic cups.

"Gentlemen, it is a bit early to celebrate, as we still have a boat with a missile on it heading for the United States. However, you have produced more information in two days than we have been able to uncover in two months; and quite frankly, you all look like crap. We are going to have a nice, long drink, sleep for a few hours, and then begin sweeping the Atlantic for everything that moves. I spoke to the director a few hours ago. Every available means is being looked at to acquire satellite intelligence that will narrow our search. In the meantime, this float has already split into four smaller battle groups to cover a larger search area as we head west."

Archer put the cups on the table and started pouring. For the first time in a few weeks, all of them were smiling at the same time. Stress levels were running high, coupled with exhaustion, and a good, stiff belt was just what the doctor ordered. They clinked plastic cups as Wyatt offered a poetic toast: "To killing those mutherfuckers." They all threw their drinks back and refilled right away.

"Your interview with Ibrahiim has been very enlightening, Andrew. It was a good piece of work. How much more do you think he has to give?"

"He's done, boss. We'll try again tomorrow after he sleeps

for a few hours, but I think he's toast. His buddy knew nothing at all. He was low-level. Just a Mujahed." He glanced at Hollahan for a second and then looked away. "He went for a swim yesterday."

Archer grunted. "We'll finish this drink, then I want you all to get some sleep. Finish with al-Bustan tomorrow early, then give me an update. We'll be all ahead full from now till something breaks. All air assets are running now, radioing back coordinates to the bridge. The commander now knows we are looking for a vessel of unknown type carrying a weapon headed for the United States. He has promised full cooperation and belayed his original float mission out here. As of now, the men in black are in charge of the largest, most powerful naval flotilla in the Atlantic. We will find the *Crescent Fire*, gentlemen, so help me God."

Archer looked at Tee. "Starting tomorrow morning, you will take our bird up and stay up until something breaks. This float has AWACs, fighters, choppers, the whole contingent, but nothing as good as ours. Plot a grid from the mouth of the Med to the central eastern seaboard of the States. We'll just start from the beginning and work until we find something."

Hollahan spoke up for the first time. "May I make a suggestion, sir?"

"Shoot," he said.

"I think we should work backward."

"Explain," he said.

"Well, we don't know how far ahead of us they are. By the time we find them, they could be there already. Why not start off the coast of the States and work our way back to the ship? We can refuel in the air if you can get us some KC-10s. I think if we start from the farthest point and work our way back to the ships, we can keep them between us and the battle group. One way or another, we'd have a better chance of finding them. Just a thought."

"Actually, that's a good thought, Hollahan. You were air intel in 'Nam, weren't you?" he asked.

"Yes, sir."

"It shows. Okay. That's it, then. We'll work our way back from the coast, but that is going to mean pilots working in very long shifts. I'll speak to the commander and see if he'll go for it. They *are* his planes, except for the one we have. We'll talk to Chris Mackey, our pilot, and see what he thinks.

With that, Archer walked out of the room. The rest of the men split up the Scotch into their glasses, threw it back quickly, and headed for their rooms for the first real night's sleep in a week.

CHAPTER 34

Washington, D.C.

Amy had invited Mitch to her apartment for lunch that same afternoon as her meeting with the director. He was pleasantly surprised, and had accepted without hesitation. When he arrived at one o'clock he found her looking extremely sexy in a winter-white knit sweaterdress. The table was set with flowers and wineglasses, and he smiled from ear to ear.

"Wow," he said as he kissed her cheek hello, "you have outdone yourself. And to think, I only took you out to a diner. I am embarrassed now."

He suddenly found himself listening to soft jazz playing in the background.

"If I didn't know any better, I'd say you were trying to seduce me," he said in a mock dramatic voice.

Amy laughed, and tossed her long blond hair before smacking his shoulder. "Oh, stop," she said in a girlish voice, obviously flirting with him. "Have a seat. I have made us a delicious lunch. Oh, shit! You keep kosher, don't you?

Damn it! I'm so sorry, Mitch, I didn't think about that!" She was totally deflated.

Mitch touched her shoulder. "Hey, don't worry . . . I stopped keeping kosher many years ago. It was impossible in my traveling, so I had a discussion with God, and He excused me if I promised to be good otherwise." He left his hand there an extra second, sort of testing her reaction, and smiled at her.

"Really? You're sure? I should have asked you."

"If it was a problem, I would have told you," he answered.

She found her face very close to his and blushed, then slipped away toward the kitchen. "Make yourself useful and open the wine. I'll get our lunch. Did you know I am an excellent cook?"

"I was already mad about you, you don't have to give me more reasons," he yelled toward the kitchen.

He popped the cork, poured two glasses, and was about to head to the kitchen with them when she came out of it with a homemade quiche in her hands. She set the white ceramic soufflé pan on the table and took off her hot mitts.

"I wanted to make something 'international' to impress you, and I don't do matzo ball soup," she joked.

"Impressive, indeed," he said and smiled. "Smells wonderful."

They both sat down, and she cut and served them lunch. He picked up his wineglass and offered her a toast. They touched glasses. "To wonderful surprises," he said with a smile. She smiled back and took a sip, enjoying listening to his accent.

They had a wonderful lunch, with lots of easy conversation, and finished the bottle of wine. They cleared the table to the kitchen together as they chatted, then moved to the couch in the small den, where they ended up sitting closely together.

They were at sort of a funny moment, deciding whether

this was a friendly lunch or more, when Amy tried delicately to get at the reason for the invitation.

"Mitch, I need to ask you a favor," she began. She smiled coyly at him and scrunched up her shoulders. She kicked her shoes off and sat on the couch with her feet under her, looking like a little kid.

He looked at her and laughed. "Gee, what a big surprise, Amy. You mean this delicious lunch with the flowers, jazz, and wine wasn't just to try and seduce me?"

"I'm serious, Mitch. We need to talk shop a minute. I am authorized by the director of the Central Intelligence Agency of the United States himself to explain a situation of global proportion to you. Of course, it is unofficial, and he would not ever acknowledge having that conversation, but it starts off with: 'Mitch, you were totally right.' See? I said it. You were right and I was wrong and I need your help."

He leaned forward, much closer to her face. "You have my undivided attention, my beautiful American spy," he said and smiled.

"Good," she said, and playfully tweaked his nose. "It's bigger than we imagined." Her voice was changing from playful to serious, and Mitch could see this was back to a business discussion. "You were correct in that many terrorist groups are working in concert to bring violence to the United States mainland. Al Qaeda, Hamas, Hezbollah, Islamic Jihad, Harakut al-Mujahidin . . . they are all working together, as you suggested several weeks ago."

"Months ago. But who's counting?" he said with a wry smile.

"Months ago," she conceded. "The *Crescent Fire*, as you said, is a ship. And now we know what is inside it. It is very scary, Mitch."

"Go on," he said, also now in business tone.

"A Scud-B missile with a sarin-filled warhead." They sat staring at each other for a moment in silence.

"Our assets on the ground intercepted high-ranking members of Harakut al-Mujahidin and uncovered a plan to acquire a nuclear warhead from Tajikistan. Thank God they never succeeded with that."

"Jesus," Mitch mumbled under his breath. "How high up the food chain?"

"The highest. Ibrahiim bin Abdul bin al-Bustan."

"You have captured al-Bustan?" He actually stood up without thinking.

"Sit down; there's a lot more. Yes, he was captured and interrogated. He gave us the port city of El-Haram in Syria as the debarkation point for the *Crescent Fire*. An Iraqi Scud is on board loaded with sarin and is headed for the United States. The problem is, al-Bustan either didn't know or wouldn't divulge the type of ship. The intelligence is at least a week and a half old, maybe more. That ship could be here anytime. We need your help with this, Mitch. And we need it now."

"Of course my country will help. I will tell the ambassador right away. He can have our prime minister contact your president immediately. Something like this should be dealt with at the very highest levels, Amy."

"That's the problem, Mitch. It can't be. I need *you* to talk to your intelligence people directly. We know you are collections, Mitch. We don't care. But we need your satellite intel. Our satellites were reprogrammed to be watching Iraq and Afghanistan the past two years. We didn't have any eyes over western Syria. We need your satellite intel, and we need it yesterday."

"Amy, I can ask for help from my government, but—"

She cut him off. "Mitch, we know you are Mosad. We don't *care*! Don't you get it? These animals are getting ready to fire a missile full of sarin at our country, and you are in a position to help. We need your help, Mitch. My country is asking your country, through me to you."

"Amy, even if I was Mosad, I am not sure how I could

convince my government to give me satellite intelligence to give to a, pardon me, low-level CIA agent. They would laugh in my face. Your director will have to speak to our Foreign Ministry directly for something as big as this."

She leaned over and kissed him quickly on the lips. "Mitch, I am asking you for a personal favor. You have to try. You *have* to."

He was obviously surprised by her kiss. He sat looking at her, somewhat speechless. "Was that official business, or unofficial business?"

She smiled and looked at the floor, embarrassed. "Unofficial," she said quietly.

Mitch stood up. "It was a great lunch. Next time, how about dinner? I have to run. It seems that I have a long day ahead of me."

Amy stood up and the two of them faced each other, only a few inches between them. "Mitch, I'm sorry to ask so much of you; I know it puts you in a funny position. If they are successful in firing that Scud, it could make nine-eleven look like a bus accident. Can you imagine a cloudburst of sarin over a city of a few million? We have to stop them, Mitch. And when we do, I will buy you the best dinner in Washington, D.C."

"I have a better idea. When we stop them, we come right back here and order in." He scooped her up and gave her a long kiss. She kissed him back with equal passion for a long moment. They stopped and stared at each other.

"You remember where we left off," he said. "I'll be in touch as fast as I can."

He headed for the door, grabbing his coat off the couch as he went, and headed out into the bitter cold December air.

Amy plopped on the couch and rested her chin in her hands. This was definitely going to make things confusing, she thought.

CHAPTER 35

Atlantic Ocean

The wind was picking up out of the west. Thirty-five-knot winds were throwing waves over the bow of the *Crescent Fire* as it pushed full throttle toward the land of the Great Satan. The seawater was freezing to the rails and metal deck of the bow, and twenty-five- to forty-foot seas kept the big tanker bobbing like a child's toy. Kareem was in the small office next to the wheelhouse, vomiting into a wastepaper basket.

Fadi was angry and impatient. "We are crawling! Make this bucket of rust move faster!"

The captain was terrified of Fadi Wazeeri. "Mr. Wazeeri, the headwind is blowing almost forty knots. The ship is light and high in the water and blows like paper. We are at full throttle, but I am afraid to keep pushing like this. If we lose an engine, all will be lost."

"Curse these infidels. You have sailed this route a thousand times. How long will the storms last?"

"It is December, Mr. Wazeeri. This is a nor'easter. It may get much worse before it gets better. The last forecast

I saw called for forty-foot seas with winds over fifty knots. The snow and sleet will continue all day and night. It is hard enough just to stay on course. Normally I would turn southwest to try to get out of this, and then return due north when it passed."

"No; we don't have time to change course. You will stay on plotted route and keep top speed. Allah will guide us through this storm, and we will give them a different rain than the one they are getting now. Allahu akbar!" he roared, and left the wheelhouse to head belowdecks, leaving his cousin seasick with the captain.

When Fadi came to the bottom of the stairs and saw his men, he was not pleased. Most of them were sitting, holding on to anything they could find, and almost all of them looked deathly ill. The majority of his men were not familiar with boats and the high seas, and they were seasick and miserable. It was cold inside the steel hull, and the men looked pitiful. When Fadi walked down into the huge hold, the men stood and tried to look as if everything were normal, but that ended quickly when the boat rocked starboard and one of the men threw up all over his own shoes.

"Allah will deliver us from this storm. We are God's eternal flame! We will shower death and terror from the sky into the heart of the infidels, and they will leave our holy lands. Allahu akbar!" he screamed. The men cheered as loud as they could. His big pep talk was not as rousing as usual, as the boat was thrown about in the angry ocean. Fadi stormed off angrily, knowing there was nothing he could do about his men being seasick. He sulked and headed to his small room.

The carrier group had split into four smaller groups, each made up of three vessels, except the group that contained the flagship carrier. The carrier group was comprised of the nuclear carrier, one battleship, one destroyer,

one fast frigate, one AEGIS-guided missile destroyer, and
one nuclear submarine. It was atypical to split the group,
and not something that would be done in a combat situation, but given the nature of the task, it was practical.

As the planes were prepped on deck, the group's commander, Rear Admiral McNamara, was alerted by the executive officer that the weather was changing rapidly.
Forecasts warned of an approaching nor'easter with high
winds and large swells. Most of the aircraft were considered "all-weather," but the plan for searching for the *Crescent Fire* called for being out over fifteen hours at a time,
with at least two midair refuelings. "Topping off the tank"
of an aircraft at three hundred knots was hairy enough in
good conditions; in a nor'easter it would be very dangerous. Rear Admiral McNamara was cursing under his
breath and headed belowdecks to find the men in black.

Dan Archer was sitting with Andrew Wyatt and Tee
when the Rear Admiral walked in. There was no "attention
on deck" or snappy salute when he did so, just three very
tired men smoking cigarettes and drinking strong black
coffee as they pored over papers and computer printouts.

"Problems, gentlemen," he said matter-of-factly.
"Nor'easter is coming fast. I can't send out planes on the
kind of mission you are talking about in this storm. There
is no way they can refuel twice with forty-five mile-an-
hour winds and driving snow. In another hour, even this
vessel is going to start rocking. I suggest we go to plan B."

"And what is plan B?" asked Archer.

"I was hoping you had plan B," he said quietly. "The
subs can keep maximum speed up regardless of the
weather and radio back coordinates and types of ships, but
that's a needle in a haystack. You need eyes in the sky, and
I can't give you that for at least twenty-four hours. I can ask
for satellite scanning of the search grid, but that may take a
while. The Pentagon doesn't have a shot of the middle of

nowhere, and it will take ten or twelve hours to reprogram the satellites. In the meantime, we will continue all ahead full, due west, and see what there is to see. We are already in the major shipping lanes, but that doesn't mean your boat is."

"Admiral, this is your boat and your planes, and I respect that, sir, I truly do. But we need those planes in the sky now, not tomorrow. Now! You want to watch Fox News tomorrow and see New York burning with sarin gas clouds killing a hundred thousand Americans?"

"Jesus! Sarin? What the hell are you guys on to?" he asked.

"As I told you yesterday, we are searching for a ship carrying a weapon headed to the United States. The rest of the story is as I just said: These people have a Scud-B loaded with sarin and intend to hit a civilian target. Now, are you going to send up those birds, or do I have to call the president of the United States myself?" Archer snapped.

The admiral sighed. "Look, I'll talk to my pilots and tell them the score. This is going to be volunteer only. A search like this requires flying low and slow, and in a nor'easter, that may be a disaster. What about your bird?"

"Our men took off last night while we were all catching a nap. They are headed for the eastern seaboard as fast as they can get there. There will be a KC to refuel them out of McGuire Air Force Base in New Jersey when they get close. Then they will start working their way back to us. That bird was made for surveillance and can search a much wider area than your planes. We also have surveillance birds scrambling out of Texas. Damn, I wish we knew what the hell we were looking for."

The admiral scowled. "Look, my pilots are some of the best in the world. None of them will turn down the mission. We have a large air wing on this carrier and can search a large area if we use all our capabilities. Let's head upstairs and brief my officers about what we are looking for and why. Weather or not, we'll have everything that can fly up and working within the hour."

Archer stood and put his hand on the admiral's shoulder. "Thank you, Admiral. Nobody said it was going to be easy."

CHAPTER 36

Washington, D.C.

Amy's phone rang almost exactly three hours after Mitch had left. She knew it was exactly three hours because she had cleaned her apartment four times and paced around like a caged tiger the entire time.

She grabbed the receiver and blurted "Hello?"

"Amy, darling! How *are* you? I haven't heard from you since Thanksgiving! Are you getting crazy at work again?" It was not the voice she had expected.

"Hi, Mom. How are ya?" she asked when the phone clicked with another call coming in. "Mom, I am so sorry—I have to call you back!" She pressed the answer button and said "Hello?"

"Hello, Amy. I am on my way back over with a friend. Be there in ten." It was Mitch, sounding like he was in a car, and he hung up.

Amy punched the numbers to Langley and the director's office. She relayed that Mitch was on the way and would advise the director ASAP. By the time she was off the phone, her door buzzer was ringing. She buzzed the

door for Mitch and his associate downstairs, and waited for
the knock at her apartment door. She opened the door, and
her heart sank a little. Mitch was standing there with a
beautiful woman. They both entered, Amy's reaction not
lost on either of them.

"Amy, this is Halia Ovlatz from our embassy. She
works for the Foreign Ministry, and I answer directly to
her." This was a tacit way of telling her that Halia was also
Mosad, or at least some branch of Intelligence.

Halia extended her hand with a strong handshake.
"Mitch says wonderful things about you, Amy. Sorry we
didn't meet before this. I was on the phone for an hour. I
ended up speaking with the very highest levels of my government. I believe they understand your government's position, although they aren't happy about it. There is no time
for a political debate about terrorists right now. We were
fortunate enough to have had satellite photos of El Haram
and the west coast of Syria. We have actually been watching that area closely for quite a while for other reasons.

"The groups that you say we should be making peace
with work out of that area with the aid of the Syrian government, and we have assets there. I am going to give you
photos and information as a gift to your country from our
country. It is the hope of our government that you will remember how we reacted in your hour of need. Our hour of
need is fast approaching as well, and we will need help
from the United States."

Halia opened her briefcase and pulled out two thick
manila envelopes, both marked in red "Top Secret" in English and Hebrew. The first was full of photos and satellite
images. The second was full of reports in Hebrew, with
sections circled and quickly translated into English. There
were four pages of pictures stapled together with one of the
translated pages. Halia pointed to the section. "I trust you
do not read Hebrew?"

"No, sorry," Amy replied.

"No problem; these four pictures are the only four large ships that moved out of the port of El Haram in the past six weeks. The port of El Haram is being dredged, and only a small portion is open. They haven't gotten many oil tankers out of there in the past eight months, except this one." She pulled another photo, this one grainier, but obviously a blowup of the same ship. "This is supposedly an oil tanker full of oil headed to the U.S., no? Then why is she so high in the water?" She tapped the waterline on the bow of the ship. "We couldn't make out the first word of the name; the second word is *King*. You can see *ent* on the first word."

Amy looked hard at the picture. "What can it be? *Orient King*? *Serpent King*? We thought *Crescent Fire* was the name we were looking for."

Mitch spoke up. "That might have been a code name for something else. But this is your ship." He pulled out another photo from beneath the first. It was dark and grainy and hard to see. "Our analysts looked at this with computer equipment. It was taken in the middle of the night. It shows something very large outside the ship. They scaled the object and all agreed it is the same size as a Scud-B mobile missile launcher, Amy."

Mitch pulled another "photo," but it was a night-vision-enhanced picture, taken with heavy filters that showed mostly just edges and outlines of objects. "This object here," he pointed. "This we believe to be your Scud launcher and missile. We had told your government prior to the war that there are dozens of these hidden in Syria. For a short time we were able to actually track them, and even offered to destroy them, but your government asked us to stay out of it, so we did. We lost them after a few months in the western desert, the assumption being that there are underground facilities and bunkers. Most likely that is where your sarin came from as well.

"I know your American media and the U.N. weapons

inspectors say there were no weapons of mass destruction in Iraq, but ten or twenty thousand Kurds will tell you differently. So will twenty thousand or more Iranians. Saddam used sarin on his own people, on the Iranians. Who knows what else he was experimenting with? The world will never know how many people you saved by removing him, but you can be sure you did the right thing."

Mitch cleared his throat, realizing he was getting off the subject. "In any case, that is your boat—an oil tanker with the name *King* in it. We have searched all registered vessels and came up with a list of almost a hundred names with the name *King* in them. It doesn't really matter anyway; knowing where the ship was registered won't tell you where it is now. Most of the crude is heading to New Jersey's Port Elizabeth or to the Gulf of Mexico. We do know the traditional shipping lanes, and that may narrow your search a bit, but who knows with these people? They may travel a different course."

Halia spoke up. "I tend to think these people are trying to look like every other oil tanker out there. They will follow the same course that most of them take. They do it mostly for safety. In the event of a problem, there is usually another ship within a hundred miles or so. The shipping lanes are busier than most people think. The wide-open ocean isn't so desolate in the international shipping lanes. Park a boat out there and you can count the container ships, tankers, and barges that go by every hour."

"Let's hope you're right, Halia," Amy said. "Look, I can't thank both of you enough. I asked the impossible, and you had it done in three hours. I was hoping for an answer of some kind today. I never expected hard intelligence so fast."

Mitch laughed. "Amy, we are a small country and a tiny agency. There is much less bureaucracy than with your CIA, no offense. If we had to jump through the same hoops as you people, the Arabs would have wiped us out a long time ago. Now, unless you have questions, we will leave you to go make your report. I am sure you will be busy the next few days."

They stood and shook hands. Amy wanted to give Mitch a huge hug and kiss and thank him differently, but they both remained cool and professional with Halia present. By the time they left the building, Amy had her coat on and her cell phone in her ear, talking to the director as she headed back to Langley.

CHAPTER 37

Atlantic Ocean

Fadi Wazeeri was standing in the wheelhouse next to the captain, holding on to a rail as hard as he could. Visibility was a few feet, with driving snow and blasting cold winds. The sea churned and smashed the railings, the spray freezing to everything it touched. The bow of the tanker disappeared into the foam, only to reappear a second later with tons of icy Atlantic water pouring off the deck back into the sea.

"We are not as heavy as we usually are, Mr. Wazeeri. It makes the trip faster, but we bounce around a bit more," said the captain apologetically.

"Just keep us moving at full speed. I am worrying about the ice on the deck. Those doors need to be able to open; they look like they will be frozen shut. I will have some of the men break the ice."

"Mr. Wazeeri, with all respect, sir, I would advise against sending anyone out on the deck until the sea calms down. This will blow over by tomorrow or the next day; then you can chop off the ice."

"If it stays like this, the ice will be two feet thick! Those doors need to be opened soon." With that Wazeeri called down to the hold, where his cousin answered the intercom.

"Get some of the men on the foredeck. The ice is building up on the doors. We won't be able to open them. Have the men chop off the ice."

Kareem was still seasick and not moving very fast. Half of his men were as green as he was, but still he yelled at them. "I need ten men! Get up on the foredeck and break the ice off of the doors. If they freeze shut, we will never be able to fire our missile." He barked out the orders as sternly as possible, even though he thought the idea was insane.

At first, no one moved. Finally one of his foremen spoke up. "You heard him, get up there." He randomly grabbed ten men by the arm and pulled them toward the stairs that led to the deck. "There are fire axes on each floor. Use them and whatever you can find. Knock the ice off of the doors." The boat heaved port ten degrees, sending everyone grabbing for something to hang on to. "Get life preservers on," he barked, knowing full well there was no way he would go out there in a million years.

The ten men looked at each other, obviously terrified to go out on the foredeck in rolling, frozen seas, but more afraid of Fadi and Kareem than the ocean. They found orange life vests and pulled them over coats and hoods. They headed upstairs, bouncing through the stairwells as they climbed to the deck in the middle of a nor'easter.

They opened the door to the deck; the door was below the wheelhouse and in the middle of the ship. It was at least a hundred yards to the frozen doors. The deck, although constructed out of nonslip decking material, was an icy mess. The windchill made it feel like ten below zero, and the unfortunate sailors struggled to stay on their feet. It was dark, except for the light reflecting off of the white clouds of snow blowing in their faces. Within minutes, their beards were frozen, and they had to scream at one another just to be heard. They ran as best they could in a single-file line, holding on to the man in front of them, as they headed out toward the foredeck. Fadi and the captain watched them move forward, but within a few seconds they were out of sight in the windblown snow.

It took several minutes to get to the deck where the doors were located. The ice had built up considerably, and the men tried to break it off with their axes and metal wrenches. They worked as best they could, while fighting the rolling deck and fifty-mile-an-hour winds. The bow plunged into a large trough and sent a huge wave blowing through the crowd of men. Instantly, the group of ten men was now three. Seven of them had been blown over into frozen blackness. The three who were left hung on to the hinges of the doors, soaked and freezing, screaming in terror for their lost comrades. They lay on their sides hanging on with their aching arms, as their legs scrambled around, trying to find footing. There was no sign of their comrades, and certainly no hope of retrieving them in zero visibility.

One of the three began shouting to get back to the wheelhouse, and the three of them slipped and crawled along the frozen deck. Several more waves crashed over them, and the last man in the line was almost washed overboard. His screaming was lost in the high winds, but his face showed his terror as he clung to a frozen side rail. His two comrades stumbled to him as fast as they could, grabbing his frozen clothes and pulling him away from the wild ocean. They managed to get back to a sealed door, where they used their combined strength to turn the locking wheel and pull it open. The three of them tumbled inside frozen and in shock, and slammed the door shut behind them.

Fadi and the captain had seen the three of them when they got back amidships, and ran down to where they entered the ship's protection.

"Why are you back already? Where are the others?" Fadi demanded.

"They are all dead!" one of them cried. "They were washed overboard. The waves are too big!" The man was hysterical, and the other two were lying in soaked, frozen clothes, too exhausted to speak.

The captain was horrified. He had never lost a man at sea in more than twenty years. "We must stop and get lifeboats out!" he cried.

Wazeeri grabbed him by his coat and pinned him to the wall, hissing at him, "You will do no such thing. This ship is all ahead full until we get where we are going. It is God's will." He slammed the captain against the wall and screamed at him to return to the wheelhouse command room. Fadi stomped off toward his room. He stopped and turned to face the four horrified men in the small hallway. "Allahu akbar! It is God's will! This storm will stop, and we will deliver death to the infidels!" His eyes looked crazed, and he was obviously enraged. He turned and moved away, his robes making fluttering noises, like an apparition moving in the night.

CHAPTER 38

Carrier Flagship, U.S. Battle Group One, Atlantic Ocean

Archer had called Wyatt and a few other "men in black" into a small wardroom, where they had communication equipment set up. It was just after lunch. Rear Admiral McNamara, commander of the group, as well as the XO and a flight officer, were in the room as well, which surprised the men in black, who had been very aloof with the ship's crew.

"I am getting ready to contact our bird. They left last night at oh-three-hundred and have been airborne heading west ever since. The storm has restricted air operations, but we have new intelligence out of Washington that greatly narrows our search. Rather than explain it three times, I have asked you all here together to listen in on my sit-rep to our bird. Mackey went out with Still, Hollahan, Tee, and the crew to find our boat. We have information that is going to make that mission easier."

Archer picked up a secure phone and called their modified De Havilland. The pilot, Chris Mackey, came on the speaker so all could hear.

"Shadow One here. Over."

"Shadow One, this is base. We have new intel to narrow your search. Over."

"We would greatly appreciate that, base. It is blowing at fifty knots up here, and I have a couple of passengers about to lose their breakfast. 'Bumpy' doesn't exactly describe the situation. Over."

"Roger that, Shadow. Storm may break in ten to fifteen hours; hang in there. Your package is an oil tanker. Confirm."

"Oil tanker? Roger that. Excellent news. Thanks, Skipper. Now we're only looking for one out of a thousand ships in the middle of nowhere instead of one out of ten thousand."

"The name of the ship may have the word *King* in it. Confirm."

"I thought we were looking for the *Crescent Fire*, Skipper?"

"Must be a code name or something. Two-word name, second word is *King*. Confirm."

"Two-word name, second word is *King,* affirmative. But I'll tell you, Skipper, until the weather breaks, I don't care what kind of eyes we have, we won't be reading any names off any ships. We are in zero visibility, flying instruments only. The crew is working our sat intel and our onboard systems as best as possible, but this storm is screwing everything up. Our refueling stop has been rescheduled to shorten their trip, but we are approaching the halfway point, Skipper. If we don't get topped off pretty soon, we won't make it back to the ship. You want us to stay out here?"

"Affirmative. We will contact McGuire and make sure you get a refill. Continue on course, refuel, and begin working the grid. We will have air assets up as soon as possible to assist."

"Okay, Skipper, but I'm telling you, it's hairy out here.

Most of their birds aren't made like ours. They are going to be useless for reconnaissance. Choppers can't fly in this, either. If it gets much worse out here, we're gonna be swimming."

Archer looked over at the commander of the group and raised his eyebrows. The commander exhaled slowly and said, "He's right. Our fighters won't be much good trying to make visuals on ships. The only thing they can do is cover a lot of ocean in a short amount of time, and if they find anything, radio back coordinates. I'm not sure how effective that is. The choppers are useless in this weather, and the range is too far. That leaves two recon planes, but they are smaller than your bird, less sophisticated, and shorter-ranged."

Archer was grimacing at being so helpless. "Admiral, what if we send up the Tomcats and let them run the shipping lanes a few times. They pick up any tankers, at least they can send back the positions to us, and we can see about getting ships, subs, or land-based air assets in closer for a look."

"Tell you what: We'll send up the fighters, as you request, and when the weather breaks a little, we'll send out our recon aircraft. I'll have the sub escorts fan out for a wider search grid. They can make visual contact if they find anything, and could also sink the bastards. In the meantime, we are all ahead full and fanned out much wider than we ever sail. We'll find your boat Mr. Archer."

Archer turned back to the radiophone. "Shadow, you will have fast movers inbound working the lanes. They will have your comm channels. Good luck. Let me drop a dime and get you some gas."

"Roger that, boss. Send the cavalry. And maybe a life raft while you're at it. Over and out."

Archer turned to the room. "So there it is, gentlemen. We are looking for an oil tanker, two words in the name, second name *King*. This boat has a Scud-B missile system with a warhead filled with sarin nerve agent headed for our homes. We believe Fadi Wazeeri and his cousin Kareem Wazeeri have put this together, and may in fact be on board this vessel. We will take them alive if possible, but make no mistake, our mission is to stop that missile launch. If that means blowing them out of the water, so be it. Any questions?" Seeing none, everyone stood and went to the tasks at hand. Archer, for his part, picked up the phone receiver and dailed Washington to arrange for refueling missions for his plane, regardless of the weather.

The admiral and the XO headed upstairs to sit down with all of the other officers and flight crews and began working out a strategy to cover a very large search area in zero visibility beyond the range of their aircraft. As the man said, nobody said it was going to be easy.

CHAPTER 39

Western Atlantic,
N 39°54´, W 50°48´

The weather had started to settle down just a bit. Bob Still was almost as white as Will Hollahan. Hollahan was a pilot, and was not bothered by the weather, but Still was quietly terrified and more than a bit queasy. Everyone else on board their cramped aircraft acted like it was "business as usual," and Still refused to be the first one to say anything about the weather and turbulence. Chris Mackey walked into the cabin from the cockpit and yelled, "Listen up!"

All heads turned toward him, and activity stopped as they waited to see what was going on.

"We have new intel. We are looking for an oil tanker. If we get a chance to read the name, it has the word *King* as the second word of the two-word name. This vessel has a Scud-B missile system armed with sarin nerve agent and is headed west to fire at an unknown target. Fadi and Kareem Wazeeri may be on board." That made him smile. Everyone in the world knew the name Fadi Wazeeri. The opportunity to blow him to Hell was something everyone on board was excited about. "So that's it, boys. Find us an oil tanker. Ears, how are you making out?"

Still was zoomed out as far as his console would go. "I dunno, man. The weather is screwing this thing up. I don't get any images. Either there are no ships out there, or we can't see them."

"All right, here's what you do. Zoom in and scan smaller areas. You'll be slower, but it will be more sensitive. Just start a grid search and stay on it. Hollahan, you work independently. If he finds something, you'll check it out, but in the meantime, just keep looking. The tankers are huge—long and skinny, nothing like a cruise ship. Just keep at it, guys." He walked farther into the back of the aircraft, where another pod of instruments was being worked by another half dozen men. "Keep running sonar, radar, heat signatures, and use the ship tracker that's online. Connect to sailwx.info/shiptrack and run the regular stuff. I doubt these guys are dumb enough to have their loran systems hooked into the satellite, but you never know. Double-check any names with *King* in them."

Turbulence sent Mackey flying. One of his men grabbed him and helped him stay on his feet. "Hey, man, you better get up there and drive this thing before we end up feeding the crabs," the airman joked. It was the nervous jokes macho guys always made when they were ready to pee in their pants.

Mackey laughed and stumbled back to the cockpit. He wasn't there a second when his man working the computer search yelled at the top of his lungs, "Holy shit! Hey, Chief! You ain't gonna believe this. I have three tankers with the name *King* in them, and they are all within two hundred miles of each other. Two Saudi and one Kuwaiti."

"Okay, run the locations to Ears and Eyes, and see if we can get closer looks at them. Don't start blasting holes in anything yet. We have to see who they are," said Mackey.

* * *

adi Wazeeri hadn't moved from the wheelhouse in three hours. He sat staring out the windows at the blizzard that was sending waves crashing over the bow of his ship. Every minute they lost because of the storm put his mission at risk. By now, the infidels would be looking for them. Headwinds and waves slowed their ship, and the captain struggled to keep them on course.

"Mr. Wazeeri, I have another vessel on our radar screen. It is within one hundred miles. They will contact us if I don't contact them. It is standard operating procedure."

"Why will they contact you?"

"It takes several miles to perform a turn with these ships, Mr. Wazeeri. For safety purposes, all of the tanker captains advise each other of their course headings."

"No! You will not tell anyone where we are headed!" he barked back.

"Mr. Wazeeri, I have to tell them something. We don't want to crash into another oil tanker in this storm. It is hard enough just to stay on course; maneuvering around another vessel would be impossible if it isn't planned well in advance. I will just give them our current course. They won't care where we are headed."

Wazeeri was pacing around the small room, making the captain nervous. Wazeeri threw his hands in the air. "Then contact him if you must, but keep it brief, and don't tell him anything more than you have to."

The captain keyed his mike. "This is Saudi vessel *Crescent King*. We are at north 39°54', west 50°48', headed due west."

There was another squawk. "*Crescent King*, this is Kuwaiti vessel *King Abha*. We are north 38°30', west 49°02', headed due west. Some storm, huh?"

"Get rid of him!" shouted Wazeeri.

The captain didn't answer the other ship.

"*Crescent King*, are you there? Everything all right?" asked the other captain.

"Yes, we are fine. Busy here. Good luck with the weather."

"Okay, *Crescent King*. Stay in touch, looks like we are on the same heading. This nor'easter should blow over by tomorrow afternoon. What is your destination?"

Wazeeri was getting furious. "Who is this idiot? Tell him you are busy!"

"I did. He is just making small talk. It is normal; they get bored out here. If we know each other's destination, it is safer, that's all."

The captain didn't answer, and he and Wazeeri just stood there looking at the radio. The ship rocked and the wind howled outside.

"You there, *Crescent King*? What is your destination? We are headed for Port Elizabeth in New Jersey."

The captain stood still, barely breathing, as he prayed this man would stop talking to him. After a moment had passed, the voice came back. "Okay *Crescent King*, you must be busy with the weather. Stay safe, and we'll see you Stateside."

The captain wiped the sweat from his forehead, even in the cool wheelhouse. "Praised be Allah," he mumbled.

"How many miles are we from Washington, D.C.?" Wazeeri asked.

"I will plot you an exact figure, Mr. Wazeeri," he answered. The captain pulled out navigational charts and called in one of his crewmen, who helped him plot the course to D.C. from their present location. The two of them worked quietly, while Wazeeri continued to stare out at the storm. His eyes burned with hatred as he watched the rain and snow freeze on his window.

The captain and his crewman conversed quietly a few minutes, then looked to Wazeeri. "Mr. Wazeeri, we are approximately six hundred and fifty nautical miles from the D.C. coast."

Wazeeri's eyes lit up. He actually smiled, showing his

long, yellow teeth. "Six hundred and fifty miles?" He
slapped the captain's back like an old friend. "You have
made better time in this storm than I would have guessed.
How long will it take us to get within five hundred miles?"

The captain looked at his crewman, and they mumbled
to each other for a moment. "Right now, we are lucky to
make fifteen knots. Quick numbers, that's ten hours. But
that's only if the storm doesn't get any worse."

"Ten hours! We must prepare ourselves!" Fadi was excited. He almost ran out of the wheelhouse as he headed
down into the cavernous hull, where his missile sat with his
crew of holy martyrs-to-be. He stormed into the hold to
find his men looking miserable. They stood when he entered.

"The hour of glory approaches!" he screamed. He expected a huge response, but it didn't sink in to the cold,
seasick men. "Do you understand? We will fire our missile
in ten hours! We shall rain death from Allah to these infidels! Your families will sing your names for a hundred
years, and we will go to Paradise, where our virgins will
await our glorious arrival!"

At that, the men did cheer, and began chants of "Allahu
akbar!" Kareem incited them into a frenzy, then continued,
"In eight hours, we will break the ice off of those doors. In
ten hours, we will open them and fire our missile. If it is
God's will, we will return to Syria. If it is our time, we will
be martyrs for Allah!" He approached the Iraqi missile
crew.

"We are six hundred and fifty miles from Washington,
D.C. How long does it take to prepare for launch?"

"Everything is ready, Mr. Wazeeri. All that remains is
opening the doors and erecting the launcher. When the
doors are open, we will need twenty minutes to raise the
missile, arm it, and fire. The coordinates were done days
ago, and the payload is ready. The missile will explode a
quarter mile above the target, and spread sarin over one or

two square miles, depending on the wind. In a city like Washington, we should expect no less than a hundred thousand dead."

Wazeeri could hardly contain his delight. He began dancing with hands over his head in traditional fashion. The men began singing and screaming as they worked themselves into a frenzy again. Morale had been horrible from the weather, seasickness, and the deaths of their comrades in the frozen ocean. Now they could see Washington in ruins, and their joy could not be contained.

The dancing and singing continued for a long time, with Kareem joining in. He had been seasick as a dog for days, but this energized him enough to ignore it. The celebration continued until Fadi calmed the men down and told them it was time to pray to Allah for help. All of them took out their prayer rugs and faced Mecca, and they prayed for a long, long time.

CHAPTER 40

CIA Headquarters, Langley, Virginia

Amy entered the director's office and handed the envelopes to one of his staff. The director shook her hand so hard she thought he was going to rip it off. He directed her to a seat in the Situation Room attached to his office.

"Amy, the satellite intelligence from Weisel was invaluable. It was more than we could have hoped for. Let's just pray it is accurate. We have narrowed our search to oil tankers only. God forbid it's a cargo ship; it'll get right past us. We simply can't watch everything at once. The lousy weather we've had the past two days has turned into a full-blown nor'easter off the coast. It is causing huge problems for our satellite images, with heavy cloud cover. It is also delaying air searches. We had two different coast guard aircraft turned back by the storm. Coast guard ships are heading to our best guesses looking at every oil tanker they can find. The problem is there are more than a hundred ships in a one-hundred-square-mile grid. We are running aircraft up and down the coast, between three and four hundred miles out. Range on Scud-B's is about three hundred kilometers, but we know they have been increasing it, so we can't be sure on that, either.

"All we can do is more of what we are doing. This is on the president's desk, the joint chiefs are all over it, Homeland Security is working, the FBI are shakin' the trees, navy and air force assets are working, and we are working. What the Hell else can we do?" He was half talking to himself at that point.

"I am sure the Israelis' analysis of the photos is correct; they are usually right on. Still, we are going to have our people go over every bit of it. We have some toys they don't know about. Maybe we can work on that name, or use the ship's details to give us more information."

The director looked at her seriously for a moment, then asked, "What did they ask for?"

"What did who ask for? The Israelis?"

"Yes. What did they want for the satellite photos? Weisel ask for cash?"

"No, sir. Actually, his boss said that the highest levels of their government were happy to help us in our hour of need, and they hoped we would remember them in theirs. Those are almost her exact words, sir."

He chewed on that for a moment. "I've been doing this a long time, Amy. I gotta tell ya, even for our allies, it's pretty damn rare that they give us something for nothing. We'll have to see down the road what they want for this. Trust me, it wasn't out of the goodness of their hearts. Still and all, he came up huge for you. He deny being Mosad?"

"Not exactly, sir. We both know the drill. We try not to compromise ourselves too much, but we work as best we can without going off the reservation, so to speak."

"Well, Amy, that was one hell of a piece of work. You tell Weisel that the president of the United States and the director of the CIA both personally thank him. On second thought, hold that praise until we get these dirtbags. The president is not going to thank him quite so much if a cruise ship sends up a Scud in New York Harbor."

He hit the intercom and told his secretary to assemble staff. Within a few minutes, agents began entering the Situation Room. Amy met half a dozen new faces and sat with large carafes of coffee. This is where they would be spending the next day or so, as reports and information came in. They would monitor satellite images, radio transmissions, phone calls, and use every means at their disposal to find their needle in a haystack.

CHAPTER 41

Six Hundred Miles off the Mid-Atlantic Seaboard

Chris Mackey radioed back to the carrier, a slight edge to his voice. "Hey, Chief, how are we doing on those KC-10s? I'm getting a little low and got a headwind killing my fuel economy. It's a little cold for swimming, and I am too low to get back to you or to make it to the coast."

Archer was calm on his end of the phone. "We didn't forget about you. You have a KC-10A Extender on the way to your location as we speak. They are coming out of McGuire and should be to your location within an hour."

"Okay, boss, thanks. But tell them to hurry. I don't have much longer than that. Give me their heading or frequency and I'll start heading in their direction."

"Roger that. Hold, Shadow One, and I will patch through to the KC." The line went quiet for about five minutes. When Archer came back, there was static in the background.

"Shadow One, this line is no longer encrypted. Do you copy?"

"Roger, base. Over."

"Shadow One, I have KC on the line for you. Go ahead, KC."

The KC-10A Extender pilot spoke up, his line not quite as clear as Archer's.

"Shadow One, this is KC-10 Topper. Do you copy?"

"Copy, Topper. We need your position and heading, and will head toward you. Situation is getting critical."

"Copy that, Shadow One. We are heading to you at maximum speed with a nice, long drink. Sorry we are late, but this lovely weather is causing some problems." The KC-10 and the De Havilland exchanged locations and headings, and coordinated their refueling location. The KC-10 was making more than six hundred knots, even in the storm, which seemed to be subsiding. While it was going to be more stressful than usual, they would arrive before the De Havilland ran out of fuel.

On board the De Havilland, Still and Hollahan were working together the same way they had for twenty years. Each knew what the other was going to say before he said it, which is why they had been chosen for this mission. They scanned the grid as quickly but as carefully as they could. So far they had checked out more than twenty ships, and gone so far as to contact the ships' captains, claiming to be another ship, to verify the name of the vessel and cross-check it against their computerized tracking system of who was out there on the water.

In the back of the aircraft, Tee was working with another crew to track the three *Kings* on their radar. The first ship was the closest to their position. It was a Kuwaiti supertanker, which, according to some research, was called the *Star King*. They had radioed the information on the *Star King* back to the aircraft carrier, where they in turn checked the information through Langley's computers. As it turned out, the *Star King* was indeed bound for the United States from the Kuwaiti oil fields, with two million gallons of crude oil on board. They verified the dates, point of debarkation, destination, course, etc., until they were comfortable that it was just another traveling gas can. Archer's crew radioed back to the aircraft and confirmed that all was as it should be with the Kuwaiti vessel.

Tee continued working to check the other two ships with *King* in the name. There were two: the *Crescent King* and the *King Abha*. Both were Saudi tankers and were traveling on the same course to the United States. It seemed unlikely that one of these was their target, since they appeared to be traveling together, but they began checking them anyway. Tee had given the names, locations, and headings to Mackey, who forwarded the information to Langley. They went through the same procedure as before, but with different results.

Archer called back to Mackey as soon as he received the call from Langley.

"Shadow One, this is base. We may have a situation here. *King Abha* is Saudi registered, one point three million gallons of crude out of the gulf. Everything checks out there, but the other ship doesn't appear to come from anywhere. It is registered as a Saudi vessel, but we can't trace it back to anyplace. According to our research, it hasn't been in service for two years. Langley is checking, and I will advise. How far are you from that location?"

"Boss, if that KC doesn't show up soon, we are *forever* from that location. That ship is directly behind us, almost one hundred eighty degrees, by almost two hundred miles. If I turn around and head away from the KC-10, we may give them a bird's-eye view of us crashing into the ocean."

Archer rubbed his temples. "Shadow One, look, this is your call. Stay on location and refuel, then find that ship. Try not to make it obvious that you are checking them out in case they are in range of the coast. I don't want to tip them off and encourage them to fire the missile. We will continue to try to track from here. I have F-14s heading to that location, but they are still pretty far out, even at supersonic.

They will require refueling as well. I can call in air support from the coast, but that will take more than an hour as well. You are the closest, maybe twenty-five minutes out."

There was a brief pause, then Mackey's voice came back. "Give me three minutes. Over and out."

Mackey left his copilot on course, but slowed to just over stall speed. He walked back into the cabin where the men were working frantically.

"Listen up!" he screamed to his crew. "We are twenty minutes out from our possible target. We can't confirm the target until we get there. The tanker is coming from the opposite direction. If we go after the target, we may run out of fuel, especially if we get there at top speed. If we don't go, it'll take the fighters more than an hour to get there, and the ship may be close enough to fire the missile. There are a few possible outcomes here gentlemen:

"We go and it turns out to be nothing and we all go swimming for no reason.

"We go and it *is* the target, and you're all just as dead, but at least we prevent the attack.

"Or we wait for refueling and go as fast as we can. I am responsible for the safety of this aircraft and its personnel, and I will not fly this mission unless it is unanimous, gentlemen. Take a second to decide, but it's all go or no go. Understand, if we go, you are buying a one-way ticket. Chances are, no one will ever know about it, either; so if you are planning on being a headline hero, forget it. I'll give you a minute."

He hopped back into the cockpit to relay his conversation to his copilot. The men in the back exchanged glances.

Still smiled his big, toothy grin at Hollahan. "Man, I knew I was fucked the minute Walker called us by our first names in Washington." He laughed his big, contagious laugh and made Hollahan smile. "You know damn well we ain't runnin' away from this."

Hollahan smiled and leaned back in his chair to see the

crewmen in the back. Still looked at Hollahan thoughtfully, then at the crew. "Time's a-wastin', fellas'," Still shouted. "If we're gonna burn fuel, let's do it wastin' these terrorists." The crew in the back all gave thumbs-up signs and nervous smiles. They may have been scared, they may have been thinking about home, but no one said a word. Mackey stuck his head back into the cabin. He found every man staring back at him with a thumbs-up signal. One of the men in the back yelled out, "Let's roll!" It was his personal tribute to another hero on another plane—that one on nine-eleven.

Mackey didn't say a word, just jumped back into his chair and hit the mike to call Archer on the carrier.

"Shadow One to base, come in," he called.

Archer replied right away. "This is base. Over."

"We are changing course to possible target ship. We have coordinates locked and will be on station in twenty minutes. We will radio all information and give you live feed from whatever we see or hear. Please dispatch nearest rescue vessels to that location. We will not have enough fuel. Copilot is radioing the KC for new rendezvous location, but that may be wishful thinking. I hope to Hell this is our boat, boss. Over and out."

Archer said, "Me, too" to himself. He felt suddenly choked up. "Godspeed, Shadow One. We will be watching."

Archer then called his direct secure phone to Langley, Virginia, where the director of the CIA himself was sitting with a roomful of assistants, including Amy Lang. He reiterated the situation to Holstrum, giving him exact coordinates of all vessels and aircraft, which Holstrum would in turn forward to the Situation Room in the White House. By now the president was with the joint chiefs and several cabinet members, awaiting the most recent information on the possibility of a missile hitting the East Coast.

* * *

Amy sat in silence with the others, Archer's voice on speakerphone in the secure room. They readjusted all the monitors in the room until they could make out two oil tankers within a couple miles of each other, heading west toward the United States. The images were lousy due to the dense cloud cover, but they could see the ships in the empty ocean.

"Can't we just fire a missile from a sub or the frigate? Why wait?" asked one of the men in the room.

"We have not confirmed that the missile is aboard that ship yet, Tom. You want us to sink a foreign vessel, kill a few crewmen, and maybe create a two-million-gallon oil slick washing up on Virginia Beach? If that was an option, we would have blown them out of the water hours ago. Until those guys can see a name or a missile sitting on that ship, we have to just sit and watch."

They all exchanged glances. Some years back, a civilian airliner went down over New York. There had been rumors of a shoot-down by a missile. Everyone at the agency and the Navy Department had been grilled. Plenty of people were convinced that either the CIA had intervened on a terrorist plot to use that plane like the ones on nine-eleven, or that the navy had simply fired a missile at the wrong target during exercises. Neither story ever checked out, but certainly the investigation showed them all how likely they were to be called in front of Congress if something went wrong today.

Archer asked for silence, and turned on the live feed from the aircraft called Shadow One. They all sat in silence, listening to the crewmen speaking quietly and calmly to each other, checking and rechecking positions and equipment. When a crewman informed the pilot that their payload was armed, several men exchanged glances.

"They have weapons on that aircraft? I thought it was observation only," said one of the men.

"That aircraft has a chain gun in the nose, similar to an

A-10 Warthog. She also carries one bomb, similar to a scaled-down Daisy Cutter."

"A Daisy Cutter? Jesus—if this turns out to be the right ship, that outta do it, no?"

"In theory, that payload is sufficient to sink that ship. Even if it didn't sink it, it would cause a massive fire and at least stop it where it is. The problem is, it's a dumb bomb. Chances of hitting that ship aren't very good. It wasn't designed for that. Those guys would have one chance to drop that thing and hit a bull's-eye. And that's only if they haven't run out of gas before they get there."

The room went silent, and each person sat quietly, listening to the transmissions and watching the boats in a very large ocean.

CHAPTER 42

The *Crescent Fire*

Fadi was up in the wheelhouse, smiling for the first time in days. The weather was breaking, and the sky was getting lighter. The winds had died down, too, and the ocean seemed to be calming somewhat. It was certainly a good omen, and a gift from a happy Allah, helping his true followers in their war against the infidels. Fadi prayed quietly as he watched the rays from the sun break through the clouds dramatically, like a religious painting. In his mind, Fadi could see the angels pushing the clouds away and holding out their hands to him. They would bring him personally to sit with Allah in Paradise, surrounded by virgins who would adore him for his bravery.

The pleasant thoughts were interrupted by Kareem entering the room. "Cousin, the weather is breaking!"

"I can see that with my own eyes," he said with a sneer, angry at the interruption of his daydream.

"The men are preparing to break the ice off of the doors. Even the ocean is calming. God is great! The men have prepared something special for you."

A gift from his men was intriguing. He followed Kareem on the long walk belowdecks to the hold, where the missile was located. A huge yellow banner was hung inside the hold with red Arabic calligraphy that read *Crescent Fire*. Fadi smiled at the beautiful sight before him. It was true. Nothing could stop them now. They were messengers from Allah—his sword, his fury, his fire from Heaven.

"Allahu akbar!" Fadi screamed, his voice reverberating off of the metal walls and catwalks of the huge metal hold.

All his men joined in, screaming and chanting. It became a frenzy within seconds, until one of his overexcited men fired off a round from an AK-47 inside the hull of the ship. The round bounced off the walls for several seconds before it found an unknown final resting place. The crowd of fanatics went suddenly silent as they waited for a bullet to strike them dead.

Kareem ran to the man and grabbed the rifle from his hands, clubbing him with it and knocking him off his feet. "You idiot! You could have killed Fadi Wazeeri! There is a missile in here! You could have killed us all!"

Fadi, in uncharacteristic fashion, was not upset. He helped the terrified man to his feet, but the man went immediately to his knees and begged forgiveness from Wazeeri.

"It is okay, my servant. You are excited! We are all excited! The hour is at hand. Get above and break the ice off the doors!" He turned to the Iraqi missile crew. "Be ready to fire your missile! We will open the doors as soon as we can, and you will deliver death to the infidels!" Fadi was working himself back up to a frenzy again. He pulled the banner down from the beam and held it above his head, screaming again, "Allahu akbar!" The men joined in and were dancing and singing. They grabbed axes and metal tools and bundled up in the clothes against the cold ocean air. They ran up the catwalks to the deck, anxious to break off the ice that held the doors closed, each man wanting to be the one who released the doors and flung death to the infidels.

Fadi and Kareem walked after the running men, their own excitement increased by that of the men. Fadi had the large banner wrapped around him, and kept it that way until they were topside. Once there, he tied it to a steel beam in the center of the ship, not far from where the men worked chipping the ice from the huge metal doors. When it was secure, Fadi let go, and it fluttered in the breeze, boldly flapping its name, *Crescent Fire*. When the men saw it, they cheered so loudly it could be heard above the wind's whistling. The sun shone brightly on the bloodred letters, the same color that would run in the streets of America in another hour. Fadi stood on the deck, his hands above his head in triumph as he watched the ice flying through the air as the men banged away on the metal doors holding back Hell on Earth.

CHAPTER 43

Shadow One

Hollahan spoke up in an excited voice, "Hey! I got action on the ship!" Hollahan was playing the role of "Ears" and had zoomed in the microphone software on the ship's location. Something loud was going on, and the ship kept causing little flashes of light to change on his color console.

Still was "Eyes," and had zoomed out earlier to get a better picture. The close-ups were very grainy and hard to see because of the weather, but that was steadily improving, so he zoomed in again on the ship's coordinates. He continued to monkey around with the controls until he got a better view of the ship. "Roger that!" he yelled back. "Looks like a whole bunch of people are on the deck!"

The crewmen were all busy working their equipment, each trying to add a piece of the puzzle, when the plane made a loud backfire noise and bounced hard to the right. Everyone grabbed for something to hold on to, and Mackey's voice came over the intercom: "Sorry folks, we just lost an engine. I am going to try to restart it. We are

driving on fumes. If anyone knows any prayers for fuel efficiency, now would be a good time. The KC-10 called in:
They are at maximum speed and dumped some fuel to gain
a few extra knots. They are about ten or fifteen minutes
away at best. We should be on our target in about five or
ten. The weather has broken and we are looking for a visual. Stay sharp, people, and just try to ignore plunging
into the frozen ocean."

The men in the back couldn't see him smiling when he
said that, and failed to see the humor. One of the men in the
back moved forward near Still and Hollahan.

"Give me a hand, will ya?" he asked. He began opening
a hatch in the floor behind their seats.

"What's down there?" asked Hollahan.

"When this bird was designed, space was very tight. To
release the bomb in the tail, you have to go below and use
an old-fashioned bombardier sight system. It's like being
the ball turret gunner and the bombardier of an old Flying
Fortress all in one. I got the short straw. You all better hope
I can shoot straight. I've only done this a few times before
in practice, and we always considered being within a football field as a good shot. If I miss and this puppy goes into
the water, we don't get another chance." They pulled the
hatch up, he gave a thumbs-up to his friends in the back,
and dropped down the small hole to a tiny crawl space below their feet. They closed the hatch and jumped back into
their seats.

Still looked at Hollahan. "We have a bad landing, he's
got no shot down there."

Hollahan cocked his head. "Bob, there hasn't been a
successful water landing in the history of commercial avi-
ation. This is a modified De Havilland. We go into the
drink, it doesn't matter where we are sitting."

Still smiled. "Good. Now I don't feel so guilty about
lockin' his skinny ass down in that hole. Thanks."

Mackey's voice came back over the intercom. "I have a

visual! Two vessels dead ahead!" The aircraft began losing
altitude as the pilot made a beeline for his target. The crew
could hear Mackey speaking to Langley, rattling off coordinates and the visual sighting. Langley, in turn, reminded
the pilot that the ship closer to him, or on his starboard,
would be their target. The other had been confirmed to be
the Saudi tanker *King Abha*, and was not a concern.

Mackey came back on the intercom for everyone to
hear. "Attention all crew. We have visual sighting dead
ahead. There are two vessels; ours is the starboard, forward
vessel. That's the one on the right, in front of the other one,
for you FBI types. We will make one slow and low pass
over her to get a good look at her. We will not get a second
chance, so nobody blink. Watch for a name on the bow, and
a strange object on the deck, anything at all that looks out
of place for an oil tanker. I'm not exactly sure what an oil
tanker is supposed to look like, but I reckon I would recognize a Scud if I saw one. Anyone sees anything, sing out
clearly. My tanks read empty, my fuel lights and alarms are
ringing, and we may be using that other ship for an airstrip
in a minute."

With an obvious lightbulb going on in his head, Mackey
looked at his copilot. "Hey, Gerry! What about it? That
other tanker is almost as big as the carrier. What if we
parked this baby on her?"

"Are you shitting me, Captain? You want to crash-land
on two million gallons of oil? I think we'd do better in the
water." He was shaking his head in disbelief. He called
back to the KC-10 with their position, "Topper, this is
Shadow One. Do you copy?"

"Roger, Shadow One; we are tracking you on radar and
can be giving you a refill in ten minutes or so."

"Roger, Topper, we copy that. We have acquired a possible hostile target sea vessel and are going in to investigate. If we aren't here when you get here, drop us a
lifeboat, will ya?"

"Hang in there, Shadow, the cavalry is coming with gas. We are breaking a speed record, and prefer to have you there when we arrive. We will advise again in five minutes. Over and out."

The plane bounced, and everyone looked at each other. That time was just turbulence as they descended rapidly toward their target. As the ship grew closer, Mackey and his copilot were amazed at the size of the tanker. They slowed and dropped altitude even more, trying to see whatever they could with their naked eyes.

"Ya know, Skipper, if we stall out at this altitude we won't get a chance to pick her back up," said the copilot.

Mackey ignored him and began arming the chain gun in the nose of the aircraft. He had control over that trigger in his steering wheel, at his right thumb. There was a backup in his copilot's steering wheel, and the gun also could be fired from a computer system in the rear of the aircraft. Mackey rolled over on his left and swooped down over the ship, only a few hundred feet above it. They could see a few dozen men in winter gear digging in what looked like snow and ice on the foredeck. Other than that, nothing seemed too bizarre.

In the back of the aircraft, the crew was snapping pictures, shooting film, and sending everything instantly back to Langley and the carrier via live feed.

One of the men in the Situation Room in Langley piped up when he saw the huge yellow banner blowing above the deck in the picture. "Hey, Chief, freeze that!" he yelled. Holstrum hit a button and the video froze.

"Drop back a few frames. I need to see that banner," he said, trying to be calm. The agent, a fairly new arrival, was fluent in several Arab languages, and was chosen specifically for that talent. "Son of a bitch! *Crescent Fire*! That's it! That's our boat!"

"Confirm that, son. We need to be sure before we blast that ship," snapped Holstrum.

"One hundred percent, sir. That banner reads *Crescent Fire* plain as day."

Holstrum yelled into his mike to the aircraft, "Shadow One, this is Director Holstrum. Be advised, we have confirmed that ship is the *Crescent Fire*. Repeat, that is the *Crescent Fire*. You are cleared to fire."

Mackey yelled into his mike, "Roger that, we are cleared to fire!" Mackey passed over the ship and leveled off, the remaining fuel swishing in the almost empty tanks. The plane sputtered a few times and blew black smoke out of the engines, but both engines were still running, and they made a second pass. "Attention all crew, we are cleared to fire! Repeat, we are cleared to fire. That is the *Crescent Fire*, gentlemen!"

Mackey's mike squawked as the KC-10 tanker called in, "Shadow One, we are five minutes out. What is your situation?"

Gerry, the copilot, yelled back at them, "Can't chat now, fellas, we are engaging enemy vessel. Continue on course! Over and out!"

Mackey called down on his headset belowdecks to his bombardier, A. J. Coolidge. "A.J., this is Mack. That's our boat down there. We have one shot. I will go in low and slow and try to give you a full-length shot in case it bounces. I can probably make two passes and after that, who knows? We are out of gas, A.J. Be ready—"

Still's yelling cut into their conversation. "Hey! The floor is opening!"

The other crewmen looked out the windows and checked the video pictures of the ship to see what he was yelling about. Sure enough, what had been the deck of the ship was opening like Bombay doors. Two huge metal doors slowly opened from nowhere, as snow and ice fell off onto the deck and bounced into the frigid ocean. The men on the ship were now aware of the plane that was buzzing over their heads and were scrambling around below them. Several of them picked up weapons and began firing at the aircraft, although they were out of range for effective damage.

"Goddamn! Those people are shooting at us!" yelled Mackey. He spoke to his copilot. "Listen, Gerry, when we drop that Daisy Cutter, I'm going to use that weight loss to bounce for some altitude. Three thousand pounds falling out of here should give us some lift. You tell that KC-10 to meet us at eight hundred feet and stay there unless they hear different, okay? A.J., you copy?"

"Roger, Skipper. I have opened the door and I'm sighting the target. We are armed and operational. Bring us in low and slow, and I will drop this in their laps."

A loud backfire announced the loss of the same engine that had gone out before. There would be no restarting it this time; it was bone dry.

"We have one shot, gentlemen, God help us. I am lining up at twelve o'clock to take a nice, straight run at their bow like it was a landing strip. Everybody sit tight and prepare for small-arms fire."

Fadi could not believe his eyes. A black plane had come from out of nowhere as soon as the doors had been freed. He was a lunatic, screaming at his men to shoot it down. As they scrambled for weapons, which were only AK-47 assault rifles, he ran belowdecks to his missile crew.

As soon as he could see them, he began screaming, "Fire the missile! Fire it! Do you hear me? Fire that missile!"

The missile crew couldn't hear Fadi's ranting over the sound of their engine. They had started the engine to power the hydraulics that raised the missile to its upright firing position as soon as the doors began opening. The cold, semidark hold of the ship was bathed in sunlight, and the missile very slowly began to move as the hydraulics lifted the great object. One of the men was standing on the back of the launcher when he saw Fadi running to them screaming. He yelled at the other crewman to stop, misunderstanding Fadi's animated rantings and not hearing him. The confused man cut the elevator control, and everything stopped as they all turned to look at Fadi.

"What is it, Mr. Wazeeri? What is the matter?"

"No! You idiots! Don't stop! Fire that missile! The Americans are here!"

The Iraqi crewmen immediately restarted the firing sequence, and the missile slowly began to move upright again. Above them, their comrades fired frantically at the large black plane that had circled above them and was now returning low and slow, coming directly at them from the bow. They were out of range, but borderline hysterical, and continued to empty clip after clip at the target, which was still out of range.

Archer was radioing back to Mackey, "Shadow One, we have missiles standing by on the frigate and sub. Impact would be ten minutes out, and they appear to be getting ready to launch. Our fighters won't make it in time. This is all up to you, Mack. Good luck. All ships and rescue aircraft are en route to your position."

Mackey simply said "Roger. Out," and concentrated on the ship fast approaching. His thumb pressed the red button on his steering wheel, and showers of white light flowed out of the nose of his plane as tracer rounds and explosive, armor-piercing bullets poured toward the tanker like Fourth of July sparklers. The men who had been firing at them disappeared in clouds of blood, body parts, and shrapnel as they were cut to ribbons. The plane was almost at stall speed as they floated over the oil tanker in what appeared to be slow motion.

A. J. Coolidge spoke calmly into his headset to his pilot, "Hold steady, Mack, hold steady. Preparing to fire. Three, two, one, firing!"

As the huge bomb fell out of the belly of the plane, Mackey pulled up as hard as he could and accelerated hard, burning precious fuel as they bounced off the loss of the huge anchoring weight. The giant bomb fell with the grace of a Greyhound bus, but sailed right into the open doors where the nose cone of a Scud-B missile began to appear. Fadi Wazeeri was standing with the missile crew when the Scud went fully upright, waiting for the exact moment when it would lock into position and the missile would fire. He was staring up at the nose cone of the missile when the blue sky above the doors filled with the sight of an object he couldn't understand at first. What was that large shape filling the doorway?

The long wand of the Daisy Cutter pressed against the Scud's nose cone, and for a fraction of a second the two opposing bombs kissed in farewell salute. The flash of light filled the hold of the ship, and the single-hulled tanker expanded ever so slightly for a brief second before exploding into a fireball of death. No fireball had ever entered the Earth's atmosphere with such a light show. The ship lifted out of the water slightly as the hull filled with the giant fireball. The secondary explosion of the Scud's rocket fuel was the final straw as the huge ship split into four large pieces and thousands of tiny ones. The wreckage began its slow ride to the ocean bottom, where it would become a reef for fish to live in some years down the road.

The crew on board the aircraft cheered as the plane was lifted by the weight loss and the concussion of the huge explosion. The fireball helped to lift the aircraft to its destination of eight hundred feet, where a KC-10 called out from behind.

"We have you in view, Shadow One. You made one hell of a mess down there. Open your fuel door and hold at two hundred knots for refueling."

"That is a big affirmative," said Mackey with a smile as he settled back in his chair. He was completely soaked with sweat and exhausted.

It took several minutes before the boom of the KC-10 moved into position above their aircraft, but the fuel free-flowed into their tanks as they burned the last remnants of the emergency reserve. They all sat in silence, awaiting a plunge into the ocean that never came as the KC-10 kept them in the air. The knocking of the hatch at their feet reminded them that A.J. was still down in the crawl space below. They all hopped up and immediately opened it as fast as they could. A dozen hands lifted him out of the hatchway and hoisted him into the air as they began cheering and hugging him. Some were crying with joy, all were overwhelmed, as they hugged and high-fived each other.

The sound of the second engine restarting was the final assurance that they were all still alive. Mackey's voice calmly came over the intercom, "Congratulations, gentlemen. You have just saved the world."

Still leaned over to Hollahan and whispered, "Again."

"We are returning to the carrier, where we are promised a lobster dinner and a cold beer," Mackey said. That got another cheer from the crew. It took a while for the KC-10 to finish topping them off. When they were done, Gerry and Mackey both thanked the flying gas station for saving their lives and a very expensive piece of aircraft. The KC crew had joked that they weren't even sure if the black, unmarked plane was one of ours.

Mackey looked at Gerry and asked, "Do ya think we could have landed on that other tanker if we had to?"

Gerry shook his head and said with a laugh, "I am so glad that we never found out, with all due respect, sir."

When they finished refueling, they flew over the area a second time and scanned the ocean for a while. The *King Abha* had seen the huge explosion from its location two miles away, but hadn't been close enough to see any exchange of gunfire. Aside from the *King Abha*, the ocean was empty for another hundred miles. Only a yellow rag floated in the ocean where the *Crescent Fire* had once sailed.

CHAPTER 44

CIA Headquarters, Langley, Virginia

All of them had watched the events unfold like looking at a Hollywood movie. They had seen, on more than a dozen monitors, the exchange of gunfire, the tracer rounds, the *Crescent Fire* blowing to a million pieces. They hadn't cheered; they had merely watched in silence. Another day at the office, another mission, this time with a good outcome.

They took a collective sigh of relief. Archer stood up. "I will need full reports from each of you by tomorrow morning. Everything that went right, everything that went wrong. Details, people—the next time we get one of these, we need to be ready. Let's learn from this and get better. It was a good piece of work, people, particularly the intel from you, Amy. I will brief the president in two hours, and again with a full report tomorrow night." He exhaled slowly and gave a weak smile. "Good job, everyone. Dismissed."

Amy stayed an extra minute after the others had left the room. "Sir, may I brief Mitch on what happened out there today?"

The director nodded. "Yeah, go ahead. You don't give him everything. Shadow One is top secret, and so is the interaction between agencies, but without him, I hate to think of what tonight's leading news stories would have been. You extend him our thanks, please."

"Yes, sir, I will do that," she said with a smile. She had her own ideas of how she wanted to show her appreciation.

Epilogue

The network news droned on in the background of Amy's apartment as she waited for Mitch to arrive. There were flowers on the table that he had sent over, the card simply reading "Looking forward to dinner and dessert." As she put on her mascara, she heard a story that got her attention:

"An oil tanker sank approximately five hundred miles off the coast of Virginia last night. The nor'easter was most likely the cause, and the coast guard continues to investigate. The ship is believed to have been a Saudi tanker, but that is awaiting confirmation. There is no word of any crew members surviving the stormy seas, and there does not appear to be an oil slick in the area of the disaster.

"In a related story, fishermen have reported a large fish kill not far from the area of last night's oil tanker disaster. No word yet on what is apparently killing large numbers of fish."